"Mr. Barnett?" Her voice was orange-blossom honey flowing around him, slow and easy and sweet.

"That's me." He smiled with no amusement. "What'd I do, sugar buns? Park in the mayor's spot?"

She frowned and then took out a pad and clicked her pen. Watching him, she paused for a moment.

Sullivan stared right back. Let his eyes drift over to the white plastic name tag located above her breast. It said Maggie Webster. He waited.

She cleared her throat. "Mr. Barnett, I have to ask you a few questions about the threats you've received in the last three weeks. I know about the car bombing nine months ago—"

"Good for you, sugar buns. You've done your homework. I'll let the chief know what a hell of a job his boys—" he paused "—and girls are doing."

"Men, Mr. Barnett. And *women.*"

"Yeah, women." Sullivan sneered. "So I've noticed."

Dear Reader,

There's lots of exciting stuff for you in the Intimate Moments line this month, starting off with Linda Turner's *Gable's Lady*. This American Hero title is also the first of Linda's new miniseries, The Wild West. Set on a ranch in New Mexico, it's the saga of the Rawlings family, whose children are named after movie stars. It's no secret where Gable got his name—and in the future you can look for *Cooper, Flynn* and sister *Kat*. You'll love them all.

We're starting another miniseries this month, too: Romantic Traditions. Each Romantic Traditions title will be written by a different author and will put an Intimate Moments spin on one of your favorite romance plots. This month Paula Detmer Riggs offers up a marriage of convenience in *Once Upon a Wedding*. In months to come, look for Marilyn Pappano's *Finally a Father* (a secret-baby book), Carla Cassidy's *Try to Remember* (amnesia) and more.

We've also got another new author featured in a reprise of last year's successful "Premiere" promotion. Her name's Kylie Brant, and her irresistible book is called *McLain's Law*. All this, plus new books from Heather Graham Pozzessere, Lindsay Longford and Marilyn Cunningham. It's another don't-miss month from Intimate Moments.

Enjoy!

Yours,

Leslie Wainger
Senior Editor and Editorial Coordinator

SULLIVAN'S MIRACLE

Lindsay Longford

Published by Silhouette Books New York

America's Publisher of Contemporary Romance

SILHOUETTE BOOKS
300 East 42nd St., New York, N.Y. 10017

SULLIVAN'S MIRACLE

Copyright © 1993 by Jimmie L. Morel

All rights reserved. Except for use in any review, the reproduction or utilization of this work in whole or in part in any form by any electronic, mechanical or other means, now known or hereafter invented, including xerography, photocopying and recording, or in any information storage or retrieval system, is forbidden without the permission of the publisher, Silhouette Books, 300 E. 42nd St., New York, N.Y. 10017

ISBN: 0-373-07526-X

First Silhouette Books printing October 1993

All the characters in this book have no existence outside the imagination of the author and have no relation whatsoever to anyone bearing the same name or names. They are not even distantly inspired by any individual known or unknown to the author, and all incidents are pure invention.

®: Trademark used under license and registered in the United States Patent and Trademark Office and in other countries.

Printed in the U.S.A.

Books by Lindsay Longford

Silhouette Intimate Moments

Cade Boudreau's Revenge #390
Sullivan's Miracle #526

Silhouette Romance

Jake's Child #696
Pete's Dragon #854

LINDSAY LONGFORD,

like most writers, is a reader. She even reads toothpaste labels in desperation! A former high school English teacher with an M.A. in literature, she began writing romances because she wanted to create stories that touched readers' emotions by transporting them to a world where good things happened to good people and happily-ever-after is possible with a little work.

Her first book, *Jake's Child,* was nominated for Best New Series Author, Best Silhouette Romance and received a Special Achievement Award for Best First Series Book from *Romantic Times*. It was also a finalist in the Romance Writers of America Rita contest for Best First Book.

To my friends

From Morton: Mary Riden, Linda Stebbins,
Maryon Tilley, Rita Baar, Marge Gamboa,
Camille Salerno, Marie Perry—for all the years and
shared sorrows and joys, thank you

From the neighborhood: Jan Renaud, Mary Biller,
Cathy Lundman—because you're family

And to Darlene Patten for listening to me whine and
still being my friend—friendship indeed!

Grateful appreciation to John Stebbins,
Peter Lisagor Award-winning journalist;
to CJ, who prefers to remain anonymous but is
Chris's dad, for help in chemical engineering;
to Trooper Clifford Dreyer, Illinois, and
Major Ken Pearson of Manatee County, Florida, for
police procedural information; and to Senior Chief
David Roberts for sharing information about the
Navy SEALs: Thanks, guys, the stories and
information were fascinating—thanks for sharing
them with me. Any errors are mine, not theirs.

Chapter 1

November, The Beginning

Driven by the storm, the waves of the gulf roared shoreward. Streaks of red and purple lingered low between sky and rolling water. Mary Elizabeth thought about walking out into that darkness, deeper and deeper, until it bore her up and carried her away.

There would be an end to it.

No more struggling.

Thundering onto the sloping beach before her, the surging waves warred with the blackness of the ruby-smudged twilight. Elizabeth let a handful of powdery white sand sift from her fingers as she stared at the sky. Only the toss of white spray relieved the deepening purple.

A lifting up, weightless. The way it had been when she'd learned to float in these sunshine-clear waters as a child. She could feel how it would be, that lovely, lulling weightlessness—the power of the storm surrounding her, sweeping her out to that thin line marking the curve of earth into space, sweeping her into peace.

No more pain.

So easy. So tempting, that floating away to sunshine.

Her head would be a small dot in the vastness for a long time, and then it would disappear while the waves rolled on forever.

Letting her thoughts drift, she inhaled the salty air blowing around her. Cold and filled with the taste of the gulf, that air stung her lips, her eyes, and burned her lungs. She coughed.

And coughed once more, convulsively, as she breathed shallowly against the tearing pain in her lungs.

She ground her hand into the beach, fighting for breath. Grit scratched her skin as she pressed her palm even harder into the wet sand beside her, focusing her fluttering thoughts. A froth of foam as cold as the windy blasts tickled her toes. She coughed hard, chest muscles straining. When she could finally breathe, she rested her head on her bent knees, exhausted.

Retreating, the wave abandoned a curl of seaweed at her feet. Reaching toward the prickly strand, she felt it slip through her fingers on the next wave.

That was how it would be. Just an easy sliding away.

She was so tired, and there would be no more pain.

Nothing, in fact, ever again.

That, too. Never again to have Sullivan's eyes light up as he saw her, his smile erase the loneliness from his face and dull the aching in her heart.

Sand blew into her eyes. Sullivan. Hungry-eyed Sullivan with his guarded smile that warmed all the cold, frightened places deep inside her.

Elizabeth sighed and lifted her head, watching the waves crash ever closer in the deepening darkness, her thoughts circling endlessly around Sullivan. She kept her gaze on that far distant horizon until it vanished, leaving before her only the billowing night and the onrushing tide.

When the water was ankle high and her jeans soggy with sand, she shook herself out of her reverie. Shivering and coughing, she wriggled her toes, burrowing them under the sand. They looked like small, bleached prunes in the cloudy water.

She laughed as she watched her feet disappear. Here she was, fanny-deep in water and shoveling her feet under the sand so she wouldn't be cold. A laugh bubbled up again as the black humor of her situation struck her. How simple life was, really.

If cold, the body sought heat. If hungry, food. The body's needs were basic. Survival. Love.

If you were lucky.

Burying her ankles in the murky sand, she thought, too, about cowardice and fear, about the balance of pain and joy.

She couldn't remember one single time in her life when she'd ever flung caution to the winds. Not even the night Charlie, the town's self-designated bad boy, had roared up to her porch on his motorcycle and flashed his wicked grin, daring her to come for a ride. With the smell of orange blossoms rising up all around her in the night air, she'd longed to fly out of her house and shriek down the driveway with him, wind whipping her hair back from her face, her arms tight around him.

Her heart racing, she had hesitated, nudging the edge of the door with her foot, Charlie's devil-may-care grin pulling her forward. She'd finally shaken her head. But underneath, oh, underneath, how she'd longed to taste the promise of Charlie's smile.

Now she wrapped her arms tightly around herself. Who'd have ever thought Charlie would become a banker?

All those times she'd let life pass her by.

Until Sullivan Barnett, who seldom smiled and who wasn't anything like Charlie. Cynical and intense, Sullivan was everything Charlie had only pretended to be.

She rinsed her sandy fingers in the eddies around her feet. Sullivan, storming into her life, never giving her a chance to hover in the shadows, wearing down her defenses with his need for *her*. Oh, Sullivan, she thought with something approaching despair, what in the world am I going to do about you?

Drizzle from the scudding clouds mingled with spray. Sullivan had promised he'd return tonight. Turning her back to the storm, not wanting to hope, Elizabeth struggled to her feet.

She'd sworn right from the beginning she'd never become dependent on him. Not fair. A tiny part of her acknowledged that she didn't want to do that to herself, either. Equal was okay. Helpless wasn't, not in her book of rules, at least.

Coughing and shivering, longing for Sullivan with every breath she fought for, she sank to her knees in the surf, head bowed, her breath rasping in the whipping wind and spray.

Coming out onto the deck of the beach house, Sullivan saw her hunched over at the water's edge, her thin figure unmoving and blurry in the wavering dark.

A sick dread sent him vaulting over the railing. As he grabbed the rough wood, a splinter drove into his thumb, but he hurried to her, his heart hammering. His shoes crunched on the sand, echoing the thud of his heart, and she must have heard him, sensed him, *something*, because, still on her knees, she turned and lifted her hand to shove her blowing hair back from her pale face. Sour bile rose in his mouth, but Sullivan slowed his steps. She wouldn't want to see his terror.

Making his way to her against the gusting wind, he worked the sliver out with his fingers and dropped it to the sand, all the time watching her, her wind-tossed hair gleaming in the fitful light, the shimmering curve of her throat, the pale shine of her cheek turning to him.

His eyes never left her, and his hunger for her, powerful enough to rend him in two, frightened him. With her, he was whole. Without her...

Hooking his shaking hands in his back pockets, hiding his fear, he sauntered up.

"Damn it, Lizzie," he drawled, watching her pivot slowly. "Had a hell of a time getting your door open. Thing's warped to kingdom come and back. Why don't you let me put up a new one?" He saw the exhaustion in her drooping posture and with an effort kept his mouth shut.

"Hello to you, too, Sullivan." Her smile was strained, but her low tone was still sassy.

He wanted to grab her out of the damned water, wrap her in blankets and carry her all the way back to her house, but he knew she wouldn't thank him if he did. Instead, pulling her out of the whirlpool of surf and steadying her, he patted her rear end through her sopping jeans and forced a grin. "Still a kid at heart, huh, Lizzie? Can't stay out of puddles." He tugged at her pocket, which was stuffed with shells. "Bet you couldn't wait to shimmy out of your Sunday best when you were a little girl."

She smiled, her mouth a sweet arc, and the everpresent tightness in his chest loosened and let him pretend that they had forever.

"All those lights." He drew her closer, surrounding her with his arms, his chest, trying to warm her. In the semidarkness he saw the blue-gray shadows under her eyes, but he plowed on. "Hell, I could see your house halfway down the island." He rubbed at the goose bumps on her arms. "Place is lit up like a Christmas tree." He heard the harshness in his voice, the edginess curling his syllables.

A fragile weight, she leaned against him, and his heart beat heavy and slow with grief.

"So, Lizzie, here you are. Windows wide open, lights blazing..." He anchored her hair with his palms, stepping so close he could feel her breath on his neck, hear the rasp and effort as she spoke.

"*My* electric bill, Sullivan, not yours. I don't like the dark." Her voice was as soft as her fine hair blowing in the storm, touching him and making him ache in the loneliest part of his soul. "And don't call me Lizzie." Her mouth pursed, she added, "I don't like that."

"I know. Why do you think I do it?" He rubbed her nose with his, his forehead lingering on her cheek, which felt cold against his heat. As he swung her up like a child into his arms, her sandy toes grazed his thigh. A yearning as old as man and woman slashed through him. "Lizzie, Lizzie, Lizzie," he taunted, whisking her cheeks with his chin.

"Mean, you are, Sullivan Barnett." She stuck out her tongue.

Giving in to his craving, he trailed his lips down the line of her throat and skimmed the edge of her small ear as he turned to the beach house. "Damn straight. Meanest coot in town. But never to you, Lizzie." Repeating her name like a mantra, he stroked the bristle on his chin against her nose.

"No?" She brushed back a strand of unruly brown hair at his neck.

He shivered at her light touch and turned his mouth to her seeking fingers. "Never to you." He kissed the tip of her thumb.

"But mean, even so." Futilely she blotted at the rain on his face.

Her touch said everything her words didn't, everything he knew she would never say to him. He knew her better than she gave him credit for.

"And wet."

"I was in a hurry."

"Were you now?" Her fingers were summer butterflies against his throat.

"Hell, yes." He tightened his grip, and when she pressed her cheek against his sodden shirt, he laid his chin against her hair and swallowed the lump in his throat. "Had to get home to my Lizzie girl."

"Did you find out anything important?" She curled her fingertips into his shirt collar.

He wondered if she realized how that small gesture betrayed her. "Nothing as important as coming home to you."

"I see."

"I doubt it. You've never understood what I feel about you."

She sighed, a wisp of air vanishing in the wind.

A lone sea gull squawked overhead and tumbled to a landing at their feet. Holding her close to his heart, Sullivan started toward the cottage.

"Put me down, Sullivan. I'll walk," she said.

"No." He pulled her closer. "I'll be damned if you will." His tone was as determined as hers.

"Yes." She touched his face and forced him to look at her. "I'll walk."

She was only a slight weight in his arms, and he paused. Deep in her clear gray eyes, her spirit flickered like a candle in the windy darkness. Sullivan loosened his grip, his need to protect her second to her need. "You make me so damned mad sometimes, Lizzie, I could strangle you."

"I know," she whispered, leaning against him. "Why do you stick around, Sullivan?"

"Shut up." He bent over her, holding on for dear life. After a long moment he said, "Do you want me to go?"

She only shivered and burrowed closer. It was answer enough for the time being.

He cleared his throat. "You going to beat me up if I put my arm around you?" He curled his arm around her waist.

"We'll see." Her smile was shaky, but she leaned on him. "Just don't go all macho on me."

He snugged her against his hip. "Fat chance." Setting an easy pace, he tried to ignore his urge to hurry her out of the drizzle. If Lizzie wanted to do it her way, under her own steam, he'd help her. "You make me nuts, woman," he muttered, clamping her to his side. "Damned if you don't."

"I know," she repeated. Wrapping her cold fingers around his, she clutched him as they made their way over the sand and grassy hillocks to the beach-house deck.

When she stumbled on the bottom step, Sullivan muttered through clenched teeth, "Enough's enough." He glared at her. "You've proven your point. So you're Wonder Woman. Now you can humor me." Sweeping her into his arms, he took the rickety steps two at a time and kicked open the door.

"All right." Her voice was a faint rasp. "Wish I was built like her, though." Her laugh stuttered into a cough.

His step faltered.

"It's the storm, that's all, Sullivan—the drop in barometric pressure. I'm fine." She shut her eyes for a long moment, struggling for control.

"Yeah, right. Damn your stubbornness all to hell, Lizzie," Sullivan said, a low buzz of anger lending a snap to his words he didn't intend. But rage churned inside him. Not pausing to flick on a light, he strode through the kitchen to the bathroom. Stupid. No rhyme or reason, but his Lizzie had this—this *gunk* in her lungs, and there was nothing he could do. Nothing anyone could do.

Stripping her out of her sand-encrusted clothes so fast she didn't have time to object, he thrust her under the shower. As the bathroom filled with steam, through the shrouded glass of the shower door he saw her slump against the tiles. She stayed so still, her head bowed under the beating spray, that he climbed right in after her, shirt, shoes and all.

When he opened the glass door, she straightened and looked up, a weary smile lighting her narrow face. "Look at you. Now who's the kid?" Looking at his feet, which he'd nudged between hers, she chided, "You'll ruin your shoes."

She plucked the white shirt away from his chest and loosened his tie. Her fingers shook as she tried to undo the knot, and his skin tightened where her fingers lingered. It had been that way for him from the first moment he'd seen her. As he turned her to the shower nozzle and grabbed the green-and-pink bottle smelling of flowers and Lizzie, he felt the slight tremble in her shoulders.

"I can still afford to buy a new pair of shoes." Sullivan squirted shampoo into his hands and worked it into her hair, pausing where her hair divided at her nape. Defenseless, that small patch of naked skin splintered his control. He traced each vertebra gently, grateful she couldn't see his face where the skin around his eyes stretched tight and hot.

"You're crazy, you are, Sullivan Barnett." She placed her palms against the tiles and peeked at him through her dripping hair, eyes wide and fatigued, but her spirit burning, burning with a fire all her own.

He rinsed her hair as fast as he could, the strands slipping slick and smooth through his fingers, while her courage cut him like a thousand knives.

"Crazy, huh? Well, that makes us a perfect pair." He popped the door open and bundled her in a huge pink towel. "You with not enough sense to come in out of the rain and me taking a shower in my clothes." In the fogged mirror, he saw the two of them, shadowy figures without substance, Lizzie pale and slim against his darkness, fitting him the way no one before her ever had, the way no one ever would again.

Sullivan stared as he dried her. His hands were long and tanned against the pink towel, his fingers dark against her cool skin. As he worked, he knew the reality of her, felt her slender bones, touched her, while before him their ghostly figures wavered dim and unreal. In desperation, he buried his mouth against her smooth neck, tasted the clean, sweet essence of Lizzie O'Connell and held her, held her against the mocking reflection in the steam-clouded mirror.

"You break my heart," he whispered.

She flinched. He knew she'd seen the desperation in his face, felt the desolation in his touch. "I never wanted to hurt you. Never."

Her words were so soft he barely heard them. But he wished he hadn't heard them at all, because he was afraid of what they might mean. Tenderly he touched the tip of his tongue to the damp corner of her shoulder and pressed a kiss there. As her skin rippled beneath his mouth, he shuddered and lifted his head, his gaze locking on hers.

Her expression was elusive, hiding her thoughts from him. "You know it will only get worse as time goes on."

He stared back at her through the mist that still blurred their images, and he couldn't speak.

"This isn't working, Sullivan. For either of us."

She shook her head, wet strands of her hair caressing his lips, and he remembered nights with her silky locks sliding down his body, promising pleasure, the merging of their bodies bringing him closer to her than he'd ever been to anyone in his entire life, her touch completing him. The memory choked him with the cruelest pain he'd ever known.

The shower door rattled in its metal track as he slammed his elbow against it.

"Oh, Sullivan." She lifted his knuckles to her cool lips and kissed them. "Nothing's going to be any different. But I want us to be happy for now. If we can?" Clear gray pools with unshed tears, her eyes beseeched him. "I don't want to think about next week. I can't even think about tomorrow."

"Whatever you say, Lizzie." He traced the outline of her face on the foggy mirror and leaned forward, pressing his chest against her back. "Whatever you want. Always." He paused. "Forever."

She wiped away the steam veiling their faces. In the clear mirror, her gaze was strong and steady, filled with knowledge that unnerved him.

As he carried her wrapped in the thick pink towel to her bedroom, she trailed her fingers along the sticky surfaces of old furniture and warped shelves, where bits and pieces of broken shells were arranged in careless heaps and circles.

"I don't get it," he said, slipping her under the bed covers. He tipped his chin toward the bits of colored glass worn smooth by sand and water, the ridged shell fragments. "What kind of collection is this, anyway?"

"My kind."

He glanced back over his shoulder. "Yeah, shoulda figured." His Lizzie had always been a sucker for the broken things in life. The kids in her day-care center, him. Why not shells?

Fighting fatigue, Lizzie watched as Sullivan rooted through her dresser for a nightgown. What she wanted, though, was his long, muscled self next to her through the coming night. Through the open windows of her bedroom the distant *kathump* of the gulf could be heard. She lived with its sound always in her ears, waking, sleeping to the endless rhythm.

Her heart was racing threadily and her lungs labored with each breath, but the pain was endurable. She hadn't seen Sullivan for two days. This pain was nothing compared with the aching need for him—not just his voice on the phone, but *him*, his strength, his tenderness masked by teasing.

"Lift your arms."

His face was close to hers, filling her world, and she held out her arms and let him ease the flannel shirt he'd found over her shoulders. His rough fingers rasped the soles of her feet as he pulled thick white socks over them. He arranged the pink-flowered blanket around her.

She crooked her finger in the notch of his shirt. Against the back of her finger, his chest was smooth and muscled. "You need to change into something dry, too."

"Not yet." He wouldn't look at her as he ran the towel over her hair and separated the drying strands.

"We have to talk." She regretted the huskiness in her voice and cleared her throat, resisting the cough that came pushing up.

His fingers were so warm against her ear. He lifted a wet strand of hair and tugged it gently. "Yeah?"

"Yeah," she echoed. "Go change."

"Bossy woman." He leaned over her. "I'll get you some tea first."

"Don't call *me* stubborn," she muttered as he walked through the doorway.

"I heard that," he shot back.

"You were supposed to." Raising her voice took the last of her energy and she coughed repeatedly, cramming the sheet into her mouth to smother the sounds. Drained, she sank against the pillows. Her hand shaking, she reached into her nightstand and took out her pain pills. She swallowed four, quickly forcing them down when they stuck in her dry throat.

A cabinet door banged and she heard his muffled curse. Metal clanged against metal. Sullivan was only patient when he was tracking a story. Apprehension nibbled at her in between waves of drowsiness. She was worried about him. Yesterday in a catch-up-with-old-times phone call, Charlie had hinted that there were unsettling rumors connected with Sullivan's investigation. Greed could warp even the most respectable people, and Sullivan would keep plugging away at the knotted strings, seeing where they led. And who held the ends.

She had to make him see how dangerous his curiosity could become if he stayed on the story he was digging up.

And she had to tell him the decision she'd made when she'd seen the agony revealed in his face in the mirror.

Her eyelids drifted partly shut, and in the twilight moments, she watched the shadows in the corner of the room, listened to the ticking of the clock, its companionable beat a quiet sound against the roar of the gulf.

She heard the small clink of teacup on saucer and forced her eyes back open.

Carrying one of the Wedgwood teacups she'd brought from her house in town, Sullivan entered through the arch between the kitchen hall and bedroom. His wide, sloping shoulders filled the doorway. The stark light struck his face, shone on the shaggy brown hair curling onto his T-shirt. As he ducked under it, the unshaded bulb swayed on its long black cord, highlighting the angles of his face, the wariness in his alert blue eyes.

She'd put that wariness in his eyes. She loved him more than life itself, and she'd harmed him. She tried for a light note, teasing him. "You changed your clothes after all."

Hearing her, he stopped, and his lopsided smile held her transfixed. "While the water boiled." One straw-brown eyebrow lifted. "Hey, I'm real good at following orders. Yours, anyway," he added as she wrinkled her nose disbelievingly.

The light seesawed above him, shadow, light, shadow. His eyes, bright then dark, filled with the sight of her. He'd always looked at her like that, as though she were the only person in his world. She smiled back, comfort she hadn't found in the blankets seeping through her.

"Here." He handed her the tea. The wicker headboard banged against the wall and the bed dipped as he sat down. He settled her on his lap, and she grabbed the cup. Bringing her feet close to him, he tucked her in the crook of his arm. Its corded strength bunched against her breast as he turned her to him. "So. Let's talk. Bad day?"

The hard, comforting thump of his heart drowned out everything, and she yearned to stay safe in his arms forever.

"No." She evaded the see-all blue of his eyes.

"You don't lie worth squat. Don't you know that by now?" He stroked her cheek and put his ear to her chest, listening against the worn flannel of her buttoned-up shirt.

Over the living bridge of his ear against her heart, she felt her breath pass from her straining lungs into him, through him.

Frowning, he raised his head and glanced toward the corner, at the oxygen tank with the nasal cannula and tubing. "You want anything?"

"No," she said, and his slow breath of frustration tickled her ear.

He touched the skin under her eyes, watching her carefully the whole while. "I shouldn't have gone to Tampa."

"You had to. The records are at the federal court house."

"There were other sources."

"All right, then, I wanted you to go." She wadded up the bed sheet with her free hand, looked down into the teacup and tried to figure out how to tell him what she'd decided in those twilight moments, the only decision she believed possible. Still trying to keep the moment light, she tilted her head and smiled up at him. "Besides, you're a pain in the patooty when you hang around all the time, Sullivan."

"Patooty?" He cuddled her closer. "Fanny I know. Ass, yeah, that too, but *patooty?*"

"Same geographic location," she answered, wiggling her patooty as she laid her head on his shoulder.

"Now I get it," he teased as he curved his palm over her. "And a *very* nice area it is. Hills, valleys," he murmured. "Geography always was my favorite subject." His palm rested at the top of her thigh.

The cup tilted. Tea slopped onto the sheet, and she put the cup on the end table. "I'm done." His palm moved once as she continued, "I know my illness is tearing you apart. We're—"

He started to interrupt, but she silenced him with her fingers against his mouth. Sullivan wasn't used to running into immovable objects or situations he couldn't fix. If possible, he wasn't going to let her tell him what she had to.

He ran his hand up and down her arm and bent over her feet, pulling up her socks, playing for time. "Look, while I was gone, I talked to some people about this idiopathic pulmonary fibrosis thing."

Reverting to childhood, she covered her ears and shut her eyes.

"Look at me, Lizzie." He pulled her hands down, and a broad palm cupped her cheek.

Basketball-player hands, she thought wistfully, remembering an out-of-focus photograph he'd reluctantly shown her when she'd teased him once about being a man with no past.

"Don't shut me out," he said and slid his lips across her eyelids, making her open them to the pain she saw in his eyes.

"Sometimes I have to," she whispered, watching the blue darken like storm-driven waves.

"When you turn away—" he gripped her chin "—I don't exist anymore." Uncharacteristically, his words tumbled out. "It's never been like this for me. I never knew I could be so lonely until you came into my life. When you're not with me..." he hesitated, searching for words "...there's nothing." He stroked her calf, her thigh, her throat until he finally touched her mouth, outlining her lips with his forefinger over and over until she felt blood rush to fill them, felt them grow warm under his touch, felt warm *herself* for the first time in two days.

He glanced again at the cannula with its utilitarian prongs and tubing. He took a deep breath, and his chest moved against her ribs. "Lizzie, I'm so damned angry all the time. I can't think straight. I can't think about anything except you. I'm scared sh—"

"I didn't think it would be like this," she said, her throat closing with her own loneliness and fear. "I never wanted you unhappy."

"Hell, I know that." His frustration boiled over, and sh
wanted to ease his pain, but couldn't. "Where were you a
those years I was roaming the world like a lost soul?"

His pain, hers, intermingled. "Me, too." She slid her arr
around his neck. "I needed you, and I didn't even know yo
existed."

Lifting her, he brought her as close as cloth and skin coul
get. "What kind of damned world is this? Why couldn't w
have had years instead of months? I wish—"

She squeezed the old childhood words out through her tigh
throat. "If wishes were horses—"

"Beggars would ride," he finished, holding onto her as i
she'd disappear before his eyes. "I can't stand..." He stopped
"No, I can stand anything I have to." He kissed her forehead
"But watching you struggle and not being able to do a dam
thing about it, Lizzie, it's..." There was rage in the touch o
his lips. Frustration.

His anger overwhelmed her. It was more than she coul
handle. "That's why I want you to leave." The words burs
from the well of her own fears. She dropped her face into he
shaking hands, Sullivan's grief and anger exhausting her.

"Is that what you really want?" His feet hit the floor, and hi
back was to her, rigid with control.

"Yes." She made herself say the words. She couldn't mak
herself mean them—not at the most basic level, in her heart
"You said, whatever I wanted. Give me what I want, Sulli
van."

The sound he made was as close to a growl as a human coul
come. "Leave, huh? Fine. Terrific. Grab my toothbrush an
go?"

She nodded. Sobs were jarring her, but she wouldn't let then
out, not now.

"No."

Her strength nonexistent against his hard chest, she pum
meled him with her fists, trying to make him understand
"Don't you think I've tried everything? I have! I lie awake a
night thinking about how things could have been for us."

White lines scored his mouth. "Listen, I said I can deal with whatever happens. I can handle anything except losing you." He looked toward the shadows haunting the corners. "Anything but that."

Gathering her so tightly to him that she knew he was walking the fine edge of control, he was silent. In the quiet, the ticking of the clock echoed the beating of her heart. She'd always taken his strength for granted. She'd never imagined she would become his Achilles' heel.

When he finally spoke, he chose his words carefully, though his tone was bitter. "I'm not leaving. No matter what, you're stuck with me, Mary Elizabeth. I still want you to marry me. Nothing's changed for me. I want to be here with you every day, not just when you decide to let me past your drawbridge."

Her sobs slipped out. "You don't know what you're saying."

"I'm forty-one years old, Lizzie. If I don't know what I want by now, God help me." He smoothed the tears from her cheeks and raised her face. "Do I look like a man who has trouble making up his mind?"

With his bright blue eyes filling her vision, she yearned to take the comfort he so carelessly extended, but she wouldn't let him sacrifice himself. "You're the kindest man I've ever met," she whispered. "But I won't marry you."

He squeezed her shoulders. "Then let me move in."

"I can't." She twisted away. "Don't you understand? I couldn't stand it if you started feeling trapped. I don't want you growing to hate me."

"Hate you? You're everything I've ever wanted in my whole life, Lizzie. You opened your door that day I came to interview you about your day-care center, and it was like someone taking a rock and slamming it into my gut. After so many years, never expected to fall in love, but there you were, cobwebs on your nose, twenty curtain climbers screaming around you, holding a kid in a dirty diaper with one hand and blocking the door with the other. You weren't about to give an inch to some damned nosy reporter, and I felt like I'd been slam-dunked.

How can I walk out of your life? You might as well marry m
you know," he said, his words like water dripping on a ston
wearing it away.

"Sullivan, I used to believe in miracles, but happy-ever-aft
isn't in store for us."

"I'll settle for what you will give me right now. I never b
lieved in miracles, anyway. Never saw any reason to."

"What do you believe in, Sullivan?" She needed to kno
now more than ever. His world was so dark.

"Not much." He placed her palm over his heart, slid his ow
hand under her shirt and pressed his wrist, with its strong puls
against her breast, where her heart thrummed out its love fo
him. "This." His palm bumped her nipple, scorched it with h
heat. "Us. What I feel for you. Nothing else." He lowered b
head to her breast. "Everything else is bull, pointless."

For his sake, she wouldn't give him the one thing he'd ev
asked of her, but she could set him free. She knew Sullivan
stubborn persistence too well. She knew how things would b
if she gave in. "I'm not giving you a choice," she said gentl
Relentlessly, truth settled like dust motes between them. Rai
ing her hands to touch him, she dropped them to her lap in
stead. Touching him gave her more comfort than she coul
allow herself.

"Well, Lizzie, it's like this." His anger buzzed through th
room like frenzied wasps. "I didn't want to love you, but I ha
no choice about that, either. Now you're telling me to get ou
of your life, and I don't even want to live in a world withou
you. I wake up, and I can't move because I'm so damne
frightened you won't be here when I unlock that damned stick
door." He lifted the ends of her hair and slid his fingers alon
her neck. Trailing his mouth down her throat, he kissed th
fretful pulse at the base of it. The planes of his face were blea
as he said, "You can't keep me away. Nothing can. Not eve
God and all his angels." His voice cracked. "I'm begging. L
me stay."

"No."

The strident buzzing of his beeper on the nightstand shrille
and they both jumped. Sullivan swore. Glancing at the read

ut, he slammed the beeper to the floor. "It's the damned night esk."

Released from his hold, grateful for the interruption, she rumpled against the pillow and shut her eyes. "Take the call."

Picking up the phone, he punched out numbers while he rowned at her. "Yeah. It's me. Can't someone else handle it?" cowling, drumming his fingers, he listened. "Yeah, yeah. I now I'm on the spot already, but someone else will have to— Damn it, find someone."

She tugged his shirt and mouthed, *Go*. He shook his head.

"Yeah, I understand. Everybody's on vacation, but that's ot my problem. I'm not going. So fire me."

Yes, she insisted with the last of her strength.

"I don't care if I'm just up the road—"

"Please," she whispered. "I can't take any more."

At her entreaty, he stopped in midsentence and covered the eceiver. His lips thinned as he spoke to her. "Okay. But this iscussion isn't over. If you think for one cotton-picking min-te that you're getting rid of me with this damned nonsense, etter think again, sweetheart." He flattened her hand hard gainst his leg and turned to write down the address of the Quik-Deli ten minutes down the island from her cottage. Hanging up the receiver, he ripped off the piece of paper. "A obbery. Cop's shot. Hostages." His eyes were grim as he wined his finger gently in the strands of her dry hair.

"I'm okay," she murmured, answering the tenderness in his ouch. "I'll be all right." She took as deep a breath as she could hrough pain and heartache. "But I mean it. Don't come back, ullivan."

"Damn you, Lizzie." His voice was ice. "I could almost hate you for doing this to us."

"See what I mean?" She wrapped her arms fiercely around im. "We can't go on like this. It's destroying you."

"I'm a big boy, Lizzie. Let me make my own decisions. Let ne have whatever time we have left."

So hard, harder than she'd dreamed to let him go. "I don't want what we've had spoiled. Let me believe that you'll re-member me a little, that your memories won't be ugly ones—"

She couldn't go on without squalling like a baby. "Let me hav
my pride. It's all I have left."

Sullivan saw her exhaustion and knew he had to give he
space, at least for the moment. "Lizzie, you can have wha
ever you want. Your pride. My liver, my nose, my toes. Any
thing except my leaving."

Her watery half sob broke his heart. He would have given he
everything he had. But the fates had decided differently.

"A toe transplant. Wouldn't I look darling in my sanda
with ten extra toes on each foot?" It was the humor that ha
first drawn him to her, but her chest vibrated with the move
ment of her straining lungs, reminding him.

He would leave now because she was at the end of her en
durance, but he wouldn't think about never seeing her sma
toes in sandals again. "Here. Lean forward." He lifted the ta
of her shirt and wiped her face. "We'll do it your way."

For now, he'd give her what she asked.

He spread his hand over her throat, his thumb warm agains
her frantic pulse. "But don't leave me alone, Lizzie. I'll neve
forgive you if you do."

"Later, Sullivan, when you've forgotten all this, try to for
give me." Tears slipped down her pale cheeks.

"Forgotten?" he said. He was furious. "You're the one wit
no faith. You *never* believed enough in what we felt to marr
me. You're a coward, Lizzie, but I love you more than you'
ever know. Somehow I'll find a way to forgive you, but it'll tak
me a long time."

His kiss was hard, filled with angry despair, and he tasted th
bitter salt of her anguish on his lips. "You know the beepe
number if you need me, but one way or another, I'll be bac
before midnight."

Leaving her was the hardest thing he'd ever done, but hi
anger was so all-consuming he was afraid of what he might sa
if he didn't. He couldn't inflict his anger and fear on her whil
she was so ill, so he kept going. Shutting the warped door be
hind him, he leaned against it, looking up at the rain-darkened
empty sky. There were no answers there, either. Slamming hi
fists into his pockets, he walked to his car and sagged agains

the wet metal. Sliding to the ground, he rubbed his burning eyes with his knuckles.

Off in the distance, an ambulance siren wailed as it approached him, heading to the far end of the island. Red lights boiled past him in the streaming rain. It was as if the whole world were crying for his Lizzie and he could only sit dry-eyed, scorched by a fury against the heavens too hot for tears.

Inside, Lizzie heard the thump of his shoulders against the door and jerked. If he came back, she'd never find the courage to send him away again. She couldn't fight Sullivan and her own longings.

The thunder of her heart was loud, shaking her apart. She fumbled in the drawer for her pills, opening the bottle with her teeth. In her hurry, she dropped it. White pills rained to the sheets.

As she leaned over, there was a sudden burst of pain and a rushing of pulse in her ears, until she didn't know whether she was hearing the roar of the surf or the pounding of her heart, louder and louder until light flared around her and she was drowning, drowning in light and silence. But still the slow thud of her pulse mingled with the oncoming tide outside her window.

And she was free of pain. Free as she hadn't been for so long that she'd forgotten how wonderful it was to move lightly, swimmingly. Moving faster than she could ever remember doing, she raced toward that swelling light that promised peace.

Suddenly, agonizingly, she remembered *everything*. Everything she'd wanted and never had. Sullivan. Children. Unbearable, that sense of loss, because all she'd had to do was reach out, take a leap of faith, and she hadn't.

Sullivan was right. She'd been a coward.

So much she should have told him. She'd never told him she loved him. Anguish whipped through her as she remembered everything left unsaid. She had to warn him about . . . something.

He was in danger.

A yearning so strong that it was unendurable pierced her, slowing her headlong flight. Slowly, slowly, she turned.

In all that radiant light a flash of brilliance, blue like the blaze of Sullivan's eyes, streamed through her. Indescribable joy. "Ah," she murmured over the slamming of her heart as she reached out, trying to tell him she'd been wrong, so wrong about everything.

Too late, too late, the wind whispered. *Too late.*

Struck by her out-flung hand, the teacup fell to the wooden floor, rolling end over end. It rattled against the floorboards for a long time until only the roar of the surf and the ticking of the clock filled the room.

Chapter 2

Sullivan slid the scrap of paper with the phone number back and forth on his desk and watched the cop scope out the newsroom.

Her deliberate perusal piqued Sullivan's interest. Even now force of habit caused him to take mental notes. Summer-weight uniform. Cop hat at regulation angle. Macho Sam Browne belt holding the gun and swagger stick. Shoes polished to a blinding shine. Pausing, the cop looked around and spotted Hinky Tom gone ballistic at his terminal. Always pushing deadline, Hinky, at least, was working on a story. Sullivan's story had fizzled. Or been scuttled. He still didn't know, didn't much care.

The cop bent over and asked Hinky a question. The electronic hum of computers, the distant and constant ring of phones, the buzz of the light tubes behind the plastic—white noise covered voices and conversations, providing a measure of privacy. Hinky's skinny fingers flipped vaguely toward Sullivan.

Still leaning over Hinky's compulsively neat desk, the cop glanced toward Sullivan, then she straightened. The snap of her head as she asked a question wobbled the rigidly placed hat. The cop thumped it into place again as Hinky nodded.

The cop's slow stroll through the aisle formed by desks and computer stations would have been impressive if it hadn't been for the slight hip sway.

Sliding down on his tailbone and propping his sneaker-clad feet on his desk, Sullivan waited. Mildly curious, mostly bored, he played the paper around his fingers as he watched her. Dropping from her narrow waist, the dark blue stripe lining the side of the blue pants drew his attention to her gently rounded hips. To her long legs, which looked good even in the stiff uniform. To the slight rise of her breasts under the white shirt. She'd have had a lot of trouble putting together some kind of uniform back in the old days. He looked away.

Suddenly, two desks away from him, she stopped, and her hand flew to her throat. Her mouth opened and he caught a glimpse of white teeth, but she didn't speak, just kept looking at him in bewilderment, as if she'd momentarily lost her bearings.

Maybe it was the look of confusion in those huge brown eyes peering out from under the damned hat, he didn't know, but something pulled Sullivan slowly out of his chair, light-headed from the blood draining from his brain.

The air was thick around him and he was having trouble catching his breath as she stared at him, but all his senses were so heightened that he heard the rasp of her fingernails as they caught on the white cotton of her shirt and slid down the blue pant stripes, heard her inhale, heard the loud click as the clock hand moved. He clutched the edge of the desk, crumpling the piece of paper in his shaking hands. Connecting him to her, an invisible wire twanged and whirred, electric with possibility. He tried to free himself from the strangeness of the moment, but something stronger than steel chains kept him rooted where he stood.

Stuffed under her hat, her wildly curling hair floated with a will of its own around her face. Thick and glossy as melted chocolate, unruly strands framed her square face with such rich color that it was all he could do not to touch the cloudiness crackling like dark lightning around her face.

Despite the crisp uniform and her arrested stance, she gave the impression of movement, of being propelled by a life force so powerful that it brightened the air around her, and from the dark cave where he'd buried it, a raw and primitive need came prowling out, snarling in its fierceness.

In spite of her long legs and curves, she was small and delicate, her flushed skin shining. A gleaming drop of perspiration slipped down her throat, to where the slope of her neck disappeared into her starched white shirt. Glittering over the steady beat of her heart, it hung between skin and collar, pulsing, pulsing, pulsing with her erratic breath.

Sullivan watched the glitter of that shining drop and let all his rage slam through him, hating her because she'd awakened a dark, frightening urge in him, an urge so primal that he could have taken her right there, standing up, in the most elemental mating of his life. Hating her because she was alive and she wasn't Lizzie.

Didn't look like Lizzie, didn't remind him of Lizzie, wasn't Lizzie, and he couldn't bear it.

He sank to his chair and buried his face in his fists.

"Sully! You got a visitor!" Hinky's voice whined.

Taking a deep breath, Sullivan placed his hands palm down on the desk. A distant corner of his rational self noted the trembling of his fingers. He unfolded the crumpled paper that held the phone number and flattened it over and over while he wrestled with the bitterness that was his second self.

He'd thought he was getting better. He'd made himself believe that he could get through the empty days without Lizzie, but he was crazier than he'd realized if he could overreact to a small, brown-eyed, brown-haired cop.

He wanted to yell at Lizzie and tell her how ticked off he was with her for leaving him behind in a world that had no meaning without her.

But his Lizzie wasn't there and he couldn't yell at her or touch her.

Sullivan moored the paper under the facedown, empty picture frame. Working late around Christmas, missing Lizzie so badly he was sick with grief, he'd torn her photograph out and ripped it into so many pieces that when he'd flung them away in the parking lot, they'd drifted down like some strange snow flurry, taunting him in the serene night.

The cop was standing in front of him when he finally looked up. Wariness had replaced the lost look in her enormous eyes. Guarded, cautious, she was pure cop and all-business.

"Mr. Barnett?" Her voice was orange-blossom honey flowing around him, slow and easy and sweet.

"That's me." He smiled with no amusement. "What'd I do, sugar-buns? Park in the mayor's spot?"

Her hands hovered over the buttoned pocket holding her notepad while she studied him. She frowned and then took out the pad and clicked her pen. Watching him, she paused for a moment.

Sullivan stared right back. Let his eyes drift to the white plastic name tag in a metal frame over her breast. Waited. His throat was dry and he wished he still smoked. Wished he had a double bourbon in front of him.

She frowned again and cleared her throat. Once more honey and sunshine poured around him as she spoke. "Mr. Barnett, I have to ask you a few questions about the threats you've received in the last three weeks."

"I didn't ask for—"

She stopped him with an outstretched, square palm. He noticed she'd bitten her nails to the quick. "I know about the car bombing—" she looked at her notes "—nine months ago?"

"That's right. December. Good for you, sugar-buns." His anger was making him as mean and nasty as a rattler kicked up from the brush. "You've done your homework. I'll let Chief Jackson know what a hell of a job his boys..." He stopped, drawing out the pause. "Sorry, boys and *girls*—"

"Women, Mr. Barnett. And men." There was grit under the honey, but her face was expressionless. The lift of one silky brown eyebrow could mean anything—or nothing.

"Yeah." Sullivan pushed himself away from his desk. He wanted to erase that bland cop look from her face. "The car bombing's old news, sugar. I'm busy, and you should be. So why don't you just hustle off and make your parking-ticket quota?" He wanted her out of his sight, off his turf and away from him.

Her peat-brown eyes glinted as she considered him. "I'm not a meter maid."

"Congratulations." He picked up the wrinkled square of paper and the phone. "Look, Officer—" he peered at her badge "—Webster." He looked again at the rectangle above her right breast and let his eyes linger before looking her right in the face. "Maggie."

Even under the heavy cotton, the tiny movement of her breast as she inhaled was visible. A foot farther away and he would have missed the infinitesimal trembling of the badge. She wasn't as poised as she appeared. The meanness coiled in him full-time now, and he realized he liked making her uneasy. He stifled the niggling voice telling him he wouldn't like himself when he thought about this scene later. "Look, Officer Maggie, I'm on deadline here," he lied. "I have to make a phone call. I told the detective who was here in December everything I know. Go root out his notes. Talk to him, not me. I don't have time."

"Mr. Barnett." She clicked her pen a couple of times, annoyance in each careful click.

Turning his back, Sullivan punched in the first three digits. So he was being rude. So what? He shut his eyes. It wasn't the little cop's fault he couldn't stand looking at her. His problem, not hers, that looking at her ate at him like acid with all that he'd lost and would never have. Tough. But too bad for her that she'd landed in his personal hell. He punched in the last number and tucked the receiver between his ear and his hunched shoulder. He listened with absorbed attention to the recorded time and temperature. Ninety-seven degrees at four p.m., a hundred percent humidity. Typical August afternoon in Florida.

A slim index finger severed the connection. The click of her pen punctuated the snap of the notepad onto his desk. Sullivan gaped, no longer interested in whether the mercury would hit 99 degrees or not.

Her hat was skewed to one side and dark curls pushed it farther off center as he watched. Across her pale cheeks, a sprinkle of cinnamon freckles stood out. "Mr. Barnett. Sit down, shut up and stop acting like a jerk."

Sullivan sat. He shut up. Her finger just missed jabbing him in the chest.

"Now—" she leaned forward and the soap-clean scent of her hair made him want to bury his face in its swirling darkness "—I have a job to do, and I can't do it without asking you some questions. Think you can drop the tough-guy routine for a few minutes so we can both finish our jobs?" She narrowed her eyes as she leaned close to him. Anger sparked in the brown depths.

He couldn't believe he'd sat down. He never backed off from cops. Or other authority figures. "I don't like bully-boy—" he smiled nastily " —or bully-*girl* cops."

"Fine. We're even. I don't like wise-ass journalists."

That faint perfume of sun-hot skin chilled by air-conditioning, and her own woman smell, vaguely familiar, drifted to Sullivan. Before he realized what he was doing, he was breathing deep of her bittersweet fragrance, taking it inside, where it circulated through his lungs, his blood, became an aching part of him. He'd read somewhere that every breath a person took had been shared with everyone else who'd ever lived. He was breathing the air that Officer Maggie exhaled, the air Lizzie had breathed, all shared in an intimacy too poignant to think about.

Suddenly so weary he could barely keep his eyes open, he leaned back. "All right. Ask your questions. Get on with it." He splayed his fingers against his eyes and tried to forget that Lizzie, too, had smelled of that same sweet soap-clean fragrance.

Officer Maggie picked up the pad and pen. With his toe, Sullivan hitched a chair over for her to sit down. He positioned the chair as far from him as he could without looking ridiculous. He didn't want to breathe in her fragrance, didn't want to be close enough to touch that springy soft hair swirling around her face.

He was walking too near the edge of control, and he was scared. Too little sleep, too much brooding, too much unending grief. He'd stayed away from liquor's easy sleep during the long, waking nights. Chalk one up for him. He rolled his shoulders. When Maggie-the-Cop left, he was going to go to Lizzie's beach house and swim until he was so tired that dreams and loneliness wouldn't keep him awake. He rubbed his eyes. "What do you need to know that I didn't tell the other cop?"

She ran her finger under the edge of her hat, resettling it. Sullivan caught once more that elusive fragrance.

"Detective Kelly's been taken off your case. I've been assigned to it."

Her gaze was impersonal, but the edge to her voice made Sullivan ask, "Why you? Why now?" A shadow swam through the depths of her eyes, turning them deeper, darker. "You're not even a detective."

"I've been promoted." The shadow flicked away. "But I'm qualified to handle the case." She didn't move or look away from him, but she clicked her pen rapidly until she saw him glance at her fidgety fingers. She stopped midclick. The final *pip* jarred her. She winced.

"All right." Sullivan scratched his chin reflectively. All his instincts were stirring; something didn't make sense to him. "Look, I didn't file a complaint. I didn't ask for an investigation. Detective Kelly called back twice after the bombing and indicated there hadn't been any progress and probably wouldn't be. Nothing that could be tied to anyone, at least. So, for all intents and purposes, the bombing investigation was closed."

Sullivan had never believed the policeman when he'd insisted that no traceable evidence had been found. He'd been there, and the explosion had thrown him flat on his face onto the gravel driveway. He'd seen metal chunks soaring sky-high in the night, fiery-red periods against the blackness. He'd smelled the burning hair on his arms, and he'd seen the snake-skin cowboy boots as someone stood near him and laughed. No, he didn't believe the police had come up empty-handed, and he thought it was real curious that the little cop had shown up now. As far as he knew, nothing had changed, but something must have. He reckoned he shouldn't trust her any more than he could pitch a piano through a basketball hoop.

"So tell me, Officer Maggie," he drawled, watching every nuance of feeling in her expressive eyes, "how'd y'all find out about this new batch of letters? Who said anything about threats?"

"Your editor did. Somebody values your skin even if you don't." Her smile was like quicksilver, flashing through her eyes, curving her lips and disappearing.

He wished she didn't look so vulnerable when she dropped her guard and smiled. Cops weren't supposed to smile like that, like sunshine fire burnishing the gulf with radiance. He swung his feet up onto his desk and rolled his chair farther away from her. "Yeah, that figures. I reckon Walker hopes I'm going to win him and the paper a Pulitzer one of these years, but can't if I'm six feet deep in a metal box. Walker's a little sentimental that way." Tapping his feet together, he continued, "Anyway, doing what I do, I get these threats all the time. My job's to find out who's got his—or *her*—" he corrected with a quick glance at Officer Maggie "—hand in the cookie jar. Can't turn over a rock or a log and not stir up maggots. Nothing new, so why're you being handed a case that's virtually busywork?"

He almost missed her wince, but he was so used to weighing everything people said, watching their every reaction so that he could sift out lies from truth, that he caught the imperceptible tightening of her eye muscles. Maggie Webster was making him very curious. Barely wet behind the ears, she had an inner steel. He was beginning to wonder why Jackson—or someone else in the good-ol'-boy network—had sicced this baby cop on him. Sullivan looked at the fine tracery of lines at the outer edges of her eyes. Maybe she wasn't such a baby cop after all. He didn't like what he was thinking one little bit.

"This investigation isn't busywork. I'll find out as much as I can. Maybe more than you want me to know." Her voice was official and smooth, the honey warmth just under the surface and not quite hidden by that iron determination. "You should never ignore death threats, Mr. Barnett. Particularly when someone's already tried to blow you up into unidentifiable bits and pieces." Notebook in hand, she shifted in the metal chair, and once more her fragrance floated in the artificial office chill. "So tell me, *Mr.* Barnett. What rock have you been poking under lately? Who's trying to kill you?"

"You want the short list or the unabridged one? You name 'em, they're on it somewhere. I have a talent for making enemies in this town, Maggie Webster. Check out any corner downtown near city hall or the courthouse. You'll find somebody who wouldn't mind one little bit if I wound up as sushi for sharks.''

"I see." She jotted something in her notebook. "What if this latest series of letters is related to the bombing? You don't seem concerned in the least."

She was cutting too close. Sullivan sighed. "Frankly, my dear," he said, mockingly, "I don't give a damn." And he really didn't. Didn't care anymore. Didn't give a damn anymore about anything.

She frowned, and the wariness in her eyes disappeared for one quick moment. "Why don't you care? Why aren't you worried about someone out there with you in his—or *her*—" she smiled with an edge of her own "—sights?"

"Sugar-buns, making friends isn't part of my job description."

She gripped her notebook at the *sugar-buns* but stayed silent, flipping her pen against one small finger.

Sullivan gave himself another point and wondered, not for the first time, why he was bothering to rattle Maggie Webster's cage. "The more people hate me, the more I figure I'm doing something right."

"Mr. Barnett." She paused for a minute before tapping her pen on the pad. "I'm going to save your rear end in spite of yourself and your smart-alecky attitude. That's *my* job." She poked her finger at him. "But let's clear up one thing first. You're not going to call me 'sugar-buns' again. You hear?" Her own drawl thickened with each syllable, like heavy cream in a mixer. "Not. Ever. Again." Tap. Tap. Tap.

"Tough lady. I'm shivering in my boots." Sullivan yawned and stared right back at her.

Without breaking their gaze or glancing at his feet, she corrected him, "Sneakers." Rising, she buttoned her notebook in her pocket and examined him for a long moment, her eyes wide and thoughtful as she added, "Maybe you're not shivering in them yet, but you will be. Count on it." She smiled so sweetly it was an insult.

The words hovered between them until she turned and walked away.

His head resting on the back of his chair, his feet still crossed at the ankles, Sullivan watched her long, narrow back and tight behind as she left the newsroom, smooth stride marked with that giveaway sway. Stopping once at Hinky's desk, she thanked him with a nod of the head, and then was gone, the automatic door swishing silently behind her blue-and-white form.

He figured she'd look back in triumph.

She did.

But triumph wasn't what he saw on her face. He saw something else, something so disturbing he couldn't put a name to it, but Maggie Webster's last, almost-shy glance left him thumping the toes of his sneakers together thoughtfully.

Outside, heat blasted Maggie in the face. Shimmering in blinding waves off the concrete sidewalk, it enveloped her. Her eyes still retained that last image of Sullivan Barnett leaning back in his chair, watching her with an unnerving emptiness in his blue eyes.

In spite of the heat, she shivered.

The reports could wait until tomorrow. She was going home. She was going to pour a tall glass of iced tea, turn the air-conditioning on high and forget about a surly, cantankerous reporter too thin for his height. Trying to generate a breeze in the humid air, Maggie shut her eyes and fanned her face with her hat. An image flashed. He'd scraped all that shaggy hair back from his angular face and secured it with a rubber band.

A red rubber band. She could see it looped around that light brown hair that clearly hadn't seen the inside of a barber shop in months.

She opened her eyes. It had been a long day. She was tired of playing games. Everything she'd done in recent memory had involved game playing, so she shouldn't be surprised if Barnett was one more player in a game where the rules changed too fast for her. Her life these days was like a life-and-death chess game on a computer. She couldn't think fast enough. She didn't trust her own reactions any more, because sometimes she felt as if she were looking in a carnival mirror where everything was changed, distorted.

Maggie stuffed her hat back onto her head. She would deal with it. She'd have to. She'd managed everything else. She could live with this nagging uneasiness. She could.

She had no choice. But no matter where she was, no matter who she was with, there was always that bewildering sense of—of *wrongness* lurking at the edge of her consciousness.

Something even more troubling had happened with Barnett. When she'd looked at his long, scowling face, reality had blurred for unending, frightening moments. She jammed her hands into her pockets. She'd lost her sense of who she was, where she was. Caught off guard, she'd covered her confusion—surely she had. But she couldn't afford any more lapses like that around him.

Taking her hands out of her pockets, she reached up and stuffed the hair sliding down her cheeks back under her hat. Keeping her guard up with Royal was hard enough, but Royal wasn't Sullivan Barnett. As smart as he was, Royal saw her the same way he'd always seen her. Barnett could complicate her life.

He saw too much. She'd hate to have him really curious about her. Right now he was annoyed with her, but he'd leave her alone to do her job.

She hoped.

"Took your time, babe. What kept you?"

She looked up into Royal's smiling face. Sunglasses masked his eyes. Surprised, lost in her thoughts, Maggie had the unsettling notion that she was looking at a stranger. She blinked, and reality slid back into focus. "Subject wasn't cooperative," she finally answered.

"Are reporters ever?"

"Not to cops." She struggled to return his smile. "What are you doing here?"

"Told you I'd pick you up when you were done."

She grimaced. "I forgot. I'm sorry, Royal."

His reply was slow in coming. "Feed me and I'll think about giving you a pass." He hung his sunglasses onto his jacket pocket and rested his broad hand on the nape of her neck.

Uncomfortable, she murmured, "Don't."

"No?" He looked down at her. For an instant, frowning, he tightened his hold. "Whatever you say, babe."

His touch was light, barely there, but despite his words, he didn't move his hand.

"Just the heat, Royal, that's all." She didn't know what else to say. She shrugged.

His hand fell away and he stepped back. "You don't like me touching you anymore, do you, Mags?"

He'd finally brought it out into the open. In a public place, at a time when she was still shaken from her encounter with Sullivan Barnett, Royal had decided to confront her.

Sleek red-gold hair, green eyes and a killer smile. Long legs in double-pleated cream slacks threaded with a slim black belt, broad shoulders under a light navy jacket cut loose enough to hide his shoulder holster, he was leaning casually against his restored '68 Mustang.

The tension in his folded arms gave him away. "It's been a long time for us, you know," he said in his deceptively easy-going manner. "Matter of fact, seems to me things have been real frosty between us since—let me think now..."

She knew to the minute when things had changed.

He unfolded his arms and straightened. "Since the accident, right, Mags? Wasn't it around then?" He waited. "Come on, Mags," he coaxed. "No cop ever forgets a shootout. Since then, right?"

Heat-stunned, frayed from the skirmish with Sullivan Barnett, she couldn't think of a solitary thing to say. Her brain had abruptly gone to sleep.

Royal pulled his sunglasses out again and swung them back and forth. "It's the truth, isn't it, Mags? Been since the accident?"

"Can we talk about this later, please?" Her mouth was chalky dry.

"Ah, but that's the whole point, right, babe? We *don't* talk about *it* anymore, do we?" He shook his head. "You can't keep putting me off, Mags, and expect me to think everything's hunky-dory."

"No. I know. But not now. Not here. We're in the middle of Main Street, Royal. This conversation—" She paused, not knowing what else to call what was coming. *Disaster,* maybe? "—can't it wait a little longer?" Looking around at the passing shoppers staring at them, Maggie added, "We've waited this long."

He pushed his glasses back onto his face, covering his cool eyes. "So we have, babe. We'll postpone it."

Relief pouring through her, Maggie sighed.

"Until we get to your house," he added gently. "We can't put off talking about what's happened any longer. I've missed you."

Stubbornness made her say, "We've seen each other almost every day."

"But it hasn't been the same, has it? You never used to keep me at arm's length and now you do."

Interrogation was Royal's strength. He'd keep at her and at her and at her and she'd finally tell him.

She took a deep breath. "You're right. I haven't been fair to you, have I?"

"We'll work our what's fair. Come on, let's get you home. Get you a cold beer. You'll feel better then."

She stroked the hot metal of the car. "Tea. Very cold. Lots of ice."

"Tea it is, then."

The sleek metal burned her fingertips. She'd loved this car from the first time she'd seen it dismantled in Royal's garage. "The car looks good. You've really worked hard on it."

"You helped, too."

Puzzled, she glanced at him. "That seems so long ago, but it wasn't, was it?" She touched the red car again. "It's really beautiful. Great paint job. Really." Thinking of the evenings in his garage, she swallowed.

Royal's fingers brushed her cheek, but she couldn't look at him.

"Don't force it, Mags. We'll wait and see, right?" He opened the car door. "Hop in." He yanked her hat off and flung it into the back seat. "It'll be okay, Mags." He tapped her lightly on her nose. "I promise."

She touched his arm as he started to shut the door. "You're a good guy, Royal."

He propped his forearms on the roof of the car and looked down at her. She wished she could see his eyes, but she was looking into the sun. Even without sunglasses, his eyes would be unreadable. She wished she knew what he was thinking.

"Bet your boots, babe," he said and smiled. "Nobody better. So long as you keep me out of temptation's way." His grin went a mile wide. As he opened the driver's door, he added, "Don't worry, we'll work this out. After all, I taught you everything you know about being a cop."

She wanted to cry.

He slid in beside her and started the engine. Adjusting the visor and removing the *Police Business* sign, he turned to her, his left hand looped over the steering wheel. His right hand lay on the back of the seat within touching distance of her arm. "I wish I'd been with you that night. You took a stupid chance stepping into the middle of that holdup." He reached out, but dropped his hand when she moved. "You were lucky." He threw the sign under his seat as he edged the car into traffic. "I should have been there."

"Why?" She shook her hair, hiding her face while she braided it into a controllable plait. Using one of her elastic ties, which she'd found on his car floor, she worked the curling tendrils into the plait, her fingers moving quickly. She concentrated desperately on her task, wanting him to drop the subject.

"If I'd been there, it wouldn't have happened."

She didn't like to talk about that night, especially not with Royal. "You couldn't have done anything I didn't do, right?" She twisted one stubborn strand into place. "Or are you telling me that I messed up and that a *guy* wouldn't have gotten himself shot? Is that what you're saying, Royal? Is it?"

He didn't answer.

Maggie wrapped the elastic tie around the end of the curling strands. The elastic was red, like Sullivan Barnett's, and she ripped it off, wincing as loose hairs caught in it. "Because if that's what you're implying, don't you *ever* say so anywhere in my hearing, Royal Gaines, or I won't be responsible for the consequences." She threw the elastic back down on the floor. "Understand?"

"That bastard shot you." Royal's mouth was a tight line. "You almost died."

"*Almost* is the key word here, isn't it? Isn't it?" She gripped his arm. "I survived."

She shook his arm. "Cops take risks. Cops get shot. I did my job. I got shot, but I'm still a good cop. I'm the same person I was before. I can still outshoot ninety-eight out of a hundred guys at the target range.''

"But not me," he said, sparing her a quick glance in spite of the traffic. "You've never outscored me, not under any conditions or with any gun," he reminded her in a grainy voice. "I'm better, and you know it. That's why if I'd—"

"I haven't changed," she interrupted, desperately trying to convince him, or herself, she wasn't sure which. She just knew she had to make Royal believe her. "I want to do my job. I can do my job if everybody will back off and leave me alone."

"Anyway, when did you rescore to qualify?" He raised his hands briefly. "All right, all right. Nobody's bugging you, Mags," he said, and his smile was good-natured. "Least of all me."

"No? It sure feels like I've got the whole department breathing down my neck! I'm tired of people watching me, *watching* me all the time, waiting for me to make a mistake, to fall apart." Her voice was shaking now no matter how many deep breaths she took, and Royal sent her a probing glance. "Okay. I was shot, I was in the hospital for a long time and now I'm fine. I'm fine!"

."Easy, babe, you're pushing it again. You don't have to convince me. I'm your partner, remember?" He pulled into the driveway of her apartment building. "After we've eaten, right? Then we'll see where we are." His smile dazzled her, but she knew she would feel better if she could only see his eyes. "In the meantime, babe, where we are is home. Your home, that is." He slid out of the car. "And you owe me a meal."

Maggie grabbed her hat and reached for the door, but he was there before her, opening it and waiting for her to get out. He never opened the door for her when they were on duty, but off duty he'd always held doors for her, taken her arm and treated her with an old-fashioned courtliness. This time, though, he didn't touch her.

He waited, as he'd promised, until after they'd eaten the hastily scrambled eggs and microwaved bacon.

His coat was off, hung neatly over a chair. He'd rolled up his sleeves while helping her scrape dishes and load the dishwasher, but he'd kept his shoulder holster on.

Folding the dishrag, he kept his back to her as he said, "I bought the ring, you know. I got it before you were shot, but afterward I never found the right time to give it to you." He snagged his jacket and fumbled in the inner pocket as he turned.

Royal had never fumbled anything in the two years Maggie had known him, and she hurt for him as she watched his fingers close around a small velvet box.

"This is as right a time as any, isn't it, babe?" He reached her in one stride and tugged her close, the ring box bumping her chin as he tilted her face to him. "Let's have one kiss, Mags, for old times' sake, and then we'll decide if you should bother opening the box."

He was moving her backward into the living room in a dance she recognized with her mind but not her heart, and she couldn't find the words to protest. She could remember loving him, but she couldn't remember *un*loving him. Sometime during the lost months, this sunshine-haired man anchoring her head and taking her mouth had become only a friend.

Frantic with loss, she pressed against him, pulled him even closer until the strain was awkward. His arousal was hard against her belly, and she moved in a pantomime of desire, willing it to sweep over her. But as she touched his smooth, corn-gold hair, she remembered Sullivan Barnett's rumpled brown shagginess, his somber, hostile face etched with lines of pain. Under her stroking fingers she felt Sullivan Barnett's rough dark hair, not Royal's sleek gold.

Royal moved his mouth urgently, seeking entrance with the teasing movement of his lips, using his tongue to coax her participation, and she tried, she tried. She wanted to love him the way she dimly recalled doing, and so she opened her mouth to the heat of his tongue, yielded to the pressure of his arms lifting her against him and pinning her to him. He moved one hand down her neck and unbuttoned her shirt, slipping his fingers inside, against her skin, and moving them in such skillful, inventive ways.

He groaned when he touched her nipple, tugging at it.

And Maggie felt nothing. Nothing at all.

Royal was the one who stopped. "It's not happening for you, is it, Mags?"

"No," she whispered, embarrassed for them both.

"That's what I thought. Making love should be a little more than one hot body and one reasonably accommodating one. You can't fake the feeling, babe. You can fake the motion, but not the notion." He ran his open palm once over her hair.

Maggie wanted to say something, but words wouldn't alter what had happened, and she owed him honesty.

Carefully holding her by the arms, he set her back from him and buttoned up her shirt. "Guess that's that." When he reached the top button, he pulled her close to his chest again in a tight embrace that said more than his words.

"I don't know what to say, Royal. I wish I could explain what happened, but I can't." She rubbed her face into his chest, finding comfort at last. He was, after all, her friend, her partner, and had been, for a brief, unreal time, her lover.

"My fault, too, because I've known all along it was over, and I didn't want to face it. I'd look into your eyes, Mags, and I couldn't find you. I hoped things would return to normal once you got out of the hospital and back on the job, but this is normal now, isn't it?" He rocked her against him, and Maggie hoped he, too, found solace in the touch.

She could have lied when she saw his eyes, could have pretended that she'd felt *something*, but honesty cut cleanly and was, in the long run, kinder. For everything he'd taught her, she owed him, and so she nodded, ending whatever they'd shared. "It feels . . . wrong, Royal."

"How can it be wrong, babe? Who are we hurting?" he asked, misunderstanding.

"Wrong for me." She knew she couldn't make him understand the odd sense of falseness that left her unresponsive to his clever touch. "There's nothing there for me."

He rested his chin on top of her head. Close to her heart, his chest rose as he sighed, and his heart slowed to a steady, reassuring beat. "That's what I was afraid of," he said, breaking the silence. He stepped back, rolling down his sleeves and fastening them before he looked at her.

Stooping, he scooped up the gray velvet box. He dropped it and grabbed it again, grinning ruefully. "It was a swell ring, babe. You would have liked it." He tossed it up and down in the air, finally lobbing it her way. "Why don't you keep it?"

Catching the tiny, rounded box with both hands, she couldn't answer. If anything, she was afraid she'd say too much, too little, and so she clutched the small package in shaking hands and waited. Her eyes filled.

"Don't cry, Mags. It's not the end of the world. I'll survive. It's only a ring," he said, his voice light with amusement, but she'd seen the clumsiness that had earlier betrayed him.

"I know." The velvet was soft against her fingers. She handed him the ring box. "But why can't I feel the way I used to? I want to!"

That was as much as she could say. If she admitted anything else to him, he'd have her in the department psychologist's office before she could turn around. She'd be back on sick leave with bills stacking up. She couldn't afford that. She couldn't tell Royal about the terrifying shifts in awareness that left her bewildered and anxious. She trusted him, of course she did—he was her *partner*. But what if she made a mistake by telling him? Torn, she said, meaning it from the bottom of her heart, "I'd give anything for things to be the way they were!"

"People change," Royal said. "That's life, Mags."

It was his smile that had her standing on tiptoe and wrapping her arms around him. In spite of everything, Royal could still smile, and that cocky grin touched her. Whatever his feelings were, he'd never been a man to wear them on his sleeve, and he wouldn't now. She kissed him as he'd said, "For old times' sake."

Brushing his hair lightly, regretfully, she said, "I have feelings for you, Royal. Can't we still be friends?"

He laughed. "*Friends?* Babe, you're something else. I don't know if we can be friends. I've never had the urge to spend long hours in bed tangled up in the sheets with my *friends*." He rubbed the velvet case against her cheek. "We'd have been something, Mags."

"Can we still be partners? At least that?" She didn't want to lose Royal from her life. He shared her past.

He snapped the lid of the case open and shut. "I guess people don't die from a broken heart."

Maggie touched his hand, closing his fingers around the ring box. "Your heart isn't broken, Royal," she said. "Not yours."

"No?"

She straightened his collar and smiled for what they'd shared. "I don't think so."

"You're probably right." His answering smile didn't quite reach his eyes. "You're asking a lot, though. We'll see how it goes." He chucked her lightly on the chin, slipped the jewel box into his jacket and walked to the apartment entrance.

Following him, she opened the door. Like a long-lost memory, night flowed in and settled around her, hot and still.

Royal rattled the doorknob and turned. Looking down at her, he grinned and shrugged, his amusement directed at himself. "One for the road, Mags, right?" He pulled her into his arms. Cupping her neck, he kissed her hard on the mouth, regret in the suddenly unpolished movement of his mouth against hers.

When she opened her eyes, she was alone in the room and her eyes were wet.

Sullivan had lost track of how long he'd stayed in the live oak-shrouded courtyard staring up at Maggie Webster's windows.

He couldn't escape the impression that he was being set up. Officer Maggie had arrived too soon after Sullivan's source had promised he could get documents linking county officials with favorable zoning regulations for certain highly placed people. In the south, old ties ran deep and strong. Like the roots of the banyan tree, those ties could erupt unexpectedly and trip the unwary. Still an outsider in Florapalma after twenty years, he knew how covert the old boys' network could be.

No, he didn't trust Officer Maggie, and seeing her with Royal Gaines outside the newspaper office had strengthened that mistrust. Gaines was literally the police department's fair-haired boy. His seemingly effortless rise through the ranks had triggered Sullivan's curiosity more than a year ago, and he'd begun keeping an eye on Royal Gaines.

Curiosity and an innate cynicism, Sullivan thought as he watched the shadows against Maggie's drawn shades. Maggie Webster and Royal Gaines. He watched their silhouettes moving soundlessly, merging, separating, merging, and remembered the sharp hunger leaping forth when he'd first seen Maggie Webster.

Mesmerized by the shadows against the shades, he couldn't look away. A voyeur to their passion, he wanted Lizzie with an unspeakable longing. Imagining the unheard murmurs, sighs, imagining the unseen touches between Maggie and the golden-haired detective, he was swamped with a loneliness so black and all-consuming that when the shadows separated one last time, breaking the connection that bound them, he hunkered down, his arms around his knees, his fists drumming against the shell driveway.

He wanted Lizzie in his arms, wanted the sweetness of her hair brushing his eyelids in the night. "Lizzie," he whispered, rubbing his empty palms against his eyes, his grief as sharp as the night he'd found her still and forever silent in the beach house.

Chapter 3

A long time after Royal left, Maggie poured another glass of iced tea and carried it to the VCR. Slipping an unlabeled tape out of a box, she inserted it into the machine and knelt down on the bare floor close to the television. Tuning to Channel 4, she pressed Play on the VCR remote control.

She'd studied the tape so often she knew it frame by frame. Tonight she needed to see it again.

In front of her in grainy, jerky motions, figures moved. Mounted high on a wall, the camera had been an indifferent observer to the tragedy it was recording in black and white.

In the corner of the screen, one small, blue-jeaned woman in a loose T-shirt stood motionless. Twenty feet away, a tall, stringy-haired man in a rubber mask stood sideways to her. He gestured with a shotgun at the clerk and the two children huddled in front of the counter.

Cautiously, her curly hair obscuring her face from the camera, the woman edged her right hand into the waistband at the back of her jeans. Pulling out a pistol, she extended it in front of her in a two-handed grip, the gun unwavering on the masked man. "Freeze! Police!" she shouted. At her words, he turned, *step one*, turned, *step two*, and fired.

Maggie peered at the screen.

Stop. Rewind. Play.
"Freeze! Police!"
Stop. Rewind. Play.
The scene never changed.

Hit in the chest, the diminutive figure of the woman spun sideways, falling, her dark hair whipping left, right, left, her lips moving, saying something lost in the explosion of shots as she fell endlessly to the floor.

On the nineteen-inch screen, Maggie saw herself struggle to her knees, saw herself brace her hands around the gun and fire twice, saw her eyes close as she slid unconscious against a pyramid of cat-food cans tumbling around her.

During her months of recuperation, she'd watched the tape several times a day. The woman who was herself—the woman with her hair, her face, her body—moved, always in slow motion it seemed, spinning, falling, spinning, with the sound of gunshots loud and real. But no matter how often she'd watched the tape during those long, confusing months, Maggie never lost the sense that the self she saw spinning and falling to the ground was someone she'd known in another lifetime.

No matter how often she played the scene and heard herself shout, "Freeze! Police!," the scene was unreal, the memory lost in her consciousness when she'd fallen to the floor, that woman with the gun alien to her.

Once more she pressed the buttons.
Stop. Rewind. Play.
"Freeze! Police!"
And the woman spun and fell, spun and fell.
The scene never changed.

In the dark kitchen of the beach cottage, Sullivan poured the last of the bourbon into the Wedgwood cup. The bottle wobbled as he put it down, then rolled to the edge of the table. He caught it one-handed.

He'd been drinking steadily over the hours since returning from Maggie Webster's courtyard, but oblivion eluded him. Rats in a flooding basement, his thoughts scrabbled ferociously to the surface and he drank to muffle their shrieks.

The liquor stung all the way down. Until tonight, he'd stayed away from liquor. Until tonight, he'd let his thoughts eat at him during the long hours from dusk to dawn. Until today, when Maggie Webster had walked into his life, he'd made it a crazy point of honor of carrying on without anesthesia.

As unlike Lizzie as two people could be, Maggie Webster had pushed him over the edge. She'd torn the lid off his submerged feelings about Lizzie. In Maggie Webster's presence, all the heartache of loving Lizzie, of losing her, of never being able to tell her he'd forgiven her the instant he'd walked out of her door, had come boiling up from the volcano of his subconscious and overwhelmed him.

As Sullivan swished the cup back and forth, it left wet circles on the wooden table. If he still believed in mercy, he would pray for blessed numbness. His Judas brain kept firing images of Lizzie, kept broadcasting sounds he didn't want to think about. He rubbed his head. Images and sounds shifted, clicked, blurred, while unconsciousness eluded him.

Under a moonless summer sky, the gulf was a flat, darker shade licking at the beach. Sullivan lifted the cup to his mouth and sipped.

He'd moved into the beach cottage because Lizzie had left it to him. Breaking his own apartment lease and boxing up his gear, clothes and computer in one afternoon, he'd shut the door behind him and headed for the cottage.

He'd moved in because it was all he had of her.

Yet there was no lingering sense of his Lizzie, not in the piles of shell fragments, not in the things she'd touched. Night after night, surrounded by Lizzie's possessions, wanting her beyond comprehension, he lay awake listening to the rhythms of the tides.

It was as if she'd never been.

But he stayed. Drinking from her cup. Rubbing the bits and pieces of sand-smoothed glass she'd collected. Sleeping alone in the bed they'd shared. What sly part of his skeptical, rational mind had let him hope some atom of his Lizzie lingered here in salt-bleached boards and sandy rooms?

The cottage was as empty as his soul.

Sullivan got up and went to the cupboard. Even in the dark he found the whiskey and opened it, drinking straight from the bottle.

Through the open windows, pine trees whispered and murmured in the night wind.

He wanted to smash the bottle to the floor, wanted to hit his head against the cabinets until he couldn't think, wanted to howl until his throat was raw.

Instead, with hands as steady as a surgeon's, he lifted the bottle again to his lips.

Air curled around his bare ankles.

A shadow drifted between the deck and the open kitchen door. In the corner of his eye Sullivan caught the movement and set the bottle on the counter. Glass rattled hollowly against ceramic tile and he edged away from the counter, behind the refrigerator. He flexed his fingers and remained still.

The rustle of pine trees, the far-off sound of a boat engine and the even hum of the refrigerator motor were all he heard.

He'd learned how to survive in six long years as a Navy SEAL, and as he moved quietly through the kitchen in the thick darkness, the shadowy figure might have been an unknown enemy from long ago, swimming toward him through muddy water.

He inhaled slowly as he cleared his mind of the blending of past and present. He waited patiently, vague curiosity stirring in him as the smell of bourbon and whiskey rose to him from his pores. The edges of his brain were becoming as mushy as jellyfish, but he would have his chance. Against the bomb planted in his car, he'd had nothing but luck. He'd attempted to manufacture an interest in the outcome, but he'd told Maggie Webster the truth. He didn't give a damn what happened to him.

Misty, the figure hovered in the dark.

Salt air and pine trees, a sweetness on the barely moving air.

"You might as well come in," Sullivan said, staying in the darker shadows of the kitchen.

Lightly, lightly, the figure moved toward him.

The wind bore that faint scent, familiar and piercing, to Sullivan as he waited. Flower-scent, Lizzie fragrance, drifting to him as he heard the heavy thud of his heart over the quiet sound of the gulf unfolding against the beach. Bewildered, he rubbed his eyes, laboring for comprehension.

Memories and loss. Fragrance he'd known in her hair, on her pillow, on his skin. Clinging to his sanity in an alcohol-induced haze, Sullivan felt his world turn inside out.

"Lizzie?" he whispered, afraid to move. The scent surrounded him, hung in the air. "Lizzie?" he repeated, reaching her in two strides.

Waking from an unending nightmare, he touched her and she was real, real, and in his arms. Doubting his senses, he touched her. Satin skin slipping under his fingers. Against his heart she fit as she always had, the touch of her flooding the emptiness in his soul.

In the darkness he saw her, knew her and was awake at last with her in his arms and the future shining ahead of them.

"I had such a dream, sweetheart. So crazy," he whispered, bending to her, shaking as he breathed in the essence of her fragrance. He ran his hands over her, slipping his hands down her slender arms to join his fingers with hers. "You'd never believe how real." Sullivan pressed her hands to his heart and closed his arms around her in the dreamlike dark. He couldn't pull her close enough and his heart was thundering so hard he couldn't hear what she murmured as he kissed her, kissed her, again and again, remembering his dream and its bitterness like salt cast on the fertile earth, destroying everything in his life.

Her lips were soft and warm. His arms were around her waist, his fingers gripping her shirt, and he was trembling with need, all the need he'd buried in his dream. She was here, chasing away the sad ghost of his dreams. Slicking her hair back, he breathed deeply of her remembered fragrance. She said something as he lifted her hair to his face, but he'd brought all that soft hair to his eyes, his nose, his lips, and he was raising her in his arms, shudders rolling through him. "Ah, Lizzie, I dreamed I'd lost you, that you'd gone and left me behind. You could never be that cruel. I should have known it was only a nightmare, not real."

He bent his head to her warm skin—how cold it had been in his dream—and took her lips again. He was frenzied in his need. Lips and skin weren't close enough, and desperate with hunger, he plunged deeply into the cave of her mouth, seeking *her.* And as he tasted her, her lips the sweetest honey as they blossomed and opened for him, it still wasn't close enough.

And like dark honey her voice surrounded him. "Mr. Barnett."

She was in his blood, his soul, everywhere. He was holding her—he could feel her heart drumming against his own—but it wasn't Lizzie's voice.

Honey sliding over him, and it wasn't Lizzie. "Mr. Barnett," he heard her say again, nothing making sense to him with the sound of Maggie Webster's voice.

Sullivan couldn't let her go. Trapped between waking and dreaming, he was lost. Dreaming. Waking. Like a bull in the pasture tormented past endurance, he shook his head.

"Lizzie," he muttered, burying his face once more in Maggie Webster's thick, springy hair.

"Mr. Barnett."

He couldn't turn her loose and he couldn't keep holding her. No, not Lizzie's voice. Maggie Webster's husky alto. In a freezing wind, he shook until his teeth chattered, able to understand only that he was pie-eyed, brain-dead drunk and he hadn't been dreaming after all.

Cruel, the awakening.

His eyes shut, he let her slide to the floor. She was smaller than Lizzie, curved where Lizzie had been thin. His palms brushed the sides of her breasts, dropped to the swell of her hips. The top of her head bumped his chest, her hair catching in the bristles of his beard. Sullivan slipped his finger under the strands. Silk coiled around his finger. He pressed a strand against his lips. The silky filaments clung, burned, drifted away as she turned from him.

"Where's the light switch, Mr. Barnett?"

Though he didn't answer, her shadow moved easily through the room and light exploded in his eyes. He blinked as he looked at her.

Her face was strained. She had one hand against the plastic wall switch. With her other hand she hooked her hair behind her ears.

Pictures clicked randomly in his head. Storm-cloud hair against one pale cheek. The other reddened by the scrape of his beard. The rose bloom of her lips where he'd kissed her.

In the grip of an illusion more powerful than reality, he'd marked her with his hunger.

Sullivan backed away until his shoulders were against the wall. Sliding down, he plunked solidly on the floor, his legs straight out. Grinding his fists into his eyes, he bent his head forward because he couldn't bear to look at Maggie Webster when all he wanted was Lizzie. He dug his fists into his eyes until stars exploded and he could finally speak. "Officer Maggie." His voice was rusty.

"Yes." She dropped her hands to her side. "I'm sorry. You were expecting someone else."

His angry bark of laughter surprised him. "I wasn't expecting anyone." Some stubborn part of his brain still functioned despite the alcohol, and he strove to make sense of what had happened. Maggie Webster had no business being on his deck, and even in his woozy state, he knew he wanted an explanation. "Did nosy little Goldilocks come looking for porridge and wind up in the wrong cottage?"

"Don't play mind games with me, Mr. Barnett. Your reporter-with-an-attitude act doesn't impress me. It didn't this afternoon. It doesn't now."

"Shucks," he managed to say. "And here I was hoping you were ready to run for the woods, Goldilocks."

Her lips tightened, rose turning white at the corners. "This isn't a fairy tale, Mr. Barnett. You're not Papa Bear, and, in spite of your best attempts, you're sure not the big, bad wolf." She jerked her chin up, and her unruly hair swung free. One strand lay dark on her cheek and she shoved it again behind her ear.

Sullivan wiped his mouth. The burn of that wild strand lingered on his lips. "To what do I owe this dubious pleasure, then, Officer Maggie?" he drawled, clinging to consciousness as his words slurred.

Her shrug pleated the red T-shirt over small breasts, and the willful curl sprang free, brushing the corner of her mouth.

"In the neighborhood, huh?" Sullivan nodded sagely. He planted his hands against the floor, preparing to stand up and show her the quick way out. "Not that it hasn't been a pleasure having you drop in—" he slumped back to the floor "—but it hasn't been. And don't try to tell me you were taking a nighttime stroll down my beach because I wouldn't believe you if you swore it on a stack of Bibles."

Two Maggies wavered in front of him. He shut one eye. "The better to see you with, my dear," he said and his head fell forward, the oblivion he'd sought so diligently finding him too late.

When Sullivan's head sagged, his fierce gaze releasing her at last, Maggie let out a whoosh of air and gulped. She felt as if she'd been holding her breath for minutes. She understood the dazed look in his eyes. She knew he was drunk. She'd seen the liquor bottles. What she couldn't explain was that anger swirling in his alcohol-blurred blue eyes.

She could understand his being ticked off. He'd said he wasn't expecting anyone, but clearly he'd lied. His reaction had been stronger than disappointment and irritation.

Deep in the ocean blue of his eyes she'd seen stark betrayal, bleak and devastating, as he stared at her in the kitchen light.

Sullivan Barnett was angry and bitter. She didn't understand him one bit, and she'd kissed him.

Shivering and hot, she'd gone still as his tongue touched hers, his touch tugging at something so basic that she'd gone under without a whimper, surrendering to his hunger, kissing him back as though her soul depended on answering his insistent demand.

She hadn't lost herself in Royal's kiss.

Sullivan's arm jerked. Maggie didn't move as she watched his twitching fingers. The beat of her heart quickened to restless fluttering as if he drummed relentlessly on it, compelling entrance. When his fingers lay quiet, Maggie touched her wrist. Her pulse was thudding as if she'd run three miles.

If she were smart, she'd turn and run back down the beach as fast as her feet could move.

She made the mistake of glancing around the cottage. White dust sugared the surface of shelves, but the sink was clean. A partially filled whiskey bottle was the only thing on the blue-and-green-ceramic counter that made an L from the sink to the refrigerator. Not even thinking, she wandered past Sullivan to the refrigerator. A grocery bag lined the blue plastic garbage container where he'd tossed a soup can and an empty bottle.

A scallop-shell magnet, its bottom ridges chipped, held a yellowing piece of newspaper to the refrigerator door. Tentatively, she touched the dried paper and flattened it.

As was usual with obituaries in small towns, it included a picture, the name in bold print underneath. Maggie thought she would have liked the woman smiling back at her from the fading picture. Thin-faced with high cheekbones, she'd tilted her head and smiled tenderly at the photographer. Falling smoothly to the base of her long, slim neck, her fair hair captured and held the light in its gleaming strands. It was one of those pictures where the eyes seemed to look directly at the observer, and behind the shyness in those trusting, clear orbs, mischief peeked at Maggie.

She touched the face, smiling back at Lizzie O'Connell. Under her finger, the vibration from the humming refrigerator made the picture seem to move.

"Got a search warrant, Officer Maggie?" The slurred drawl tickled her ear.

She froze. Dropping her hands, she turned to face Sullivan Barnett. "Do I need one?"

Swaying slightly, he'd braced himself with one hand on top of the refrigerator. With the other, he straightened the magnet that had shifted when she'd touched the picture. He didn't look at her as he concentrated on making the hinged edge of the shell perfectly level. "Oh, yes, sweet Maggie, I think you do if you're going to come uninvited into my house and search it. Yes . . ." he nodded thoughtfully, " . . . I think that's still the law. Or has the law changed since I last checked it?" His forefinger stroked the side of the picture. Then he looked right at Maggie, animosity in his brilliant blue eyes.

There was nothing she could say, but she didn't look away from his cold eyes.

"Illegal search and seizure, isn't it, Officer?" His gaze swept her from head to bare feet. "But I'll be damned if I can tell what you seized. Or did you bring something to plant?" He patted her pockets. His fingers closed around what he'd discovered there and dragged it out.

Maybe it was the remote dislike in his face, maybe the feel of his palm skimming her hip as he reached inside her pocket, but Maggie shivered, regretting the impulse that had driven her from the sanctuary of her apartment.

"Cat got your tongue, little Maggie?" he whispered, menace in his low drawl. His long arms surrounded her as he placed his closed fist on the refrigerator. "Where's all that reckless courage now?"

Carved in hard lines, his mouth was too close to her as he whispered, and she remembered what had happened when he'd kissed her by mistake. Darting under his arms before he lowered them, she grabbed the back of his belt and pushed him none too gently against the refrigerator.

"Look, Barnett, I'm not dumb. I know what you're trying to imply—"

"Not *trying*. Saying." He turned easily, freeing himself from her grip, but he leaned back on the refrigerator and folded his arms. "If you want it spelled out, I think you're trying to set me up, Officer Maggie." He held his fist to her and opened it finger by finger until he revealed what he'd yanked from her pocket.

"Seaweed? You think I'm trying to frame you with dried seaweed?" Maggie slapped the shreds to the floor.

"Seaweed," he echoed, frowning. He stared at the floor, and swayed once as he started to reach down but changed his mind.

"What did you think it was? Grass?"

"Yep." He straightened to his full height. "I sure did." He strolled past her to the kitchen table. He could almost have passed a straight-line test, but the *oomph* he made as he sank into the chair gave him away.

She knew he was trying to figure out what had happened, but even drunk as he was, he didn't lose the thread of his accusations. "Maybe you've already stashed the evidence somewhere I won't find it until it's too late."

"Don't be an idiot." She didn't want to explain what she was doing at his house or why she'd stayed during the moments he was unconscious.

"I'm skunk drunk, but not stupid."

"Really? You could have fooled me. I think it's pretty stupid to leave all your doors and windows open after you've gotten eight threatening letters and had your car blown to kingdom come."

"Stupid? Whatever you say." The expression in his eyes was so lost that she knew stupidity hadn't made him leave his house open to the wind and whoever wandered by. "But you still haven't explained what you're doing here, Officer Maggie." He kicked out the chair facing him. It teetered, and he watched it settle before he caught it with his foot and continued, "Sit down and tell me."

"If I don't?" Maggie faced him and folded her arms. She'd made a mistake, but she could handle it. Now that he was five feet away from her, she could. .

Even slurred with drink, the rhythm of his voice was smooth. "I've messed up big time the last few months." One side of his mouth drew up as he added, "But the pen—or chip, I reckon— still has some power in this town." His eyes narrowed, he pushed the chair once more toward her. "You don't want me writing about you in my column, sugar-buns."

Maggie didn't give an inch, but for the moment she ignored the deliberate provocation of "sugar-buns." "I'd survive." She smiled. "But would you? All six-foot-four, hundred-and-eighty-pound you harassed by five-feet-three, hundred-and-five-pound me? Golly gee, if that story appeared in the paper, wouldn't you look silly?" She widened her eyes in mock innocence.

"You haven't been following the reports I've been working on, have you?" He rocked the chair invitingly. "It's about corruption in beautiful Florapalma, Gateway to the Gulf." His mouth quirked again. It would have passed for a smile in anyone else, but didn't with those accusing blue eyes staring at her. "You know what I'm talking about, don't you, Officer Maggie? Corruption involving payoffs to people who have land to sell, loans to lend, protection to offer? You know, like protection by the brothers and sisters in blue?" He rocked back in his chair. "Sure you won't sit down and have a little chat with me? Might save us both a lot of embarrassment, don't you think?"

"If we *chat*, do you think you can drop the 'sugar-buns'? I've already warned you about that." She stalked to the table. She didn't know what he was talking about, but since he seemed to think she did, she'd stay until she found out what he was referring to.

Momentarily diverted, he looked at her bare legs and concentrated on them. And such concentration. If he'd slid his finger over her thighs and ankles and down to her bare toes, she couldn't have been any more aware of him. With his blue-eyed gaze moving over her so intently, she couldn't take a deep breath. Light-headed, she couldn't move, couldn't get enough air into her lungs.

His eyes lingered at the edge of her shorts and he frowned. "Officer Maggie, why aren't you in your little cop outfit?"

She wanted to tug the sides of her shorts down, wanted to hide her naked feet. If it killed her, she wouldn't give him the satisfaction of letting him know he'd rattled her. He'd finally pushed her too far. She fixed him with her best cop-on-the-beat glare. "Look, you may be drunk, and I shouldn't be here—I admit it. But I've been promoted. I'm a detective, not an officer. I'm not in my cop clothes because I'm off duty, and I'm just about ticked off enough right now to haul you in and book you."

"Ah." He pinched his ear. "Got a charge thought up yet?"

"Resisting an officer."

"Oh, Maggie, you walked right into that one." Both sides of his thin, mobile mouth lifted, but his eyes were still cold. "Neither one of us resisted, did we? I know I didn't. Seems to me you kissed me right back. Very nicely, too, I might add."

Maggie could feel the blood roaring in her ears, heating her cheeks. "You win." She yanked the chair away from his foot and sat down. "Ask your questions." She could pull her hair out by the roots, she was so mad at herself. "But you ought to think about this habit you have of shoving chairs at people."

She was furious with him, but it was herself she could smack for winding up in Sullivan Barnett's kitchen. For kissing him. Maggie hooked her toes in the rung of the chair. "Come on, time's wasting, Barnett. What do you want to know?"

"I asked already." He rocked on his chair, his long legs letting him tip dangerously.

"So remind me."

The rising wind rattled an aluminum chair on the deck. The incoming tide had a heavier sound as it rolled onto the beach.

"It's time for good little girls to be home tucked in bed. So why aren't you, Maggie-the-Cop?"

Maggie hadn't been a little girl for a long time, but she would have given a hundred dollars to be home in her own bed. She hadn't landed herself in this mess by being a bad little girl, but by being an impulsive woman who should have known better. Well, she'd known, but she'd still yielded to that stupid impulse and stepped up onto Sullivan's deck. "It's a long story," she began, sorting out what to tell him, what to omit, wary of the cynicism still sharp behind the alcohol glaze in his eyes.

"They always are," Sullivan said. His hands resting on his head cast shadows over his eyes, hiding them as he rocked slowly back and forth like a metronome. "I've never heard a short one."

"You could rile a saint," Maggie said, shifting irritably on the chair.

"But you're not a saint, are you, Maggie? You're a cop." Back and forth, back and forth, never missing a beat. "A cop who needs a real good reason for showing up at my house."

"I went for a walk." Maggie folded her hands in her lap. If she weren't wearing shorts, she'd cross her legs and dare him to think he was getting to her. Let him look at her legs and think about anything except the topic he was doggedly pursuing.

"A walk? Tell me another one," he jeered. "I know where you live, Detective Maggie. You didn't go for a walk at midnight fifteen miles from your apartment."

"No. I went shopping."

Sullivan made a rude noise.

"I needed milk and bread."

"Nothing open on the mainland?" He paused as if thinking. "Jack's Supermarket on 63rd? Andy's Swift-Serv? When did they quit staying open all night?"

"I decided to take a ride down the island, and I remembered I needed milk for my cereal." Maggie kept her hands still with an effort. She knew Sullivan was watching her closely. In his place she would have been, too. Suspects gave themselves away with the smallest reactions. But she wasn't a suspect. She simply didn't want to tell this long-legged, persistent man where she'd gone or why, and since she couldn't explain to herself why she'd climbed onto his deck, she sure didn't have a chance of making him understand.

"Keep talking." Back and forth, back and forth he rocked.

Maybe he'd get seasick. She sighed. How much longer could he stay upright? She'd give him facts, but not reasons.

"So I stopped at the Quik-Deli." She shrugged. "That's all."

Sullivan's chair hit the floor with a thunk.

He was watching her blearily, and she saw his curiosity fighting the alcohol. She knew which side she was on. His thick eyebrows rose. "Still doesn't make sense, Maggie Webster." As he said her name, he frowned. "Webster," he repeated, rolling the syllables slowly on his tongue as he fought the incoming tide of unconsciousness. "I *know* you." He struggled to stand up. "Don't I?" He thwacked his hand against his forehead, battling the tide. "I know something about you."

Maggie was married to her chair seat. With Sullivan Barnett leaning over the table, his hooded bright eyes intent on her every reaction, she knew she wasn't going anywhere until he fell asleep.

"It'll come to me. Damn." He sank back into the chair, slumping onto the table. "Something I should know." His head dropped onto his arm. "You stopped at the Quik-Deli?" His gaze sharpened and she couldn't breathe as he added slowly, "Webster. You're the cop who was shot at the Quik-Deli, aren't you?" He fought to sit upright, his bare elbow slipping on a wet spot on the table. "Oh God. I was there. I saw you." He was up and moving faster than she could have expected, and he had her wrist clasped in his fingers. "I was there when they took you off in the ambulance. The paramedic said you wouldn't make it to the hospital."

She pulled at her hand, but he gripped her tightly, desperately.

Sullivan felt her slim bones twist in his grasp as reality and shadows fused. Her pulse was rapid against his thumb. Even with alcohol fogging his brain, he grasped the one essential fact that mattered to him, the one fact that he could understand.

"Now I remember." he said, staring at her frightened brown eyes. "The shooting. It was that week in November."

She was breathing rapidly and her red shirt moved with the frantic trembling of her breasts against his forearm. That shiver of red. Her blood had been dark red against the brightly colored labels on the cans lying around her.

He leaned forward, searching for that elusive sense of familiarity. Her small, square face was inches away from his, her hair lashing him with softness and that flowery scent. Everything tumbled in his brain—sense and nonsense, half-seen images and old memories shifting into focus. "I wrote the story about you, Maggie Webster. Cop Shot. Saves Two Children. Fights for Life. I was *there.*''

He stared at her. Her wrist twisted once in the tight cuff of his fingers.

Her eyes were wide and terrified.

Chapter 4

Leaning over Maggie, Sullivan drowned in the darkness of her pupils which were so dilated they were almost black in her blanched face. They engulfed him, their darkness growing until the room filled with shadows and mystery, her eyes the only reality, her terror reaching out to him, feathering his skin until goose bumps lifted the hairs on his arms.

Under his thumb the skin of her wrist was the only warmth in all the numbing cold rushing down on him, cold filled with terror and confusion and unbearable loss.

He shivered.

Staring at the deepening brown of her eyes rimmed by that band of deep black, seeing the specter of himself staring back, he struggled to follow the thread of an idea that flickered in and out of his consciousness.

Something was wrong about Maggie's terror—too much terror for his simple questions. The idea wavered in front of him. Terror didn't fit. Sparked by an erratically firing cell in his anesthetized brain, curiosity stirred. He lifted his free hand to her chin, anchoring it as he drifted in the dark river of her eyes.

She was utterly still. The faint movement of her breasts under the thin red cotton ceased as if she had momentarily forgotten how to breathe. In a strange paralysis, his hearing preternaturally keen, Sullivan heard the rasp of his own breathing, the rattle of sand blown against the deck. Heard, too, the slide of his thumb over the soft skin of her inner wrist as he tightened his grip.

Then she blinked and he lost the shape of that illusive idea fluttering formless at the edge of his awareness. For a moment, clarity sharpened the cloudy edges, but it dissolved, taking the idea with it. Gone. He frowned, regretting the bourbon for the first time tonight. Trying to frame his thoughts, he struggled for words and failed. "I did," he insisted finally, drunken persistence substituting for logic in his tired brain. "I wrote about you."

"Congratulations. I'm sure it was a terrific article. Sorry I missed it." Her voice was pitched a tone higher, but she looked straight at him, ease in every line of her body, her smile casual and mockingly courteous, the condescension of the very sober for the very drunk.

For a moment he was sure he'd imagined that glaze of terror.

Then the skin at the corner of her eyes stretched, giving her away.

Like a dog with a bone, Sullivan hung on. "No scrapbook filled with pictures and newspaper clippings for you, huh?" He flopped her hand up and down, reluctant to release that warm wrist, enjoying her resistance that told him—what? He frowned again, feeling stupid. "Everybody keeps scrapbooks. People collect mementos." Like a windshield wiper, his thumb stroked against her skin, and he felt the jump of her pulse.

"No." She jerked her hand away. "I didn't make up a scrapbook. I don't need trophies."

"Why not, I wonder?" Sullivan watched the spread of pink over her cheeks as he continued. Her hands lay loosely in her lap, but he saw the twitch of her little finger. "It's not every day a cop saves the lives of two little kids, Maggie. And lives to tell about being shot, lives to tell about her last moments. I think you'd want to remember that day."

Uneasiness pinched her face. "Some people might. Not me. I don't think about it. It's over. Done with. In the past."

She was lying. He smelled it.

She rubbed her side and abruptly stood up. "I did my job, what I'm trained to do. Nothing more. Any cop would have done the same."

Her response was mechanical, as if she'd said the same thing so often it no longer had meaning for her. He wondered how many times she'd responded with the same words and phrases. Her answer was too rehearsed. Too controlled. The kind of answer that always hid something—sometimes something interesting, sometimes not. But in his experience, it always hid something the other person didn't want him to know, and for that reason alone her answer became irresistible to him.

She should have waited out the silence, he thought, but she rushed into repeating herself, her words again automatic. "I'm a cop. I did what I had to do. That's all."

"Is it?" On the prowl, Sullivan unfolded himself from the chair, not ready to see her leave in spite of the fatigue and confusion overwhelming him. "You've put it all behind you, huh? Damn, but I have a hard time buying that, Detective Maggie." He looked down at the heavy thickness of her hair. A silver clip jammed into the unruly curls winked back at him.

"That's your problem, not mine, Mr. Barnett."

As she took a determined step toward the door, Sullivan shifted, blocking her. No longer certain what he wanted from her, knowing only that she was lying through her pretty little teeth, and goaded by instinct, he could only keep butting his head against the wall of her resistance. Halting her quick shift away from him, he gripped her shoulders. The light threw their shadows onto the deck, merging them into one, his shadow engulfing her smaller form. Pain pierced him in an exquisite ache.

"Why don't you want to talk about that night, Maggie?" He touched the gleaming silver clip. It was cool against his fingertip. A satin-smooth strand of hair snagged on the rough skin of his finger and curled around it. Its softness surprised him, and he rubbed it between his thumb and forefinger. "Tell me about that night, Maggie." In spite of himself, his voice was scratchy with memories.

Lifting her chin, she grimaced. The strand of hair slipped free of his outstretched finger and curled over the barrette. "I don't think so." She shook her head and silver winked and glittered.

"Why not?" That sparkle of silver beckoned him like a light shining in the rich darkness of her hair.

"Why should I?" she countered, and the wariness in her voice broke the spell between them.

"Be an interesting story." Under his cupping palms, she shrugged, her movement sending his hands down the curves of her arms. He couldn't get over how warm she was. Her skin had an inner glow that seduced him, made him want to pull her close and bury himself in that warmth until he dissolved the cold knot inside him. He slid his palms upward, her warmth drawing him nearer and nearer.

Irritation quickened her speech. "That's all that matters, isn't it? The story. You're only one more reporter who wouldn't think twice about shoving your tape recorder in a man's face and asking him how he feels while he's watching his home burn down with his wife and children in it." She pushed against his chest.

Catching her hand, Sullivan closed his fist around it. So much heat and energy in that one small hand radiating into him. "I'd think twice about it."

"But you've done it." Her hair swung forward, hiding her face, but he heard the accusation. It wasn't the first time he'd heard it, and he didn't like it any better now.

"Yeah." He dropped her hand and leaned against the door. The fragrance from her hair lingered in the air around him with her every movement. He didn't think he could bear these memories flowing in with the early morning shadows and the lingering sweetness of her perfume. "And I'd do it again if I had to."

She stepped back. "Like I said, just another reporter."

"Like you said." Only the dying embers of curiosity kept him upright in his bone-dissolving weariness and pain. It was that same fading curiosity, though, that made him ask, "Between us, Detective Maggie, why won't you tell me about the rest of that night? About what happened afterward?"

"You're the one who's making it into the crime of the century, not me." She folded her arms tightly across her chest. "Why?"

"Golly gee, damn, I don't know." Growing tired of the game, he yawned. "Inquiring minds want to know and all that. Fatal curiosity, I reckon." He yawned again, his jaw popping.

Tilting her head, she studied the floor for a minute before looking up and fixing him with a steady gaze. "Well, we all know what curiosity did to the cat, don't we?"

"Oh swell, Detective, a warning?"

She rubbed that spot on her left side. The drag of the T-shirt across her breast outlined the design of lace underneath.

The idea of tough little Maggie in lace snagged his flagging attention. Sullivan straightened. "Or a threat?"

"Look, you're in no condition tonight—" she looked out at the deck, where the shadows were growing dimmer in the pre-dawn "—this morning, rather, to make sense, so I'm going to let that pass. I didn't come here to threaten you, to set you up, to trap you. I didn't come here for any of those reasons, no matter how it looks to you. I just want to solve this case, and believe it or not, I'm on your side."

"No," Sullivan said, enunciating each word carefully, "I damn sure wouldn't believe it."

"Why not?" Her challenge was halfhearted, as if she, too, were tired of the contest.

"You have too many secrets, Detective, and secrets make me itch."

"And you always scratch whatever itches, I suppose?"

In the mix of natural and artificial light, her face was tired and strained. The light emphasized lines he'd barely noticed before. She was older than he'd figured earlier today. Thirty-something, not the mid-twenties he'd assumed. In her rumpled weariness, she made him think of other mornings, mornings not spent playing head games with a cop with secrets. It was the memory of all those other mornings that burred his voice, not the sight of a Maggie suddenly vulnerable. "You bet I do. Scratch and scratch. Until the itch is gone." Deliberately vulgar, he scratched his belly and watched her eyes follow the movements of his fingers. Leaving the tips of his fingers flat against his stomach inside his jeans, he hooked his thumbs over his waistband and shifted his weight to one hip.

The unconscious drift of her gaze across his skin had him growing heavy and hot. He jammed his clenched fists under his armpits and leaned back against the door, crossing his legs, hoping she hadn't noticed his jeans growing snugger by the minute. He'd been about as dumb as a rock. The impulse to irritate her had sure rebounded on him. Served him right, he thought sourly. He'd made a mistake.

She sighed, the droop of her shoulders touching him when he didn't want to feel anything for her except annoyance. A little anger, too.

"Why do you keep picking at something that happened months ago?" She asked finally. "It's yesterday's news. Nobody would be interested now in what happened to me."

"Oh, I am, Detective. Very." Sullivan whispered the words into the stillness, her vulnerability blunting his aggression.

"Why?"

He didn't need to think about his answer. He gave the one that had spurred him as long as he could remember, the answer that made him a reporter. "I don't like secrets."

"So you dig and dig until you find someone's private hell, some pathetic little secret, digging and digging until you find the one thing someone's afraid of showing to the world? Then you write that secret in big black type for the whole world to laugh at or gossip about for an hour or two while you zip merrily off to the next story? Don't you ever get tired of digging around in the dirt?" Her anger chased away her tiredness and her vulnerability and struck an answering chord in him.

"Is that your secret, Maggie—fear? Is that what you're hiding?" It made sense to him. "You killed a man and now you're spooked? If it's not that, what are you afraid of?"

"Not one damned thing I'd tell you." She whirled away.

She moved so quickly he didn't catch her until she was out on the deck. Reaching toward her, he snagged her around her narrow waist, halting her forward rush so abruptly that her fanny jammed against the notch of his jeans and settled against the swelling under his snug zipper.

If she'd moved carelessly, bumping against him, he would have known the awareness thrumming between them had been all in his mind. It was her careful edging away that told him she was smart enough to tiptoe past sleeping tigers.

"Let me go." Ice sheathed that husky voice.

He did. He was all for letting some sleeping tigers lie himself.

After raising his hands in the universal sign of surrender and releasing her, Sullivan rubbed his knuckles over his head in exhausted resignation. As she stepped down the deck, her shoulders were as straight as if she expected to catch a bullet between them any minute. That resolutely stiff line of her spine made him ask, "One last question, Detective?"

"Yes?" Turning, she rested her hand on the wooden railing. Tilting her head, she waited, shoulders back, spine poker stiff—one tough cookie who wasn't about to let him intimidate her.

Sullivan shut his eyes against the image of big-eyed, brown-haired Maggie with that look of forlorn courage. Some tough cookie, all right. So many times he'd seen Lizzie braced against this railing, her straight, silky hair tossed every which way by the gulf breeze, her smile widening as she saw him, that sweet smile shining in her luminous gray eyes.

In the warm August morning, Maggie's face wasn't the one he wanted turned up to him.

But it was Maggie's guarded expression he saw when he opened his eyes, and so he asked his question. "What was it like, that night?"

"What was it like?" She curled her fist against her chest. "What was *what* like? Killing a man? Being shot? Almost dying? What precisely is it you're so damned curious about, Mr. Barnett?" Her voice rose in a tense whisper.

What he wanted to know was what it had been like for Lizzie, those last moments without him. In some twisted kind of logic, what he wanted was absolution from Maggie because he'd been at the Quik-Deli with her and not with Lizzie when he should have been. What he wanted with every breath he took was to have Lizzie next to him. Impossible, all of it. And even knowing, he couldn't stop himself. "Do you dream about that night, Detective? Does it haunt you?"

"No." Water lapped quietly against the beach. Looking out to the gulf, she spaced her words in a husky echo of the water against sand. "But if I do, it's my business, no one else's. Inquiring minds may want to know, but nobody buys my soul for fifty cents at the newsstand. Nobody."

Sullivan watched her throat working as she swallowed again, her face closed against him.

"You've had your question." She slapped her hand against the railing. The thump was loud in the hush of dawn. "Now I have a couple. What makes that night so important to you? Why didn't you follow up on the story before now if it was so important to you?"

He shrugged, memories of that rainy November night pressing in on him.

Damn you, Lizzie, I could almost hate you....

"Cat got *your* tongue, Mr. Barnett?" She waited until it was clear he wasn't going to answer before she hurled more questions, the words tumbling forth so rapidly that his sluggish brain couldn't keep up. "Any fears and regrets of your own that you'd just as soon stayed buried?"

It'll be a long time before I forgive you, Lizzie.

Don't come back, Sullivan.

"Why don't you think about what's going on inside your own head for a while instead of digging in mine?" She whirled away, the force of her anger sending her hair tumbling around her.

Lost in the past, he still heard Maggie's final words. Fear and regret? If there had been any laughter left in him, he would have roared at the irony. Oh, yes, he knew those two companions. Knew a soul-destroying fear that Lizzie might have been frightened without him, corroding regret for carelessly hurtful words, regret for all the things he'd left unsaid. A groan rose, gut deep.

Taking a shot in the dark, Detective Maggie had hit the bull's-eye. Oh, yeah, there were things he'd like to forget, too. He had his own ghosts. He'd let Maggie keep hers.

As for the pricking of his curiosity, well, it was a small thing, after all. He was the only one interested in that night, and it couldn't have any connection with what was going on now. He'd been there when she was shot. That explained the intensity of his reaction to her. That was all. It meant nothing.

She was what she said she was. A detective assigned to his case, nothing more. No layers of motives involved. A clear-cut, simple situation. Nothing hidden, nothing murky. Everything what it seemed.

Maybe.

But he'd never believed in coincidences.

He'd let her go through the motions, but he'd watch her every step of the way. The occasional show of vulnerability could be an act, probably was, and while he might not give a rat's damn what happened to him anymore, he found himself surprisingly reluctant to let Maggie-with-the-big-brown-eyes play him for a fool.

Stepping slowly off the deck, his knees creaking, Sullivan bent down to pick up the slash of silver sparkling in the half shadows of the early morning sunlight. Holding the barrette carefully in his hand, he watched the small, sturdy figure trudge northward, the line of her footprints filling with the incoming tide and disappearing until she vanished in the curve of island and morning mist.

For a long time he stared after her. Finally, his eyes scratchy and tired, he turned and pulled himself up the deck stairs, so drained he barely managed to make it to the bedroom, where he collapsed across the bed and burrowed his face into Lizzie's pillow, the clean smell of pine trees and saltwater filling the room, mingling with the echo of a sweeter perfume.

For the first time in months he slept, deeply and dream-lessly.

With the back of her wrist, Maggie rubbed the drop of sweat off the end of her nose. Twenty-five yards down range, she could see the target silhouette clearly, with its three new holes in the center of the chest area. Fourteen orange stickers covered the chest where she'd emptied the first clip.

She was on the second magazine and still shaking. Her palms were slick with sweat and she'd rubbed them on the seams of her jeans over and over in a futile effort to keep them dry. A thin line of sweat trickled down her spine and soaked her waistband. Her jaw ached from clenching it to keep her teeth from chattering. Although muffled by the ear protectors she wore, the constant thuds from firing had given her a headache to end all headaches.

Gulping air, she held on to the shelf in front of her where she'd carefully placed the 9 mm Smith and Wesson 459. Two clips lay next to it, one empty. After her last shot, the slide had locked back, the breech in open position. Now she flicked the safety on with hands shaking so badly she was afraid she wouldn't be able to press the button hard enough.

She could still qualify. She'd hit her target again and again. But if the sergeant in charge of the police pistol range ever saw her sweating and shaking like this, he'd have her on desk duty before she could remember her name. 'Stress-related assignment' would be how they'd put it. For that reason, she'd avoided the police range. This wasn't the police range.

After leaving Sullivan Barnett's beach house, she'd gone home, changed and collapsed into sleep. Later she'd awakened abruptly, with her heart pounding and her mouth dry. Unable to go back to sleep, she'd gone, as she had every day for the past month since she'd been back on duty, to a public range. Going to different ones, she'd hoped to avoid seeing anyone she knew. Before she showed up for her qualifying test, she had to get back to her normal self, whatever that was.

She hadn't told Royal about her forays into the pistol ranges around the county.

He would have helped her. She could have told him everything.

But she hadn't.

With two weeks until she had to qualify officially, she would make herself get over the shakes. One more challenge to face.

She didn't want to think about the stressful night shoot she'd have to endure. That would come later. First things first.

And she couldn't think about the situation with Sullivan Barnett. At a very basic level she'd known that he could get to her. She should have handled that situation better, too. She'd been off balance, though, the entire time—her fault for drifting up onto his deck and going inside. She could have prevented everything that had followed.

Foolish, impulsive, dangerous.

Her whole life was sliding through her fingers and she couldn't get a firm grip on anything.

She swept her palms down her sides again and picked up the semiautomatic. The four-inch barrel vibrated like a dowsing rod. All she had to do was touch the thing and the shaking started.

Putting the gun down, she bent forward at the waist, stretching the tight muscles of her back and neck, her hair falling forward and catching in her mouth. She puffed the strands away and stared at her sneakered feet. Anything to keep from picking up the pistol again.

The concrete floor inches in front of her nose was a lovely gray. The angled pit that trapped the bullets down at the end of the range was a lovely gray. The pitted cement walls in back of the target were also gray and lovely. Very muted and tasteful. Really, Taggart should recommend his interior decorator. Designer ranges for the upscale shooter.

Okay. She took five slow breaths and stood up. She could do this.

She adjusted the safety goggles and ear protectors and reached for the 459. The checkered high-impact nylon stock fit smoothly into her slick palm. Her thumb slid into the curved rest. She picked up the clip. Eleven shots left. No problemo. With the heel of her hand she inserted the magazine, flicked off the safety catch. The red button popped out, taunting her: *ready, aim* . . .

Twenty-eight ounces of metal alloy and plastic; such a small object to shake her from head to toe. She couldn't line up the sights, for the square of the rear notch was bobbing like a rowboat in a storm. She blinked the sweat from her eyes and stared out at the gently swaying outline of a paper man.

Concentrating so hard she blocked out the thuds around her, she extended her arms and levered the hammer back with her thumb. In the tunnel of silence enveloping her, she fired. Pulled the trigger again and fired. Again and again.

Seven to go. Hammer flipping back automatically after each shot. Fire.

Through the sweat dripping into her eyes and blinding her, she aimed and fired. Not until the sound of the trigger clicking uselessly on the empty pistol registered did she stop.

Flipping out the clip, she lined up the two empty magazines and brought out one more. In the relative privacy of the alley, separated from the shooter to her left by thick concrete, she took off her safety goggles, lifted the edge of her shirt and dried her throat and face. Her stomach was shiny with perspiration, and she fanned it, too, resignation settling on her shoulders.

At the last, she hadn't been able to see the target. She'd gone as still inside as she could and simply fired—all she'd been capable of doing at that point.

She grabbed the handle of the pulley and wheeled the target in. All fourteen shots were perfectly placed in a tight pattern. If all she had to do to qualify was show the target, she'd be in like Flynn. Unfortunately, a sweating, wild-eyed cop wouldn't pass, no matter how high the score. She traced one of the holes with her finger. It was so small. The exit wound would be big, ragged at the edges.

Working methodically from left to right, she marked the fourteen holes, the orange stickers glowing like some kind of weird skin disease on the figure. Reattaching the target to the frame with squeeze clamps, she cranked the figure back to the ready position.

One more clip and she could go home. Go home to an apartment that felt empty and alien. Not home anymore.

Leaning against the partition and lifting the edge of her shirt once more to dry her face, Maggie froze with her shirt still gripped in her hands, her heart accelerating with anxiety.

Barnett was *here*. Off to the side and slightly behind her, he nodded once to her and then settled against the wall away from the alleys, as if he had all the time in the world. Like her, he wore headgear-type ear protectors. A pair of safety goggles dangled from his fingers.

Lightheaded with dread, Maggie swung back to face the target, but she could feel Sullivan's intense gaze on her back. Her skin prickled all over with awareness of him behind her, watching, judging, *knowing*. All those questions she'd avoided answering and now he was here, and he would know that, no matter how she'd lied last night, she was still trapped in a rainy November night.

She rubbed the sweat away from her eyes and slipped the goggles on. They fogged up immediately and she took them off. Emptying her mind of everything except the mundane task in front of her, and forcing herself to move slowly, she cleaned the goggles and repositioned them, picked up the pistol, butting the clip in.

Her knees buckled with the effort of ignoring Sullivan.

Ready. Gripping the handle so hard she knew she'd leave the imprint of the checkered design on her palm, she lifted the Smith and Wesson and pointed it downrange, her teeth chattering so much that she wondered for one wild moment if Sullivan could hear them. She could sense his attention as strongly as if he were at her elbow.

Aim. She pulled back the hammer.

Fire. Dead center, the bullet slammed into the cement wall behind the target and fell harmlessly into the 30° angled trap.

The gun was greasy in her slippery fingers, and she couldn't get a firm grip. She wanted nothing more than to pull the trigger, firing until the clip was empty.

Even as she took a shaky breath and started to squeeze the trigger, pride and the promise she'd made herself stopped her. That would be cheating. Trying not to think about Sullivan behind her, Maggie repeated her ritual. This time she scrubbed her hands so hard against her jeans that her palms burned.

No matter what, she wouldn't stop. If she put the gun down one more time, she'd never pick it up again. Even with Sullivan Barnett in back of her, reaching his own conclusions, she couldn't stop.

Not if she ever wanted to be a cop again.

And she did. She wanted her life back the way it had been. She wanted to be comfortable in her own skin again, not feeling this sense of dislocation that left her uneasy all the time, a stranger to herself. Damn Sullivan Barnett.

Orange dots mixed with the sweat in her eyes. The silhouette fluttered in an errant breeze, seemed to turn toward her. Was that what she'd seen at the Quik-Deli? That flutter of movement? Through her blurred vision, Maggie saw for a brief second the serrated ramp of the front sight on the pistol. Gripping the pistol with outstretched hands, she fired in that one instant. Wobbling in front of her sweat-blurred eyes, the pistol sketched an ever widening circle on the target. She couldn't keep it steady enough to aim accurately.

Extended, her arms were rigid. She couldn't command her muscles to relax and lower. She couldn't move her thumb to the hammer to pull it back. Locked in a death grip on the gun, her fingers hurt, and she was shaking too hard to turn the gun loose safely.

She felt as if she'd never fired a gun before in her life.

A faint whimper escaped her.

In her panic, and with her ear protectors on, she didn't hear Sullivan step up behind her. He was there suddenly, his long arms over hers, bracing her hands until the gun leveled again. One of his fingers edged hers free of the trigger, taking its place.

With his palms swallowing her hands, the gun seemed a toy as he pulled the trigger smoothly and steadily, one shot after another, the 459 cracking out thirteen shots. The gun never jumped once in his firm grip, and his hard chest was so tight against her damp back that his strength and calm flowed into her. A pattern smaller and tighter than her orange stickers blossomed in the silhouette's torso.

On the last shot, the slide locked open on the empty gun.

His arms stayed around her, the gun still pointing toward the target. He stepped back as he released her hands, but she didn't turn around. She slid the clip out, the slide forward, and released the hammer to the Safe position. Picking up the clip and never looking at Sullivan, she stashed it in her purse.

Even when she rolled in the target, he never spoke.

The pattern of his shots was better than hers. Maybe tighter than Royal's when they'd competed against each other, but Sullivan had shot without seeming to take aim. He'd been fast, incredibly accurate.

Not able to look at him, she unclipped the target and showed it to him. "Nice shooting, Mr. Barnett. You want to keep this?"

"A trophy, you mean?"

At that, she looked up at him. She'd expected derision, mockery, scorn, something other than compassion in his blue eyes.

Maggie didn't know what she would have done if he hadn't helped her. She'd failed. All her old sureness and reliable instincts had vanished in the Quik-Deli.

Nothing in her life made sense any more.

She was coming apart at the seams, shattering into jagged splinters.

And in that moment she hated Sullivan Barnett for knowing her weakness, hated him with a fierce passion for the curious and unwanted glint of pity in his beautiful blue eyes.

Chapter 5

"Here." In the noisy parking lot of Taggart's, Sullivan's voice was a low burr, rough against Maggie's throbbing eardrums.

She squinted at the red-and-white can gripped in his long fingers and appearing as if by magic under her bowed head. When she didn't move, Sullivan ripped open the pull tab with an abruptness that flustered her. Her stomach churning sickly inside, Maggie surveyed him through strands of hair hanging limply in front of her face. Even her hair was wet with sweat.

"Drink it." He held the can to her mouth.

Some of the cola dribbled onto her chin as she sputtered, "I don't want—"

"You need it." Standing with one foot propped next to her on the cement steps where she'd collapsed, he bent forward, wiped the stickiness away and pushed back the curtain of hair hiding her face. Awkwardly brushing it behind her ears, he tried to anchor the strands, which curled forward as fast as he worked against them.

His preoccupation with tidying her flyaway curls stunned Maggie into immobility. His careful touch quelled her restless twisting. She opened her mouth to tell him he was wasting his time and closed it as the stroke of his hands behind her ears and against her damp hair slowed and settled the churning, lulling her into a singular stillness where traffic noises disappeared. There was only the rhythmic stroking of Sullivan's hand against her, the strength in his fingers coursing through each strand of her hair and down her body, a languid tide flowing from his hands into her, floating her away to some far shore where she glimpsed shapes and shadows in a half-remembered landscape.

Drifting in the utter rightness of the moment, Maggie watched him through half-closed eyes, her lids growing heavier with each careful nudge of his long hands against the weight of her hair.

He should have had bags under red-rimmed eyes, but the only evidence of his alcohol-soaked night was the slightly weary tension in their deep blue depths.

She saw understanding and pain of his own in those eyes, and noticed a loneliness there, too, that she hadn't seen before. Behind it all, his acute intelligence was piercing the private space where she'd huddled for nine months, faking her make-believe life.

"C'mon, sugar-buns. Bottoms up." He tapped the bottom of the can. A male trait, that kind of teasing. She recognized that jab-jabbing. Cops were good at it, too, but the hostility was momentarily absent from Sullivan's grainy voice, and the imperceptible lift of one eyebrow invited her to smile.

Maggie wished she could.

At least he wasn't grating her raw nerve endings with idle conversation.

"I swear I didn't dump a cup of arsenic in it. It's safe to drink."

She wrapped her fingers around the Coca-Cola can Sullivan handed her. The thank-you she owed him stuck in her throat. Instead, she nodded, looking at the cars rushing past on the Tamiami Trail, looking everywhere but at him. Safer that way.

With the memory of her failure still weighing her down, she couldn't handle his keen scrutiny. He'd calmed the seismic uproar inside her, but she would never forget for as long as she lived her inability to stop her trembling. Her shaking had led to an irresponsible breach of safety in her handling of a once-familiar tool.

She sloshed the cola around in the can. That was the way she'd felt in those moments. Even the way her thumb rested on the thumb groove had been alien in those frightening seconds.

"You looking for peanuts to drop in? That your style?"

"Not since—" Since when? She couldn't remember. Some of the cola slopped onto the steps in a dark line.

"Go ahead, drink. I'll make you pay me back later."

Still not able to speak, Maggie nodded again and stared at the ground. Today he was wearing black boots. She noticed in her swift glance, too, the worn fly where frayed threads separated faded denim from the metal zipper teeth less than a foot away from her nose.

"Seventy-five cents on your tab. I wouldn't want to be accused of trying to bribe a cop." A trace of amusement rippled through his words.

Coming from anyone else it would have been a joke, but Maggie didn't think Sullivan made jokes. Especially after his comments the night before, this off-handed remark sounded barbed, the amusement at her expense. She couldn't tell for sure. She hadn't the slightest clue how his mind worked.

Tilting her head back and staring up through the dull green leaves of a moss-heavy live oak, Maggie gulped down the carbonated sweetness and let her mind float free in the wide sweep of a sky bleached from blue to white by late-summer heat.

In the blistering humidity of midday, she was cooler than she'd been inside Taggart's, even with the big exhaust fans sucking out the smell of cordite and powder. The rivulet of sweat down her back had dried the minute she'd walked outside, Sullivan close at her heels, a line of darkness in her peripheral vision.

An avenging angel. The thought popped out of nowhere. Maggie set the can next to her. Rubbing her hands on her knees, she winced.

Faster than she could yank her hands free, Sullivan turned her palms over. Blisters already bubbled white against the raw redness.

"Not a pretty sight, Detective."

Collecting the shreds of her dignity, Maggie loosely fisted her palms and shrugged. "Hazards of the job."

"Yeah. I noticed." He still held her hands, his fingers coarse against hers and oddly gentle, his thumbs curled over hers. "Rough, huh, Maggie? Has it been like this since the shooting?"

"Push, push, push." Hating him for seeing her weakness, but still caught in the spell of their fragile harmony, she found peace in the linking of their hands, the comfort of connection with another human, one she didn't have to pretend with.

"Only way I operate."

"Like leopards, reporters never change their spots. I should have known." Drawn by the spilled pop, a line of red ants divided the step between her feet and Sullivan's booted toe. She grimaced as his thumb brushed the largest blister. "And here I thought you might go five minutes without meddling in someone else's business."

"Not in my nature. But don't give up. Hope springs eternal and all that, Detective." He hesitated, then rocked forward, resting their joined hands carefully on his bent knee. Haloed by his scraped-back hair, his thin face blocked her view of the parking lot. Slanted toward her, Sullivan had isolated them within the shelter of his body. Shrunken by too much time in an overheated drier, a clean but wrinkled blue T-shirt hung to the top of his jeans. Royal would have tucked in his T-shirt. *And* worn a belt, Maggie thought as her gaze slid toward that threadbare placket between empty belt loops.

Minutes earlier, his solid presence at her back had stilled the shudders ripping her apart. Now, as he slouched over her, his hands cupping hers were unexpectedly comforting, and, even as she regretted her weakness, Maggie yielded and let his strength seep into her.

She'd been running on empty for so long.

Shielded by his tall form, she was safe from the casually inquisitive glances of Taggart's clientele. An avenging angel or the devil himself, who Sullivan was didn't matter as long as no one knew what she'd been doing here.

Winging on that thought came a second. "Where did you come from?"

"I reckon my dear departed momma could answer that better than I could." He'd straightened, removing the umbrella of his protective posture.

She struggled to her feet, her knees still wobbly. "You know what I mean. What are you doing at Taggart's?"

His expression went blank and he paused.

She thought he might be working on a credible lie. "Don't tell me you were in the neighborhood."

Looking around at the cement-blanketed strip malls and fast-food joints, he shrugged. His shirt rode up over his waist on his flat, smooth belly. "No neighborhood here, is there? For me to be in the vicinity of?" He pointed at the silver-and-black motorcycle parked away from the lot in the shade of a row of passion-pink oleanders. "Would you believe me if I said I was tooling around, looking for fun in the summer sun?" There was sardonic humor in his alert face, and his eyes were those of a cat batting a toy mouse playfully, a threat implicit.

"Were you?" She glanced at the cycle. "You don't strike me as the 'tooling around' type."

"Slumming and stopped because I saw your car?" He shoved his hands through his already disheveled hair. It should have looked messy. Instead, the brown strands curving around his corded neck underscored his lean and hungry look.

"You don't know what kind of car I drive. You've never seen my car. Not that I know of."

"I followed you here." He cut to the bottom line with a vengeance.

"What?"

"Yeah. You in your unremarkable blue two-door and me on my cycle. From your apartment building and right down the Trail. You stopped for fifteen minutes at the police station. A wonder you didn't see me." He scraped the bottom of his boot on the edge of the step. Clots of dried brown mud from under his heel showered the step. That dirt hadn't come from the beach. The police station was surrounded by asphalt and grass. He'd been somewhere else before he followed her, because it had rained early in the morning before she'd left her apartment.

"You followed me?" She should have noticed. One more bad sign, that kind of carelessness. A dangerous inattention. She couldn't afford lapses like that. "Why in the name of heaven would you follow me?"

"I told you I don't like secrets." He slipped his fingertips into his back pockets. "You interest me. I wanted to know what you were up to."

"And I'm not flattered by your *interest,* trust me." Maggie resented his invasion of her privacy with a force that left a bitter taste in her mouth.

"But that's the problem, you see. Trust."

"I don't see, but at least now you know what I've been 'up to,' as you put it."

"No," he corrected gently. "I know what you were doing *today.* And why."

"You still think I'm trying to double-cross you." She was astounded by his skepticism. "You don't trust anybody, do you?"

"I wouldn't want to be caught short." Cynicism wound between the syllables of his studiedly agreeable tone. "I don't like surprises."

The tenuous link between them snapped with an almost audible pop. Words slipped out before Maggie could stop them. "I sure hope you've told all your family and friends not to give you any birthday parties without checking with you first."

His face tightened, the bones sharp under his skin, but he let her gibe pass unanswered.

"Did seeing me fall apart satisfy that itch you were talking about?" The severing of that slight connection between them left her bereft.

"Nowhere near."

Hunger and heat and loneliness stared back at her, and she remembered the feel of him against her, his arms strong under hers as he steadied her. Remembered the ravenous seeking of his mouth over hers.

It was the loneliness in his grim face that stirred her, a loneliness that mirrored her own, but she was too offended to draw back. "Are you going to let me do my job without sniping and spying and second-guessing everything I say or do?" Her outrage came as much from knowing that he understood things about her she'd hidden from everyone else as from the realization that he didn't trust her.

He reached down and picked up a stone, tossing it from one hand to the other as he answered. "I won't make any promises, but I'll cooperate."

"For reasons of your own."

He slung the stone into the weeds at the edge of the lot. "For reasons of my own," he echoed. "You can interpret that any way you want to. But if you can't handle it, let me know." He kicked a chunk of broken stone off the sidewalk and walked toward his bike. "Or complain to Jackson and have him take you off the case," he tossed over one shoulder with a lifting of his lips that was no smile.

As little as she relied on her instincts these days, Maggie knew as sure as she knew anything anymore that Sullivan had intended all the time to go along with her. He'd followed her, sure, but he'd planned on cooperating at some level with her investigation. She wouldn't forget again that Sullivan Barnett had his own agenda. Whatever it was, it would come first with him no matter what her investigations turned up.

Maggie stayed where she was, letting her voice carry to him. "I'm not going to complain, and I'm not going to fail."

"No?" He turned toward her, no real interest in his face.

"I will find out who's been sending you those letters, and I'll follow up on the bombing. Even though the case is officially closed, it's connected to these letters, and I'm going to pursue it. I've already made my purpose as definite as I know how." Perversity made her kick the stone back in his direction. He trapped the skittering pebble with the edge of his boot as she persisted, "But I'll be damned if I'll have you looking over my shoulder with every move I make."

"Tough. That's the way it'll be." Every line of his tall, muscled body was unyielding. He rolled the stone back and forth under his booted toe.

Maggie had a strong desire to jump all over his dusty boots until he cried uncle. She didn't think he would, though. That stopped her—the sure knowledge that she'd be the loser in a battle of wills with him. Biting her tongue, determined not to let him know he'd gotten to her, she snapped, "Whatever you say. After all, we cops are the servants of the community." She wrinkled her nose as if searching her memory. "And I'm almost positive that includes reporters."

The corners of Sullivan's mouth twitched.

Good enough. Maggie was pleased. Later she would remember that tiny twitch and wonder why, in spite of her anger and frustration, she'd been pleased that she'd coaxed the closest thing she'd seen to a real smile from his hard-edged face. "I promise you I'm going to get to the bottom of what's happening." The ball was in his court now.

Skipping the stone back her way soccer-style between his feet, Sullivan skimmed it to her at the bottom of the steps. When she blocked it, he nodded. "Maybe you will, Detective Maggie. But as I live and breathe, it will be a miracle if you manage to accomplish even one of those commendable goals." He sauntered over to his bike. "You'll understand, won't you, if I don't applaud until after I hear the jail doors clang?"

The blood rushing to her face sizzled the roots of her hair. "I'm not interested in trophies. Of any kind. I told you last night."

"So you did." As he straddled the bike, his long legs rested comfortably on the dirt, his boot heels braced. The V of his spread legs strained the zipper seam to its limits. "I remember that." His look said he remembered a lot of things. "Your call, Detective. What do you want to do next? Got your detecting kit handy? Ready to solve twenty crimes and call it a day by five?" The cutting edge had returned once more, and as he jabbed the temples of a pair of sunglasses through his spiky hair and settled them in front of his shrewd eyes, Maggie knew the barricades were back in place—his.

Hers.

"Fifteen, maybe."

Pushing his glasses firmly onto his narrow nose, he paused, an unwilling twitch again crooking one side of his mouth. "Only fifteen? I've overestimated you, it seems, Detective. I was sure you could knock off at least twenty and then go home and turn out a three-course meal." He half stood from the seat and reached into one pocket for his keys. With one hand in his pocket, one resting on the handles of his bike, the muscles of his thighs half bent, he was wholly male, whipcord lean.

Maggie couldn't look away from him, and his untidy masculine strength engrossed her. She wanted to smooth down that shaggy brown hair, erase the line between his eyes, touch the long length of those strong legs. Royal in all his golden smoothness had never affected her the way Sullivan Barnett did, and her fascination with him made no sense, not in this life, not in the next. She didn't even like him.

"A three-course meal?" She had to laugh. "Mr. Barnett, you've been reading too many women's magazines. The days of women doing it all are gone. Men are just as likely to cook up the grits in the kitchen." She chuckled again, amused by his never-say-die razzing.

"Yeah? I'll keep it it mind the next time I find myself in your kitchen, Detective Maggie." He kicked the starter and fired the engine.

Maggie's face flamed. He hadn't been talking about cooking. But she knew it was still part of the game he played with her—because she was a cop or because something about her in particular got under his skin, she didn't know. But she'd die before she let him know he bothered her. "My kitchen? Oh, I don't think so," she said sweetly. "I rarely cook."

He stared at her for a second, measuring her. Then, over the roar of the cycle, he said, "Truce, Detective. What's the next step?"

She walked closer so that she wouldn't have to shout. She didn't want the whole parking lot to hear what she said to him. "I want to follow you like a burr on a hound dog for a few days. I need to see what your pattern is, who you talk to, who contacts you and how people act around you. And I want to see first where the car bombing occurred."

He interrupted. "You don't need me along."

"I want to see it with you so that you can answer my questions."

"Detective Kelly—"

She stopped him. "I know. He went over the details with you. I read his notes. However, I haven't gone over it."

The engine noise almost drowned out his wry comment. "You'd make a good reporter, Detective. Nosy."

"Really?" Maggie smiled up at the dark circles of his glasses. "And you're so suspicious of everyone, you might make a good cop."

"Truce didn't last long, did it?" Thumbing the gears on the handles, he looked over the top of his glasses, holding her gaze for a long moment before sighing. "Sorry. My fault." He lowered his head, contemplating the dirt under his feet, where a few pink oleanders were crushed. "Look, if you're going to handcuff me—"

"Only if necessary." She forced a smile one last time.

"All right. Fine. But I have an errand to run first . It doesn't have anything to do with the bombing. Or the letters."

"I'll follow you."

He quirked an eyebrow. "Think you can keep up?"

"Oh, if I can't, I'll pull you over and give you a speeding ticket after we arrive." She turned her back and strode to her car, where she'd stashed the bag with her pistol and gear as soon as she'd left Taggart's. She'd never made it back inside to the bathroom, to throw up in privacy. Instead, Sullivan had found her collapsed on the cement steps outside.

She might have known he'd do the unexpected. He waited for her to pull up behind him before he signaled for a southbound turn onto 41. As sedately as any of the blue-haired snowbirds driving the crowded highways during the winter, he putted along, making a mockery of the sleek power of his motorcycle. No lane changing, no zippity-do-dahing, but straight-ahead, picture-perfect driving until they pulled into the side streets of a palm-lined area one block off the main highway.

He stopped in front of a cyclone-fence-enclosed yard, where children were lined up noisily in front of one big slide and three swings. On the front steps of the large, two-story house, a tall woman with her hair cut in a tight asymmetrical wedge called out, "Tommy Lee, wait your turn, now, hear?" The bantam-size redhead opened his mouth, but the woman put her hands on her slim hips and said, "Something you want to say, Mr. Gilbert?"

The redhead shuffled his feet in the grass in back of the slide. "No'm. Reckon not."

"I didn't think so." Her smile was brilliant. "Everybody has to take turns, Tommy Lee. You'll get yours. You know the rules."

"Yes'm." But Tommy Lee made a face at the back of the little girl in front of him and muttered something under his breath.

Staring at the two, the woman shook her head. She took a breath as if she were going to impart one last warning to Tommy Lee, a child most certainly with trouble on his mind, but she didn't.

Climbing out of the car, Maggie noted the pleasure in the woman's face when she turned away from the preschool drama and saw Sullivan.

"I wondered where you'd been the last few weeks." She stepped lightly, gracefully down the broad wooden steps from the porch to the sidewalk, meeting Sullivan halfway. "The children have missed you."

Maggie blinked. Sullivan and children. Truly, a mind-boggling concept.

Sullivan hugged the woman tightly. "How you doing, Alicia? Things cool enough in this heat?"

"The downstairs air conditioner you sent over helps a lot. The kiddies can actually sleep during nap time now." She scrutinized his face. "How you doing?" Patting his gaunt cheek, her hand a shade darker than his tanned face, she said, "Same ol', same ol', huh? No better?"

He shrugged but didn't answer.

Watching the two of them, Maggie thought about the newspaper clipping under the magnet on Sullivan's refrigerator, the careful precision as he'd straightened the magnet after she'd touched it. Remembered, too, the hunger in his kiss when she'd walked into his house. Remembered—and wanted to forget—his desperation.

"I keep hoping you'll..." Alicia hesitated, searching for words.

Patting her back and halting her sympathy, obviously trying to avoid the subject, Sullivan still didn't answer. His attempt at a smile held so much bleakness and emptiness that Maggie's throat tightened. Nobody, not even cynical, sarcastic, usually rude Sullivan Barnett, should have to work that hard to summon up a smile.

Unquestionably a woman to be reckoned with, however, Alicia wasn't easily shunted aside by Sullivan's brush-off. "I thought after all this time—"

Before she could finish, several children spotted Sullivan and gathered in an ear-splitting, shrieking knot around his legs, pulling on the knees and pockets of his jeans. Hitching up his waistband and patting one thumb-sucking girl absently on the head, he scooped a small boy high up into the air with one arm and swung him in loops. When the boy was finally giggling so hard he couldn't shriek anymore, Sullivan settled him on his shoulders, where the boy smiled triumphantly down on the rest of the kids attached like sandspurs to Sullivan's knees.

As if holding onto the reins of a horse, the boy yanked enthusiastically at a handful of Sullivan's hair.

Maggie winced.

Though the giddyap pulling had to hurt, Sullivan only reached up and adjusted the small fists clinging to him. "Easy does it, Skipper."

Resting his dirt-smeared chin blissfully on Sullivan's head, Skipper thumped his raggedy sneakers enthusiastically against Sullivan's chest.

"My turn." The thumb sucker's whispered plea around her firmly entrenched thumb had Sullivan kneeling down, Skipper swaying like a metronome on his shoulders. She gazed solemnly into Sullivan's face, now only a few inches higher than hers. "Me next. Please. And thank you."

"Of course, Katie. Right after Skipper has his turn." Sullivan's words were so reasonable and calm that, listening, Maggie couldn't believe he was the same man who couldn't spend five minutes in her company without turning into a porcupine.

And then she remembered his understanding at the pistol range, the compassion in his eyes, the slide of his fingertips through her hair.

As if her thoughts had triggered his awareness, Sullivan swiveled on his heels and stared at her. Steadying Skipper with one hand, tucking Katie's hand into his own, he stood up. "Uh, Leesha, this is—" He frowned.

"Hi," Maggie held out her hand. "Maggie Webster." Name, no rank or serial number. She'd let Sullivan reveal anything else. He could fill Alicia in on whatever he wanted her to know.

"*Detective* Webster, Leesha." Worlds of meaning in the first three syllables. He slid Skipper off his shoulders and hoisted Katie in place. Unlike Skipper, Katie rested her hand lightly on Sullivan's neck, sucking her thumb in quiet contentment.

The man actually blushed! Watching him, the tall woman grinned. Turning to Maggie, she said, "Nice meeting you, Detective. I'm Alicia Williams."

"Leesha owns the Sunshine Day-care Center."

"Partly. Mostly I run it." Her smile vanished, and her response was polite but reserved, her quick glance at Sullivan the only indication that some message had passed between them. "How can I help you?"

Reaching into the depths of her purse, Maggie whipped out her notebook and pen. She didn't have any specific questions for Alicia, but the woman was bright, observant and cautious. She'd be a good source of information. "Right now, Ms. Williams, I'm simply tagging along after Mr. Barnett. Could we talk later? If it's convenient with your schedule?"

Another lightning exchange of glances between Sullivan and Alicia. "Sure. Whenever. Let me herd this crew in for their snacks and settle them down for naps." She waved and gave a whistle to the few kids still around the slide and swings. "Some of these kiddos have to stay until 6:30. Makes a mighty long day for them at this age."

She opened the door and stood to one side as the kids lined up. "Y'all go on in and Lala'll give you your juice and cookies. Sullivan will read you a story when you're done. Okay?" Pulling a tissue out of her skirt pocket, she stooped. "Don't wipe your nose on your sleeve, Tommy Lee. Here."

Tommy Lee's honk was formidable.

Alicia's blazing smile at the small terror made Maggie blink.

Holding the tissue with a thumb and finger, Alicia nodded approvingly at the knee-high child. "Wow. I'm impressed, Tommy Lee." She walked over to a wastebasket behind a potted palm and discarded the wadded-up scrap. "Go on, now, you hear?"

A macho strut in his four-year-old stride, Tommy Lee went. He went—but he poked Skipper in the back.

Maggie laughed. "Sorry." It was the first truly spontaneous laugh she'd had in months, and Sullivan's frowning glance made her feel awkward and self-conscious. Her chuckle stuck in her throat. She couldn't decipher his expression.

It wasn't exactly condemnation in his harsh face, though. The absolute concentration in his motionless pose reminded her of the way he'd touched her at Taggart's, the way he'd shut out everything except her need. In the shadows of the porch, his narrowed eyes were unreadable. She wished he'd look somewhere else.

Ignoring him, Maggie gestured in Tommy Lee's direction as she spoke to Alicia. "A handful, isn't he?"

"Ho. There's the understatement of the decade. That child's going to make a name for himself one way or another. Not a mean bone in his body, but he's got more ways to stir up a classroom than any kid his size ought to have. I hope we can get him to realize doing well is more fun than making mischief, but we'll have to see. Little rascal's only been with us a couple of weeks. We have a chance. Unless his mother has to move again," she added to Sullivan and Maggie in a quiet aside.

"She having more trouble with her bastard of a husband? He beating her again?"

Glancing at Maggie, Alicia waggled her hand sideways. "I'll tell you later. Wait for me in the office." Alicia took three long steps to catch up with the line of toddlers. Tommy Lee had worked himself up to the third position and was making his move toward the head of the line. She locked onto Tommy Lee's arm. "Whoa, hotshot. Last in the door, last in for juice."

"I'm helping Lala today." The feet kept pumping, but the rest of Tommy Lee stayed in Alicia's grasp. "I will pass the cookies."

"Nope. Don't think so." Alicia gently held Tommy Lee by her side, waiting for his original spot in line. As he squirmed, she bent to his level and turned his face to hers. "Don't worry, sugar. We've got plenty of cookies. And juice. Hey, if we run out, Sullivan'll scoot over to the store and buy as much as we need, right?"

His face scrunched up until his mouth was nothing more than a grimy button, Tommy Lee cast a doubtful glance at Sullivan, who nodded and said, "Nobody goes hungry, kid. Not here."

"You can pass the cookies tomorrow, sugar, if you check first, okay?" Alicia said, patting Tommy Lee's arm as she watched the line. "It's your turn now. Go on." She smiled at Maggie and Sullivan. "Catch you in a few minutes."

The door slammed behind her as she hurried after the children, leaving Maggie and Sullivan alone on the suddenly quiet porch.

He glanced at her and away, too quickly.

She pulled at the edge of her shirt, rolling it between her palms.

"Look, I—"

"Why don't you—"

They tripped over each other's words.

"Ladies first," Sullivan said, all lightness vanished from his lean face. Hunched on the porch railing, which ran around the old house, he looked as though he'd been flayed alive.

Maggie needed to ask a hundred questions, wanted, with a surprising need, to wrap her arms around him and take away the pain gouging lines around his mouth. Instead, she said only, "Why don't I wait out here for you?" She pointed to a royal poinciana tree, where branches heavy with scarlet petals bent low, offering a canopy of shade in the heat. "You and Ms. Williams have things to discuss first. When you're finished, I'll talk to her. Then I'd like to walk over the bombing site." She looked out at the peaceful street. "I thought it was near here . . ." She flipped open her notebook.

"Right. Close." He nodded but didn't move. "Yeah. Leesha and I need to talk." He nodded again.

In the thick silence, his whispered, "Damn, damn, damn" was nothing more than a breath lingering in the still air.

But Maggie heard. "Sullivan?" She started toward him.

"Don't. Maggie, don't." His head was bent and he gripped the railing so tightly his knuckles went white. "Leave me alone. Go away. For a minute. Please."

Go. Stay. Maggie didn't know which to do, but she knew she couldn't walk away and leave him alone with his pain.

Walking over to stand next to him, she covered his hand with hers. He could reject the gesture if he wanted. He probably would.

The door opened again.

Big eyes and a tiny mouth surrounding a thumb peeked around the door edge. "Su'van?"

Lifting his head against a weight Maggie couldn't imagine, Sullivan looked at the three-year-old emissary. "What's up, Katie?"

A toe nudged the door back and forth. "Leesha said you c'n read. If you want." Aware of the importance of her message, she enunciated her syllables very carefully, finally abandoning the comfort of her thumb.

"Sure. I want to. You know I always read when I visit," he said, straightening slowly.

"Tommy Lee said you wouldn't read to us. He said guys don't read baby books. I'm not a baby. Tommy Lee is the baby. He don't know nothin', does he? Poor Tommy Lee," she crooned, shutting the door behind her and shaking her head mournfully.

Katie's thumb served the same function as a sink plug. With it out of her mouth she was a fountain of volubility, words spurting forth. But she approached the adults tactfully, taking in their joined hands as she edged between them. "I told ol' Tommy Lee I get to sit on your lap sometimes, but he could today."

She wiggled between Maggie and Sullivan. Her shoulder was hot against Maggie's arm. "I told him it's okay. Right?" Katie beamed at Sullivan, a small earth mother righting the wrongs of the world.

"Right." Sullivan curled her into his arm. "Whatever you want, Katie-o."

Leaning against Sullivan's long thigh, Katie rubbed her head against his knee. Thumb plugging her round little mouth once more, she murmured, "I wuv you, Su'van."

Maggie didn't know she'd made a sound until Sullivan lifted his head from Katie's and stared at her, his expression shuttered and remote.

As clearly as if he'd shouted the words, Maggie could read his expression now. *Back off.*

Chapter 6

Staring out the upstairs window of Alicia's office after he'd finished story time, Sullivan watched Maggie wander through the yard, her pale T-shirt flashing in and out of shadows, catching his gaze again and again.

He wanted to ignore her. He couldn't.

He should never have forced her to come with him to the day-care center.

Seeing Maggie here in Lizzie's old home was a peculiar torment.

Everywhere he looked he saw Lizzie. He missed her past explaining, and a desolate weight settled in his chest where she'd once filled his heart. As he watched Maggie in the bright sunshine, a cold fog of gray loneliness wrapped around him, muffling everything, leaving him, as always, alone.

It had been so long.

And now Maggie with her vibrant hair and soft breasts was here in Lizzie's place, confusing him.

He looked at Maggie and shattered inside with longing for Lizzie. He looked at Maggie and *hungered* to touch her, to run his palms across her silky warm skin and lift the fog shrouding him, to bury himself in her softness and at last find oblivion.

Touching the windowpane, Sullivan found himself tracing the outline of Maggie.

When Alicia had hurried in after the children, leaving him and Maggie alone on the porch, he'd looked at Maggie's gentle curves in her tight jeans, remembered the shape of her leaning into him at Taggart's, remembered, too, the unconscious pleas for help in her dilated, shocked eyes, a poignant appeal he hadn't resisted. In that moment on Lizzie's porch, he'd wanted Maggie with such ferocity that he'd been appalled.

Every time he looked at Maggie, the kernel of pain in his chest twisted, grinding deeper and reminding him of all he'd lost with Lizzie. And yet with the twisting pain came a different aching he didn't intend to satisfy.

But what if he did?

Unbidden, the thoughts flooded in.

What if he yielded to the obsession to wrap her hair around his throat, spread it over his chest, breathe in the scent of her skin, drown in pleasure?

Unwanted images of Maggie coiling beneath him, brushing his mouth with eyelash kisses, sliding sleekly beneath him and drawing him deep into her warmth . . .

The sweet forgetfulness of hot, wild sex.

He longed for Lizzie and craved the touch of Maggie Webster.

While never taking his eyes off Maggie, Sullivan pressed his face against the window and clenched his fist.

There was no explanation for what he was feeling. Lust was simple. He could understand lust. What he didn't understand—couldn't understand—was the unpredictable feeling of tenderness Maggie stirred in him. Couldn't understand and didn't like. Not at all. He drummed his fingers on the window.

Maybe he was still hung over.

As the afternoon drowsed on, Maggie wandered through the yard. Following a well-worn path to the west side of the house, she found herself in a courtyard, where a hummingbird feeder hung right in the center of a vegetable plot.

Under the partial shade of a large Brazilian pepper, the waxy white flowers of a gardenia mingled its heady perfume with the smells of earth and honeysuckle. Enormous old oaks and shrubs absorbed the street noises, muting them to a distant hum, making the courtyard an island of serenity in the lazy afternoon.

The pepper tree would have large bunches of berries at Christmas. Maggie wondered if Alicia and the children would make wreaths and mantel decorations with the deep red fruit.

Looking around, she smiled in delight. Picnic tables and child-size chairs were scattered randomly on the brick-paved patio, where clay pots filled with petunias, tomatoes and strawberry plants testified to the children's gardening interests and attempts.

Fingering a pole bean plant staked to a yardstick marking its growth, she nudged aside the leaves at the bottom and saw Katie's name neatly printed in ink with a red-crayoned *K* staggering off the card. Sweet, practical Katie had a yen for red.

Thinking about Katie and the way she'd nestled against Sullivan, Maggie started as Alicia caught up with her in the courtyard, her rapid speech breaking the sleepy quiet.

"Whew. Sorry you were left to conduct your own tour, but this is a busy part of the day."

"I'd guess your whole day is hectic." Maggie sat down in one of the preschool-size rockers facing the house. Ground-eye view provided a whole different perspective, she found as she looked up at Alicia.

Laughing at Maggie's wry grimace, Alicia folded herself into an Adirondack-style chair and unselfconsciously draped her slim legs over the side. "Better?"

"Much. Thanks. This—" she indicated the chair "—isn't good for my image. And I'm not wearing my power clothes today, either."

"Shoot, I'm tall enough without you sitting in these itty-bitty chairs, Detective, even if you were decked out in a nifty buttoned-down suit."

"I think you could be formidable," Maggie conceded, wrinkling her nose at the image of herself in the rocking chair. She swayed back and forth, the curved wood rockers underneath her squeaking cheerfully. "Yes, it's the height and the no-prisoners-taken look you get on your face every now and then. Very intimidating, I'd think, to most people," Maggie said, letting Alicia know it hadn't worked with her.

"I know." Alicia's smile was a flash of white, an acknowledgment of sisterhood. "But I try to save intimidation for special occasions—like squeezing funds out of the city council and fence-sitting rich folks." She flipped a file back and forth, her finger picking at the edge of the manilla folder. "Or sometimes for parents who don't have the sense God gave a banana."

Maggie saw a silhouette in one of the upstairs rooms overlooking the courtyard. Sullivan. Watching her. Or Alicia. She cleared her throat. "The kids don't see that side of you. They're crazy about you."

"Vice versa. Usually. Not always. I don't expect unconditional love and adoration from these kids. I don't need that from them."

"What do you need?" Genuinely curious, and liking Alicia more than she'd expected to, Maggie stopped rocking and leaned forward.

"I need to believe that some of them will leave here with a fighting chance in the world. Nothing more." Alicia's sculpted mouth curved down. "Fifty percent success is enough to make me jump up and down and click my heels." Fanning herself with the file, she said, "Now. Sullivan told me you're following through on that bombing and checking out some letters he's gotten recently?"

"Yes."

"He told me to answer any questions you had."

"I see. That explains the thaw." Maggie smiled to take the sting out of her comment, but she'd taken careful notice of the reserve in the woman's initial, quick assessment.

"Sullivan's my friend." Straightforward truth shone in Alicia's level gaze. "I wouldn't even talk to you if he didn't want me to. Not if it would hurt him. We've been in the trenches together."

"He's lucky to have you for a friend."

"Again, it's mutual." On her guard once more because of Maggie's comment, Alicia had resumed her professional attitude. She wouldn't reveal anything carelessly.

The children and Alicia were shining a light on Sullivan's character that Maggie hadn't expected. For a man who said he didn't care about anything, Sullivan definitely cared about the people at the center. A loner, he was still bound up in the lives here.

Not knowing where Sullivan was taking her when they left the pistol range, Maggie hadn't prepared any questions for Alicia, but meeting the day-care director and thinking about her friendship with Sullivan had given Maggie several ideas. She pulled out her notebook and shrugged as Alicia eyed it. "One of the tools of my trade. How long have you known Mr. Barnett?"

"Since shortly after Mary Elizabeth O'Connell hired me to help her start this day-care center. I had the college degree. She had the money and the house." Alicia swung her long legs back and forth, setting a rhythm for her clipped phrases.

"This house?"

Nodding, Alicia fanned her long, elegant neck, which was gleaming with a hint of perspiration. "Some house, huh?"

Maggie could imagine a family drinking iced tea here in the courtyard with the sun sliding behind the trees. It would be cool then. Even now in the blaze of afternoon, a sense of imagined coolness muted the heat. The evening sun would be red, a dying fire in the tops of the trees, then gone, leaving the people in the courtyard in a mellow twilight. For an instant, Maggie tasted the lemony tea, saw the fire glow and rocked tranquilly in a time long past.

"Her folks left it to her. She took every bit of her money and plowed it into this place. Said she was the luckiest woman who ever walked the earth, and sure as God made sour green apples, she could afford to make life easier for kids who didn't have much of a future ahead of them." Alicia was silent. "She purely loved these kids."

A dragonfly landed on Maggie's knee. Its wings fluttered dreamily, and then it lurched skyward toward the sun, pulling her gaze with it to the dark profile of Sullivan framed in the window. She wondered what thoughts kept him a solitary prisoner behind the window. Jumping as Alicia continued to talk, Maggie tried to put Sullivan out of her mind. Yet the image of that remote figure lingered on the edge of her awareness.

"We'd been working for several months and had about forty kids at that point. We were trying to arrange for funding through some of the city and county agencies. See, this center is primarily for kids whose parents can't afford full price for child care. That was Elizabeth's whole point in starting the Sunshine Center."

Spread against the glass, Sullivan's palm seemed to reach out to her.

"Anyway, he came banging at the door—checking out some tip that we were understaffed and in violation of some nit-picking zoning ordinance. Elizabeth opened the door, and that was that. They were together almost every day after that until she died."

Mary Elizabeth. The woman whose picture Sullivan kept on his refrigerator door.

Alicia stroked the wooden armrest of the chair. "She talked him into writing a story that brought in funding like you wouldn't believe. Frankly, I think the city council gave us the money to save their political necks."

"A biased story?" Maggie was surprised. She shifted in the diminutive rocker.

"No way. Man, that Sullivan could blister the hide off an elephant if he had a mind to. Nothing but cold hard facts, one after another, piled on so thick even the councilmen—and women—had to see that it was in everyone's best interests to make this center work."

"I don't get it." Maggie underlined *city council* in her notes.

"There's a lot of migrant labor in this area, a lot of single parents working at the juice plant, packing plants. And parents who both need to work just to pay the bills and keep food on the table. Lord, they don't have a wad of extra cash to shell out for day care, no matter how worried about their kids they are. The kids have to go *somewhere* when folks don't have relatives and they're in a financial bind. 'Course, some of the little guys stay in the family's pickup truck or in the housing developments with older brothers or sisters."

"What about school?" Maggie thought about earnest little Katie. She wanted to pick her up and cart her home. And Tommy Lee, with his determination to get to the head of the line one way or another. "Don't the truancy officers check up on them?"

"Bureaucracy's always a step or three behind. Some of these kids move around so much, they're lucky if they get any schooling."

"Who had the most to lose if the center became successful?" Maggie had to quit thinking about the children in the house behind her.

"Well, there was a group of buyers interested in zoning this area for commercial development. Some talk about another plaza or mall. They'd like to see us fail. There's always talk about this or that council member hand-in-glove with some development group, but I don't know any names. The center does stand in the way of some big-money projects, I know that. Elizabeth had contacts in the community through her family and she was able to put some pressure on, with her sweet, coming-at-you-sideways approach."

"What was she like? Who was she?"

A long shadow fell across Maggie's knees and onto the patio.

"She was..." Sullivan paused, looking down at hard-working Maggie, her knees bent into her chest. *Oh, Lizzie, who were you? Not my mistress, not my wife. No words for what you were to me, Lizzie.* He scowled. "She was..."

He saw Alicia clamp her hands together, saw the puzzled tilt of Maggie's head as she waited. He wasn't going to make it.

"She was..." *Everything. My life. My soul.* "My Lizzie," he finished through a tight throat. "My Lizzie."

Maggie's question bridged the awkwardness. "Did she make enemies who would have tried to get at her through Barnett?"

"Mary Elizabeth? The bombing happened after..." Alicia raised her shoulders.

"I see." Loaded with perception, Maggie's drawl sent shivers down Sullivan's spine.

"Anyway, nobody could hate her even if she ticked them off. Right?" Alicia took his hand and tugged him closer.

"She wasn't a saint." He turned to Maggie and lifted her notebook out of her hand, inspecting the neatly written notes in her private shorthand. "Very industrious, Detective." He shoved it back into her unresisting fingers, her untypically patient acceptance of his rudeness fueling his confused irritation. "You want to take a look at the bombing site now, or have you solved the case?"

"Sullivan . . ." Alicia's warning left him unmoved as he looked down at Maggie.

Everything was mixed up in his mind, and he wanted to go home, go to the beach house where he wouldn't have to see Maggie Webster's rosy face half in sunlight, half in his oppressive shadow.

"You coming or not?" He shifted his weight irritably. Maybe she wouldn't come. Maybe she and Alicia would sit and talk the afternoon away. Yeah. That would be terrific, with Alicia having decided Maggie had passed some female test incomprehensible to men.

"Give me a second." Maggie rose in a fluid shift of muscles and held out her hand to Alicia. "Thanks for your help." She nodded. "Oh, before I forget. Detective Kelly's notes indicated that none of you here at the center heard or saw anything before the explosion? Anybody who didn't belong in the neighborhood wandering around?"

"No. We were all back in the kitchen. Lala was showing us how to make brownies. You can't hear back there with all the noise."

Sullivan ignored the way Alicia glowered in his direction.

"You come by the Sunshine Center anytime you want to, Maggie, she went on."

First names. Must have been a real cozy chat, he decided.

"Thanks. I enjoyed talking with you."

"We can always use an extra pair of hands if you have some free time to volunteer," Alicia added with a sly smile in Sullivan's direction.

He could have strangled her. And she knew it. Alicia was way too smart not to realize he didn't want Maggie anywhere around the center, even if he had messed up royally by dragging her here in the first place.

"You know, I might do that. Let me think about the idea," Maggie said, her slow stuffing of the ever-present notepad into her purse evidence that she was seriously considering the possibility.

A momentary impulse on her part. She wouldn't follow through. He hoped. Would have prayed if he'd been a praying man.

A cosmic joke on him if she pitched camp at the Sunshine Center.

"I'll meet you out front. If it's all right, I'd like to slip in and say goodbye to Katie."

"Sure." Alicia pointed to a side door. "Right through the kitchen."

Maggie strolled off. Her enormous shoulder bag looked ridiculous in proportion to her slight figure. Stopping at the door, she raised her arms to the sky, her spine pulled tight and elegant as she stretched. She looked like a pagan woman offering herself to the sun.

He could see her with all her pale skin burnished gold by the sun, her hair streaming around her, coming to him out of the blue gulf, shining drops sliding over her, clinging to the indentation of her navel . . . With a stinging, barbed pleasure, desire rocketed through him. Sullivan turned his back and dropped his arm around Alicia's shoulders.

Staying close to him as they walked to the front, she groused, "I like her, Sullivan. She's good people. I want her to come back."

"I don't. You know that." He scowled at her. "I know Lizzie left the center to you and that was the best decision she could have made. But Maggie here, in Lizzie's—" He turned her to face him. "Alicia, I swear, I'm going 'round the bend." He squeezed her shoulders. "I don't understand what I'm doing or why. I'm a son of a gun, I know that, always have been, but with her—" he gestured with his head toward the kitchen door and gripped Alicia even more tightly "—I've gone beyond mean. I can't stand being inside my own skin anymore." He hadn't realized he felt that way until the words burst forth. He wouldn't have confessed his mental chaos to anyone, hadn't ever talked about his feelings with anyone except Lizzie, but Alicia's disapproval of his behavior made him try to explain himself.

"Sullivan, you have to get past your grief. I loved Elizabeth, too. I miss her every day, still do, but she wouldn't . . ." Alicia touched his cheek lightly.

He struggled to explain. "It's more than grief. I could get on with my life if that's all it was."

Her thin eyebrows rose in puzzlement.

Sullivan made a fist against his chest. "There's this hole. Nothing fills it up. It doesn't get smaller, it doesn't go away. It's just always there, this ripped-out place inside me."

"I'm sorry." She looked at him, pity welling into her eyes.

He labored with his thoughts, thinking that if he could make it clear to Alicia, he could then understand himself, but he couldn't untangle the snarled tangle of his malaise after all. Shrugging, he bent and picked up a fallen poinciana blossom as they passed the tree. "Have you ever loved someone, Leesha? Loved that person until you didn't know where you began, where you ended? That's how it was for me with Lizzie, and now—" He stopped, words deserting him. "Now there's nothing inside me anymore."

He saw the front door open. Waving to someone inside, Maggie propped the door ajar with her rear end. At her thighs, the crease of her jeans tightened, drawing the denim glove-taut across the round curve of her fanny, outlining the narrow line of her bikini panties.

"I'm sorry," Alicia repeated, the hesitation in her step telling him she, too, was fumbling her way through the discussion. "I've never felt that way. I don't think, personally, I'd want to be that consumed—"

"Neither did I. Life doesn't always give you nice, clean choices, Leesha, so bolt the door to your heart. That's my advice." He shredded the blossom, four scarlet petals and one yellow-white-and-pink one with red spots falling behind him on the ground in a Hansel-and-Gretel trail.

Maggie slammed the door shut with her rear end. She was balancing a white box in her hands and trying to keep her purse on her shoulder.

"But—" Alicia forged ahead, choosing her words with the delicacy of a surgeon "—if I did care about someone that way, I'd think it would be a once-in-a-lifetime feeling. And I'd hope the joy was worth the pain."

He tried to smile, but his lips wouldn't move. "Smart lady, but you don't have a clue, Leesha. I'd like to believe that joy and pain balance out. I try. And I remember all the good times—I can't stop remembering them—but nothing fills up this Grand Canyon Lizzie left inside me."

"Maybe not," she conceded as Maggie hurried to them.

He'd given something away in his quick glance toward Maggie.

"You're attracted to her." She also looked Maggie's way.

"Yeah." He watched Maggie's quick walk, the subtle hip sway. "Not surprising. Everything's still in working order."

Alicia chuckled. "There's hope, then."

He knew she truly didn't get it. "No. Because there's nothing working except testosterone. And that, after all's said and done, is nothing more than a cheap thrill." He exhaled heavily, despair weighing on his chest. "Doesn't fill the gnawing vacuum. If it could, I'd line up for the carnival ride."

"Take care, my friend." Alicia kissed him briefly on the cheek. "I wish I could help."

"Me, too."

Thrusting the box at Sullivan, Maggie dug inside her purse and pulled out a bright green-and-violet scarf before resettling her purse on her narrow shoulder. "Does Ms. Lala send everyone home with a box of cookies and peanut butter-and-honey sandwiches?" As Maggie talked, she twirled the scarf, reducing it to a narrow coil. Her fingers were quick and talented, moving smoothly over the material as she pulled her hair back and under the control of the scarf.

"No. This is a first."

Leesha didn't have to stare at him so pointedly. So Lala wasn't usually friendly. So?

"Goodbye, Alicia." He let his formality carry his message as he trudged to Maggie's sedate dark blue chariot.

"See you soon?" Leesha wasn't any more daunted than Maggie had been.

"Soon. Bye." He slammed Maggie's car door after putting the food offering on the back seat.

"See y'all around." Cheerfully waggling her fingers Alicia hurried into the center.

Sullivan took Maggie's arm to hurry her across the street. The sooner they were through, the sooner he could rid himself of her. He dropped the smooth knob of her elbow right after his fingers, with a life of their own, molded themselves to the delicate curve, his thumb on the tender inside of her arm, Chinese silk to his callused grip. "Sorry," he muttered, scarcely knowing what he was apologizing for.

The fact that he'd taken her arm? His mulish self? The slip of his thumb against her skin?

"Where was your car?" She looked up and down the block, her gaze halting where the street intersected with a four-lane road. "Down there?"

"You're standing where my car was parked. When it blew up." He stepped upon the curb beside her. They both looked across at the Sunshine Center.

"Here?" She crouched to examine the old brick road. "I hadn't realized . . ." Rubbing the scorched edge of a brick with her toe, she frowned and then looked back at the center. "So close," she murmured, and leaned nearer to the bricks.

Sullivan no longer noticed the charred marks. Forced to look at them now with Maggie, he was surprised by the extent of the stain. A strand of Maggie's glossy hair, freed from the scarf, caught on the rough red brick, its shine bright and alive against the scorched and worn roadway.

"Where were you?"

"At the curb." He'd been about to open the car door. He'd turned to watch Katie swoop high on a swing in the playground. He'd taken a step toward her. Several. He'd been about to tell her to . . . to be careful. He'd forgotten that he'd turned to speak to Katie. Those steps had saved his life.

The bomb had been meant for him. Should have blasted him to kingdom come and back. He couldn't thank little Katie for calling to him at the wrong minute.

"The bomb-and-arson guys indicated it was a remote-controlled device."

"Yeah." Someone had been too eager.

Maggie walked around the area, reaching into her purse for a metal measuring tape. "Hold this end, please."

He did. The metal ribbon quivered between them, a tangible connection. "Kelly went over all of this."

"I know," she repeated patiently, caught up in her task. "I like to do my own work."

"Excuse me. Of course you do." He dropped the tape as she pushed the return button. The tape clattered against the bricks.

"Do you think someone was trying to warn you off the story you were working on, or do your instincts indicate that he was trying to kill you?"

Kelly hadn't asked that question. Thinking of the snakeskin boots beside his head that night, Sullivan stalled. "He?"

"Or she. Whoever. Out of all the thousands who'd like to see you silenced." Maggie's cheeky grin packed so much magic it would have alchemized steel into gold.

"Either way, what difference does it make?"

Shoulders hunched up around her ears, she pushed her tape measure back into her purse and retrieved her notepad, clicking the pen. "Don't know. None, probably. But it could tell us something about the person who set the explosive. Or ordered it set. Motive, opportunity. Personality. One type of personality delivers a warning, another goes for the kill. I'd like to know which we're dealing with."

"Someone stood there laughing, that's about all I remember. In those double-damned snakeskin boots."

"Boots?" She flipped her pages back and forth, searching, not finding the information. "Boots?" she repeated, her nose wrinkled in frustration. "Did I miss something?" She rummaged through her pages again.

"I don't know." But he did. He'd told Kelly about the boots. Kelly had nodded and scribbled on his notepad.

Reflecting, she clicked her pen several times, her intelligent face meditative as she sorted through her information. "There was nothing in the report I saw about anyone coming up to you after the explosion."

"Someone did," he said, letting her digest that information. Satisfaction curled in him. Either she was faking her bewilderment, or Kelly hadn't included that fact in his report. Before she could ask, he volunteered, "And no, I didn't recognize the boots. And no, I don't know if anyone found boot prints and made casts. If no boots were mentioned in the report, I'd reckon the county sheriff's department didn't make any casts?"

She shook her head, rubbing her nose with the end of her notebook. "No. Nobody ordered ground casts. But they should have been taken anyway," she acknowledged under her breath. "Kelly's report indicated some residue and metal fragments were shipped off to the state crime lab, but the follow-up report only confirmed that it was a radio-controlled, not an ignition device."

"Well. Doesn't matter. A hundred and one ways to finagle bombing supplies. Black market, renegade ex-military missing the adrenaline of action." He'd loved that part of being in the navy, the rush. But he was older now and he'd seen too much destruction. "Law-enforcement people."

Over the notepad, Maggie's gaze never faltered. She didn't even blink. Loyal, ignorant or deviously crooked. He couldn't make up his mind about big-eyed Maggie, with her soft mouth and on-the-edge vulnerability. Part of him wanted her to be as crooked as a corkscrew. She was too bright to be ignorant about the shenanigans going on around her.

But part of him stubbornly insisted on seeing her as foolishly loyal.

Sullivan rubbed his eyes. Her cool disregard of his last statement didn't do anything to reassure him. Should he take her with him to meet his source? He didn't want to drag her out to the river. He'd already miscalculated when he'd insisted she come with him to the center. The less time he spent around her, the better. For him. For her.

He couldn't have foreseen the way she'd affect him. He understood that. Couldn't have predicted that she and Alicia would become sisters under the skin. He rubbed his burning eyes again. "I don't care."

Her damned pen went *clickety-clickety* again. She had stopped and was staring at the center.

Contemplating the gate and playground, Maggie said, "You loved her very much."

Sullivan stopped in the middle of the street, knowing he was staring at her as if he'd lost the power of speech and thought.

She stepped up onto the curb near the driveway and faced him. Her face still below his was serious and reflective, the tough facade absent. Green-and-purple scarf ends lay against the side of her neck, silk against silk.

Or maybe acetate against silk. Or nylon. Sullivan concentrated on the fluttering fabric. He didn't want to talk about Lizzie with Maggie Webster.

Reaching out, he drew the scarf between his fingers. Slippery smooth like her hair, her skin. Fixing his attention on the rolled edge of the fabric, he brushed the sliver of material across her ear. Her mouth softened.

But she was still speaking. And he could still hear her question.

"Mary Elizabeth O'Connell. Your Lizzie. You loved her." Husky and warm and velvety. And relentless, that voice with honey running through it.

He let the ends of the scarf slip away. They lifted in the slight breeze for a moment and then lay in a long parenthesis against her neck once more.

"Yes. I love her."

Her pen rattled against the curb.

"Love. Loved." He released the syllables. While she solved her case, Maggie was going to carve her pound of flesh from him.

Picking up her pen and rolling it between her palms, she didn't look at him as she said, "Past tense. It's like crossing out someone's name from your address file, isn't it? Nothing changes until you erase the name."

"What difference does it make to you?"

"None to me. It makes a difference to you, though. It's why you don't lock your beach house. It explains why you don't care who set off the bomb in your car. Why you don't give a damn about the letters someone's sending you."

"Bull." He stalked to his motorcycle.

Her small, capable fist caught the edge of his T-shirt and wrapped itself in the fabric.

He pivoted, pebbles scattering like shot with his abrupt turn. "I don't need your analysis, Detective, and I don't want your 'detecting.' Now let go."

Her face was flushed with fury. "You asked me last night how I'd felt when I was shot. You wanted to know if I felt anything when I flatlined? When I was clinically dead?"

He couldn't move. The light pressure of her knuckles against his bare ribs wouldn't have stayed him for a nanosecond, but her words, oh, they held him in his tracks.

"I'll tell you, Mr. Barnett. Flatlining is *nothing*. That's what it felt like. Nothing. I felt *nothing*. I *knew* nothing. I was shot, I collapsed to the floor. If I died—and my doctor told me I did—death is an ending, a beginning. I don't know. Just... nothing." She gripped his shirt tighter, rising up on her tiptoes.

"Stop," Sullivan said, her words bringing torment he hadn't expected.

"No, listen to me. *Life* is what's important. It's everything. It's a gift most of us only get once, but I was lucky. Every day I wake up grateful for the rain in my face, the hot cement under my feet, the idiot dawdling in the passing lane. Grateful because I got a second chance to make my life mean something. I was that close—" she snapped her fingers "—to nothing. And you're a fool to treat life like a cheap present you can exchange at the mall if you don't like the way it comes wrapped."

She dropped his shirt and one slender fingertip caught inside his waistband, a point of unforgiving heat. Her words ran together, the drawl slurring them into one long rush of sound. "And if you don't give a damn about the gift of your own life, think about these kids." She brushed two furious tears from her eyes. "Think about *them*. Someone's out there trying to kill you. You may not care if he succeeds, but Alicia and these kids care."

Catching Maggie's flailing hands, Sullivan tried to stop the torrent. "But I—"

The words continued to pour forth. "And if that doesn't matter to you either, then think about what could have happened if Alicia and the kids were walking to the corner—" she freed her hand and pointed to the ice-cream shop at the corner not far from where his car had been parked that day "—and the bomb had gone off then? Or what if he keeps trying and one day you're in the playground with Katie and, oops, too bad, poor Katie was in the wrong place at the wrong time."

"All right." He flung her hands from him. "I *didn't* think about endangering anyone else. It never occurred to me. I should have realized..." His words trailed into silence. He was sick with a different kind of fear now. "But I didn't."

"Someone's going to keep taking shots at you until he—or she—succeeds."

"I'll be more careful." Acid boiled into his mouth. He'd never once thought about the kids.

Maggie ran her raw palms down the side of her jeans. A fleck of blood touched the seam. "If you don't help me figure out who hates you enough to kill you, you're responsible if one of these kids—or Alicia—gets caught in the cross fire.''

"I won't come here again."

"You won't come here? Won't go to work? Won't go to the corner for a newspaper? You're a walking time bomb, Mr. Barnett. You'd better start caring whether you live or die because if you don't, you're going to get some innocent bystander killed. And maybe he—or she—unlike you, will care. About living."

"Help me, Sullivan," she pleaded, her eyes huge and shining with unshed tears. "Help me. Life is *everything*. It's all we've got, the one sure thing. Make it count. There's nothing else," she whispered, her breath a sweetness on the air, filling his lungs until he tasted the very essence of her. It still wasn't enough.

Chapter 7

Not until Sullivan slid into the cramped space of her compact car, glared at her and then hid behind his sunglasses, saying only, "Drive," had Maggie dared hope she'd penetrated his who-gives-a-damn attitude. "Head north on Route 41 to the Palma River," he'd continued, his thin mouth a slash in his gaunt face. "I'll tell you what to do when we get there." Staring out the window at the flatland ranches passing in front of him, he hadn't spoken since.

She'd struck out, appalled at what might have happened, furious at the waste of Sullivan's life, slashing at the cynicism that let him believe his life was worthless, that it didn't affect the wiggle of the earth one iota if he lived or died.

He was wrong. Short-sighted. Plain ignorant, that's what. She might not have said anything if she hadn't realized how close the bombing had occurred to the day-care center. She'd never forgotten a poem she'd read in school about the tolling bell and each person's death diminishing everyone else. She knew about that tolling bell, and that's what she'd tried to make Sullivan see—that life truly was a rare gift.

Checking her mirror, she accelerated, passing a semi loaded with shiny new cars angled into the steel structure rising off the flatbed. A long *buh-wuh, buh-wuh* saluted her. She waved and shot forward, the speedometer needle edging toward the top of the circle. She saw Sullivan eye the needle over the rim of his glasses, lift an eyebrow at her and fold his arms across his chest, sliding down into the seat on his tailbone as if to say, "What the hell."

Maggie loved driving fast. She was still a good driver. Unlike the business with the Smith and Wesson, she was her old self—whatever that was—behind the wheel of her car. She'd been driving a lot since she'd been released from the hospital.

Even with her world turned inside out since the shooting, she'd learned that each day was precious, each minute a coin to be spent wisely. Not squandered, but not hoarded, either.

Bent like a pretzel into the passenger space, Sullivan looked miserable. His knees bumped the dashboard even with his legs slanted toward her. Self-condemnation and overwhelming guilt had blazed into his eyes earlier.

Hidden behind the mask of his sunglasses, that tormented blue haunted her.

Fighting an errant wave of sympathy, Maggie tried to ignore his morose presence. She would have felt guilty if she hadn't been sure she was right. Sullivan needed to see the ripple effect of his actions. She didn't feel sorry for him, not one little bit. Not her. No way.

But she turned to ask him if he wanted the air conditioner on when he shifted uncomfortably. His brooding glance kept her mouth clamped shut. She pressed the accelerator. The needle swung to the right, past the seventy mark.

He could suffer. She preferred fresh air, herself. Air rich and redolent with the pungent aroma of cow dung. Drawing a deep breath, she tried not to cough. A good, healthy stink.

Sullivan sat up, peering through her bug-spattered windshield. "Turn right at the next crossroad."

The next crossroad streaked into view as he spoke. Checking her mirrors even as she turned, Maggie deftly spun the car east, farther inland and away from the gulf.

"Thank you, Mr. Barnett." She wanted to tell him to give her a little warning next time, but instead she nodded her head regally, graciously accepting his direction. She knew it would annoy the bejeebers out of him.

If glowers could burn, she would have been a heap of ashes.

Casting a rapid look sideways, Maggie permitted herself a very private, very smug smile. Sullivan was better off getting ticked with her. Much better for his health than brooding.

Braced against the door, Sullivan watched Maggie's square, competent hands control the car through its slide after the turn. She was an exceptional driver, but he should have given her advance warning. He'd been lost in his thoughts, back at the center—images of Katie laughing, her sneakered toes pointed to the sky; Skipper with ice cream melting and dripping down his shirt.

The boom of an explosion and metal spearing the sky.

They would have been waiting on the curb for their ride home if the explosion had happened an hour or two earlier.

"So, Mr. Barnett, where are we going? Or are we playing What's My Destination and I have three guesses?" Maggie flashed him another one of her teasing grins, the tucked corners of her bottom lip quivering.

She'd stripped off a piece of his hide like a platoon leader after a botched parachute drop during his SEAL training, all her detached professionalism peeled away by the strength of her worry about the kids at the center. Passionate in her attack, every inch of her trembling with alarm. Passion, hot and searing, heating her skin, branding him with her touch, her accusations.

"I won't report you if you break down and call me Sullivan," he said finally, fidgeting into a different position, equally cramped.

"Really?" She swerved smoothly around a large chunk of rubber retread. "Okay. I'll call you Sullivan. You can call me Detective." Again that quiver at the corners of her mouth. The defining V of her upper lip was barely there, the bottom lip a long, full swoop of rosy softness. "But you haven't told me where we're going. Not that I mind chauffeuring you around the county, but I'd hate to run out of gas back here in the boonies."

Was there any harm in revealing where they were headed? Sullivan lifted his glasses and held them between his hands, thinking.

"You're going to have to trust me sometime, you know." Her voice was quiet.

"Why?" Trusting was dangerous. He'd learned that during a nighttime live-fire exercise. Expecting the guy behind him to cover, he'd leapfrogged to the next belly-down point. In the dark, under the frightening and real gunfire, the man had panicked. Sullivan had spent some down time in the base hospital. He shifted position again, his knee brushing her denimed thigh. And being a reporter had only intensified his basic belief that people were seldom what they presented themselves to be. "Trusting people can get you killed. Why should I trust you?" he said to Maggie.

Lizzie hadn't trusted him, hadn't believed in the strength of his love.

"Because sometimes you have to have to take a leap of faith."

Jerking bolt upright, Sullivan slammed his head against the ceiling. "What the hell did you say?"

She frowned, flicking her short fingernails against the steering wheel. "Every now and then you have to reach out." She grinned. "You know—reach out and touch someone." Her voice trailed off and she frowned again. "You might as well take a chance, Sullivan Barnett, and trust me. You may resent me, but at the moment you need me."

"I don't need anyone." He never had. Not until he'd met Lizzie. And then she'd taken half of him with her and left him with this never-ending soul sickness.

"Look, at some point, you're going to make up your mind to trust *me,* regardless of your suspicions about the department. I won't have a chance of discovering who's threatening you if you can't give me a little trust. And that's the bottom line, tough guy." She pulled off the road and shut off the engine, half turning in her seat and facing him, her movements crisp and decisive.

A Rubicon. He could cross it or not. She was leaving it up to him. "You're asking for a hell of a lot, Maggie Webster."

"I know." In the heat, tendrils of hair frizzed, framing her earnest face. Next to the delicate lobe of her right ear, the green-and-purple scarf ends hung limp in the humidity.

They weren't being tailed. He'd watched. She hadn't made any phone calls after they'd left the Sunshine Center, and they were in her personal car, not a department-equipped vehicle, so she didn't have a radio or cellular phone. He'd noticed that before he crawled into the car. Reaching a decision, he nodded once. "Yeah. I reckon I'm going to have to trust you. Sure as hell I can't get rid of you." He'd planned to, but she'd sand-bagged him.

She frowned.

Tapping her cheek, Sullivan said, "It was a joke, Maggie. A joke."

"You don't make jokes."

Her cheek was peach soft. He flicked the scarf tail against her earlobe, where a gold ball shone against her skin. "Well, I just made one."

"Now what?"

He wondered if she realized she'd turned her ear to his touch. The gold earring was satiny and cool. It moved once under his light touch, and he dropped his hand. "Now you keep driving until the first gas station. Fill up. We'll need it for the round trip. I don't want to be stranded where we're going, either."

"Which is?"

He wiggled the steering wheel.

"Aw, c'mon, big guy. It's not that hard," she encouraged, a sassy tip to her chin.

"Yeah, actually it *is* that hard. For me." He meant trusting her wasn't easy, but in the silence of the open country, her cheek tilted toward him, his hand still warm from touching her, the words hovered between them, taking on an old meaning, and he stumbled over his words.

She blushed, her glance sliding away from his.

"I didn't mean—"

"I didn't think you—" She played with the ends of the scarf, grew pink again, and turned loose the fabric as if it had burned her.

She pinched her mouth and didn't say anything else.

Sullivan hadn't felt this embarrassed with a woman since he'd been thirteen and the janitor had caught him necking with Carly Thibideau in the girls' washroom after school.

Back then, he'd said things like that and thought he was be-ing a stud. Wouldn't have been okay then, either, but it was understandable. Or if he and Maggie were casual friends, they could have joked about the way they'd both responded to the unintended double entendre. And if they were lovers...

Therein lay the problem. They *weren't* lovers. Weren't going to be, and yet this constant, insistent awareness sang between them like a note struck on a tuning fork.

Somehow, being forty-one made his blunder more embarrassing.

Like a rude noise in a public place, the incident was best forgotten. He took a deep breath and doggedly ignored the charged moment, getting back to business, where they would both be less ill at ease. "We're going fifty miles upriver to Seth's Landing. I'm meeting a source there." It was hard to teach an old dog new tricks. The cliche, like most, held a nugget of truth. He didn't intend to tell Maggie the name of his source.

Pink still shading her cheeks, Maggie fiddled with the keys, avoiding looking at him as her thumb stroked one serrated edge. "And?"

There was no escaping the turbulence she created in him. Shifting, Sullivan rearranged himself once more, his blood pooling thick and heavy as her thumb slid along the key.

"He says there's an illegal toxic waste-dumping operation going on up here. He says he can hand over papers and names that will document the connection between this operation and a supposedly legit real-estate group."

"What?" The keys clanked against the steering column.

"Hanky-panky, Detective. Add greed and money and, abracadabra, you have hanky-panky."

"But this dumping situation isn't the story you were originally working on?" She hauled out her handy dandy notepad.

"No, the toxic dumping came up after I'd already gotten several letters."

"Why did you first get interested?"

"Four companies getting excessively favorable city contracts. It seemed simple enough. Usual quid pro quo. Payoffs, you know. But one thing led to another. I kept running into several names over and over—in the corporate records of those companies, on the records of large land buys that later became megamalls or exclusive housing developments."

"I don't see how it ties into the dumping. Anyway, the real-estate stuff doesn't seem illegal."

"It's not. Unless someone paid a city council member or a county commissioner under the table for zoning changes, for instance." Taking her hand and holding it palm up, Sullivan handed her a nickel from her jumble of coins in the car console. Carefully lining it up on her life line, he continued.

"Unless that someone is also involved in illegal low-bidding deals for city contracts. Unless that someone—or several someones—has a long-range plan for condemning certain privately owned land and rezoning protected acreage for commercial development." He dropped a dime and a quarter into her palm with a clink.

"Unless someone pays off the police to turn their heads when stuff is going on, like destruction of supplies at rival building sites." Opening his hand, he let a rain of coins fall into her palm. He rattled the remaining coins in the console. "Then it's real illegal. Money, as they say, talks, Maggie. And I'm always curious when I hear that little green voice chattering away in my ear."

Looking out the open window at the empty landscape, Maggie closed her fist tightly around the coins. "All of this is happening?"

"That's only half of it. I've been digging for months. I've checked corporate records to see who owns what companies. I've gone back and forth between tract indexes and abstract books to see who owns the land or buildings these companies use. I've checked divorce records to see if Jack and Jill are reporting the same assets. Sometimes they aren't, and I have another paper trail to follow." He tapped her fist holding the change. "All kinds of greed, Maggie."

She dropped the coins back into the console. "All kinds of reasons to kill you, Sullivan."

There was nothing timid about Maggie Webster.

Her mouth was tight. She slapped his arm. "To send you threatening letters. To blow up your car. How *could* you have ignored these threats?"

He held her small hand flat against his leg as he reminded her, "Because I was doing my job the same way you were! Because I like the rush it gives me to nail these schmucks. Because, by the time the bombing happened, I plain didn't give a damn anymore."

"So the payoffs led you to the toxic dumping?"

"Yeah," he admitted. "I had a phone call from this guy who insisted on staying anonymous, so I couldn't use him in my pieces. But he told me details about some of the land deals that I was able to check out and verify through other means. And then he started handing me little teasers about a company that's supposedly passing itself off as an approved toxic-waste-disposal outfit, but in fact isn't. Instead, it's busily cooking up a poisonous chemical stew somewhere out here where no one knows what's happening. There's an unbelievable amount of money involved in this. Eventually millions."

"For someone." Maggie's pen skittered across the page. "Your source is in danger, isn't he?"

"God. I hope not." Sullivan thought for a minute about the county clerk who'd begun calling him late at night to pass on information, the man's voice shaky at first but determined. The clerk had had enough of crooks and corruption, he insisted. "I don't think so. He's cautious, and I haven't written about the dumping yet. As far as I know, he's the only one who knows I've hooked on to it. The letters might have something to do with this new development, but I think they're related to the payoffs and bribery." He raised his shoulders. "Maybe not."

The quiet was oppressive, and Maggie glanced back down the road they'd traveled. Nothing but heat-silvered concrete running east and west.

Damn, damn, damn. Not caring what happened to himself, he hadn't given other people much thought either, Sullivan realized, figuring they, like his source, were responsible for themselves. The human being at the other end of their electronic connection had been only a shrill treble, only a ripple in Sullivan's endless night. And now, looking at Maggie and seeing again in memory the glint of tears in her eyes when she'd torn into him, he cursed his self-centered blindness to everything except his own despair.

Maybe the clerk had been smart as well as cautious.

Sullivan hoped so. If the man had trusted anyone with the meeting arrangements... But he wouldn't have. That would have been stupid. The man hadn't been stupid. The proof of that had been in the kind of material he found and delivered.

"Could he be setting you up?"

Sullivan looked at her. "You think I wouldn't double- and triple-check and then check again everything he handed me?"

Resting her forehead on the steering wheel, Maggie murmured, "It's all tied together. The payoffs. The zoning. The toxic dump."

She sounded dazed.

"Yeah." Sullivan reached out to touch her narrow shoulder slumped against the wheel. He wished he knew what she was thinking. He was thinking he'd been too careless with other people's lives.

Slowly she lifted her head. "And you need these documents from your source in order to write the story?"

"That and his identification of the dump area. He didn't tell me where it was. He'll take me to it from the landing."

The slope of her shoulder was fragile under the weight of his palm, fragile and infinitely poignant. Big-eyed Maggie was carrying a lot on her slim shoulders, and the curve of her bones under her skin suddenly made him afraid for her. He didn't like the zing of fear any more than he cared for the way he seemed to need to touch her every chance he could. The pink T-shirt was new, its cotton stiff to his touch. Carefully, he rubbed the cotton against her skin, straightening it where he'd made wrinkles.

"And you're absolutely sure nobody knows who your source is?"

A flash of anxiety quivered deep inside him. "No one knows. No one could. I haven't even told my editor."

"The source. Would he tell?"

"I'd bet my life he's kept his mouth shut."

Maggie laughed, her throaty chuckle strained, and Sullivan let his finger trail down her arm, down the tiny pale hairs and back to the dash as she parroted, "You'd bet *your* life on it? That's not very encouraging, you know, Sullivan, not with your recent record."

"Yeah. I reckon you have a point." He hit his fist against the dashboard. "Maggie, I never thought about putting those kids in danger, not once. There's nothing I wouldn't do to keep them safe.'' He wanted her to believe him, needed her to understand that he'd been lost somewhere in an unending night of the soul where there'd been nothing except his pain and loneliness and loss. ''But I won't let them be hurt. Do you understand?'' His voice was harsh with his regret for his selfishness.

A breeze sighed in the nearby pine trees.

''Yes,'' she whispered.

He twined the end of her ponytail around and around his finger, turning her face toward him, not stopping until he felt the smooth skin of her neck under his wrist.

In the hot afternoon her skin bloomed under his touch. Her neck was smooth and silky under his palm. Everywhere, silence and heat and memories oppressed him.

''I want to kiss you, Maggie.'' The words slipped out. He hadn't meant to say them.

''I know,'' she whispered again, motionless under his touch.

''Will you let me?'' He slid his hand down to the top of her T-shirt. Under the heel of his palm her heart thrummed against him.

Silence and heat, her heart beating so fast under his hand. The scent of her skin, her hair, rising around him, clinging to his skin, sapping his will.

The slight swell of her breast was under his forearm, the tiny point of her nipple pebbling against him as he brushed it, a sweet dot answering his hunger. ''Please?''

His breathing was harsh, hers quick and wispy. Close to his mouth, her eyes were the warmest brown, her lashes spiky in the heat. Down between the curves of her breasts he slipped his wrist, watching her all the time, lifting her shirt with each slow slide. Her bare skin was smooth and slightly damp from the heat, her stomach shivering as he touched it, his fingertips rough on her silkiness. With one hand, he tugged on her ponytail, urging her backward. Skimming the midline of her stomach with the back of his wrist, a slow, exquisite stroking, he murmured again, ''Please?'' and pressed his mouth against her quivering skin, lost in her perfume, lost to the need pounding through his blood, driven.

Her scent enveloped him. Nudging her shirt higher, he nuzzled his open mouth across her sleek skin, the taste of her overwhelming him as he moved up from her stomach to her breasts. Reaching the soft curves, he took her into his mouth, closing his mouth fiercely around her, biting gently on her lace-covered, delicate nipple.

She arched, a tightly strung bow to his mouth.

Her slim arm was around his neck, her fingers scrabbling under his shirt.

A whisper of sound in the heat. Hers.

A shudder. His. And the pulsing need as he took her nipple deeper into his mouth, his, all his.

He was lost to everything except the taste of her, the supple, sleek feel of her skin against his lips, and in his ears the only sound was the rhythm of her heart beating with him.

Her small hands curled around his neck, brushing his throat, and he shivered.

Everywhere he felt her light touch against him, an awareness of her even where she was separated from him by cloth and air. Slanting her to him, one palm cupping her hip, the other still tangled in the unruly mass of her hair, he had an image of her against him as if she were lying over him, his hands running down her sides to the slight swell of her hips, the dip of her navel quavering under his thumb as he pressed against it, his fingers spanning the slope of her belly, his little finger resting in the beginning of soft curls, and in his ears the sound of the tide running as fast as it would in a storm.

Horn blaring, a semi racketed past. Sullivan blinked. Dazed, he lifted his head slowly from the satin of Maggie's skin.

Pine trees and a bleached-out concrete road, Maggie's pink T-shirt bunched around her neck, her face flushed and blurry soft.

He could still taste her sweetness.

"Boy, Sullivan, that's your definition of a kiss?" There was sleepy teasing in her smile when he'd expected a verbal slap in the face.

"Not exactly." He realized she was working hard to keep things light between them and was grateful to her because he couldn't. The moment had shaken him to the core.

There'd been more than lust in his hunger.

"For future reference, should the question come up again— not that I expect it to, you understand—" she was talking so fast she was tripping over her words "—but I think I'll take a pass on kisses, okay?"

In the bright sunlight her skin was glossy pale, woman warm. Over the slope of her breast, lace dampened by his mouth clung to her nipple, shaping the burgundy-rose point. And a hand's breadth to its left a puckered scar, red and raised, bisected her slight chest. "Aw, Maggie," he muttered, hurting for her. He touched the scar again. Such devastation a piece of metal could work.

Maggie felt the even pressure of his finger tracing her scar, all the way to its end. In time the scar would flatten and become only a faint line.

Above her, the bones of his cheeks were hard, his expression somber as he returned her gaze. His right eyebrow lifted in question and he stopped, his finger lingering between two ribs. "Did you have someone to sit by your side and hold your hand during those long hours? Or were you alone, too? And frightened?" He bent his head, his shaggy rough hair brushing her stomach, and kissed the ruched skin where the bullet had entered her and changed her forever.

Much as Katie had done, Maggie rested her forehead against the top of his head, leaning into him, an unexpected peace moving in her like the slow, opening notes of a symphony.

"Most of the time I was alone."

He lifted his head and she moved away from him, the separation leaving her melancholy. Easing her T-shirt down, he covered her hands, his fingers sliding between hers, linked. "No family?"

"No." She was quiet. "It was all right. Royal came to visit as often as he could. Chief Jackson twice."

"No one else?"

"No," she repeated. "Funny, isn't it? I think I must have been so busy that I never realized I hadn't yet made any friends in Palmaflora. The job must have been enough, I guess." She shook her head. "I don't think I cared, one way or the other. But I don't remember being lonely." During that drug-muzzy twilight when light and dark mingled and shifted, terrifying her, she'd slipped in and out of a gray nothingness, fighting its tenacious pull, reaching out for consciousness. But she hadn't been lonely.

"Frightened." He flipped the ends of her scarf back over her shoulder. "You would have been scared."

She nodded. That grayness had been a powerful undertow, sucking her down until she thought she'd never see sunshine again.

"And now?"

That was the question she wouldn't answer, not for Royal, nor for Sullivan Barnett. She wouldn't admit to the fear stalking her in the quiet moments of her nights, when she was alone—the sense of something over her shoulder, at the edge of sight. "And now I'm doing my job."

Smoothing the curling wisps around her face, he said, "Keep on repeating it, Detective, and maybe I'll believe you."

The tender sarcasm almost broke her. She wanted to lean on his shoulder and weep.

Instead, she turned the car key to the right, the engine a purring animal she could control. She swallowed. "Where's the first gas station?"

He told her.

When they stopped to fill up, he uncapped the gas tank and dug into his side pocket. She put her hands behind her back when he handed her the wad of bills.

"I have my charge card. I'd rather put it on my bill." Keeping it business defused the impact of that maybe-it-was, maybe-it-wasn't kiss, lessened the invitation of his tenderness.

Rotating the metal handle, he set the gas pump. "Take it. Charge cards leave a paper trail. I'd rather not have one."

Maggie took the money. Stopping first at the washroom, she splashed cold water on her face and made a pit stop. Washing her hands again, she looked at the battered phone on the wall.

If she wanted a good time, she could call Hank. Or Bronco Bud.

She didn't want a good time, but she wanted to let Royal know where she'd disappeared to.

They were supposed to meet at four to compare ideas. She couldn't leave him waiting, feeling like an idiot with no word from her. She'd already hurt him enough.

Eyeing the greasy receiver, Maggie decided that if she couldn't reach Royal, she wouldn't leave a message that anyone else could see. She'd talk to Royal or no one.

Sullivan didn't want a paper trail. She shared his concern. But she could trust Royal. He was her partner. She knew him inside and out—his strengths, his flaws. Maybe she hadn't told him about her reactions after the shooting, maybe she didn't want him knowing about them, but, at rock bottom, he was her best friend. And he was a good cop.

She owed Royal the courtesy of not leaving him stranded.

Dialing quickly, she punched out Royal's car-phone number.

Carrying colas and peanuts, she sauntered up to the passenger side of her car and handed the packets and cans to Sullivan. "Food."

"Loosely defined."

Her eyes flew to his.

"Like the kiss, Maggie. I was trying to make a joke." He sighed. "I reckon I'm out of practice, huh?"

"A little." She laughed. "Third time's the charm, tough guy. I'll recognize the next one, I promise."

Swinging open her car door from the inside, Sullivan said, "Want to pour the peanuts in the can?"

He was almost smiling. More than a twitch. A definite almost-smile.

"Sure." She fastened her seat belt and drank from the can he handed her. "I got us both the real thing—no diet colas, just pure sugar water undiluted with chemicals." Peanuts plopped wetly into her mouth. They had a solid crunch, but they'd be soggy before long. "How far to the meeting place?" She pulled out onto the highway, leaving the oasis.

"Twenty miles up the road. You'll see a big orange Park sign where we have to turn left off this road and head north again on a dirt road."

"You checked the meeting place out already, didn't you?"

"Yeah." He swigged cola, then mashed the can in his hand. "Want to tell me how you knew that?"

"Woman's intuition?"

He shook his head.

"Because you don't like surprises, and it's smart to scope things out beforehand?"

"Could be." Rolling the can back and forth between his palms, he said, "Is that how you knew? A lucky guess?"

"Nope." She couldn't resist sticking out her tongue. "You chunked dirt off your boots when we were at the range. I knew you'd been somewhere after the rain and before you showed up at Taggart's."

"Smart aleck."

"Told you I was a good cop." She hunched down in her seat, settling the cola can on the console. "How will you recognize your source?"

"Except for us, he'll be the only human with all his teeth stupid enough to show up back here with the rattlers, cottonmouths and gators. I'll know him," Sullivan said grimly, staring ahead at the road running flat and endless before them.

As the miles ticked over on the speedometer, Maggie grew silent. Away from the neon and gimcracks, Florida was still primitive, with its own heart of darkness deep in the marshes and swamps where camera-laden tourists never ventured, even though their swollen bodies sometimes floated up in the bayous.

Not a place to take one's leisure when the sun plummeted below the horizon, leaving the southern night black and filled with the shrieks and squeals of creatures on the prowl.

Night comes late in the tropics, but the shadow of her car passing over the kudzu along the road was already long and thin when she turned north at the orange sign and exited from the highway onto the dirt road. Moss-strung trees crowded together alongside the muddy, rutted road. Passing underneath, Maggie shivered as overhanging branches blocked out the last of the afternoon, plunging them into an early twilight.

They were at Seth's Landing.

Somewhere off in the deepening dark, the Palma River cut a channel through the weeds and brush. Seth's Landing was an abandoned dock where passengers in the early 1900s had disembarked for a day of picnicking, returning to town after elaborate buffets as they chugged back upriver during the evening. The actual landing had rotted from disuse after the county bought the land, leaving it untended. The landing was now only a name on a map, accessible only by the dirt road and the sluggish Palma.

Sullivan leaned over to her speedometer and checked it. "All right. Now drive exactly one mile and pull off under the trees. We'll have to walk from there."

The hairs on her arm were rising the farther she drove down the road. She had an impulse to raise the windows and turn on the air-conditioning, isolating them from the brooding darkness on either side of the car. Yet she wanted to be able to hear anything that was out there. "Your contact has been careful."

"Yeah." But Sullivan was edgy, bending forward and staring through the increasingly heavy gloom. He glanced behind them. "He'd see anybody following him."

Maggie didn't like Seth's Landing.

When the speedometer turned over at the end of a mile, she pulled the car into the brush, where Sullivan pointed to a stand of palmettos and cabbage palms. The car was no longer visible from the road.

"Wait a minute," Maggie gasped as her sneakers sank into the spongy ground. "I want to get my hiking boots out of the trunk. You came prepared." She scowled at his boots as the mud cleaving to the bottoms of her shoes threw her off balance.

"Hurry up, Maggie," Sullivan said, pacing back and forth, his head turning as he watched the road.

The urgency in his muttered order squelched Maggie's retort. She lifted the trunk lid and pulled out the boots, bracing herself on the back bumper as she threw her sneakers into a plastic bag and back into the trunk. "Are we late?"

"No." He stopped pacing and cocked his head, listening.

Maggie grabbed a flashlight, tucked her wallet and keys into the side pocket of her jeans, and retrieved her notepad before plopping her purse into the trunk and closing it quietly. Whether it was Sullivan's pacing or the rustling around her, she didn't know, but she had an urge to tiptoe and speak in undertones.

"I don't know. Something doesn't feel right."

"You're telling me? This place scares the heck out of me," Maggie whispered as she walked beside him.

Checking the compass he held in his hand, Sullivan headed off through the ankle-grabbing underbrush, Maggie close behind him. She had no intention of losing sight of him, not out here. The edge of a sawtooth slapped her cheek, scratching it.

Sullivan turned at her "oomph" and touched the spot. "All right?"

"Sure. But get me out of here as fast as you can. This ain't Kansas, Tin Man."

"For damn sure." He checked his compass and stopped. "The river's over there." He pointed through a particularly vicious patch of jungle. "We'll have to go down to this spot on the river and wait." He brushed his hand across the scratch on her cheek. "I shouldn't have brought you."

"You didn't. I talked you into letting me come with you. No big deal, Sullivan. Don't sweat it," Maggie said, fighting an urge to walk right up to him and beg him to hold her. "Lead on, Captain."

They struggled through the brush to a wide bend in the river. Rotting vegetation and the stench of decay burned Maggie's nostrils. A smell of rotten egg hung like a mist in the air. She covered her nose and breathed through her mouth.

"Please say we aren't going to be here long," she begged.

"Maggie, stay close. I don't like this." Sullivan moved slowly from tree to tree, holding her tight to him, moving her with him closer and closer to the river's edge.

And the entire time his head rotated left, right, left, his eyes piercing the gloom, searching, watching.

The man lay sprawled facedown in the muddy water.

Half an hour later they would never have seen him.

Flipping him onto his back, Sullivan said in a voice so filled with fury it shook, "And hanky-panky sometimes adds up to murder, Detective." He was gripping her hand so hard Maggie was afraid her bones would crack.

"Somebody knows who your source is," she murmured, her throat dry.

"Was, Maggie." Sullivan looked around him and then hunkered down, his boots squelching in the mud. "Who he was. He's been shot."

A cawing crow circled overhead and then vanished, the metallic violet on its back swallowed up by the dark.

Chapter 8

Sullivan battled the urge to pick Maggie up in his arms and run like hell away from the mud and the river and the bloody face of the man lying loose-limbed in the rancid muck of the Palma River.

He recognized him. A clerk in the courthouse, he'd pulled records for Sullivan several times. The sandy-haired man had never said more than, "Hi" or "That about it?" and Sullivan would never have picked him as a possible informant. But this particular man turned out to be a clerk who had had access to both the city council and county commissioners' offices, where both boards met in the courthouse.

This man would have been virtually invisible, a wisp moving through the old courthouse, hearing, seeing things he shouldn't have.

Lord only knew what he'd discovered.

And now he was dead because he'd volunteered to supply that information.

Sullivan's stomach twisted as he surveyed the area. He was careful not to disturb anything. No papers littered the ground, not even gum wrappers and condom foils. No empty beer cans or liquor bottles.

Nobody came to Seth's Landing.

But somebody had.

His bum knees protested as he rose, and he shook his head at Maggie, who was aiming the flashlight. "Don't turn on the light."

"Oh." Only her smothered gasp gave her away. "Of course not. We'd be sitting targets."

"Right."

"You think someone's still—" Her shaky inhalation was so imperceptible that it wouldn't have revealed anything to him if he hadn't seen her earlier at the pistol range.

But he knew her now.

Taking the flashlight from her, Sullivan jammed it into his loose waistband. The metal poked him in the ribs as he folded his fingers around Maggie's rock-steady hands. Rock-steady, all right, but cold and clutching him for an instant before she snatched her hands free, as if embarrassed by that second when she'd clung to him.

"How long has he been dead?" She fumbled in her back pocket and pulled out her notepad and pen, scribbling something in the gloom.

"Half an hour?" Sullivan stooped and looked again at the wound in the clerk's forehead. He lifted the man's arm and studied the flex, the blood coagulated on his face. "Hard to tell. I'm not a coroner, but I had some experience with gunshot wounds in the navy, and this looks like a contact wound. I couldn't swear to it in court, but from what I see, I'd guess he was probably killed not long before we showed up."

He believed they'd missed coming face-to-face with the killer by minutes.

Not a comforting thought.

"Congratulations, Barnett. You used as many qualifiers around your opinion as a coroner would have." Maggie's voice was barely audible as she ridiculed him.

Admiration raised his glance to her pale face. She was coping.

She clicked her pen once and then looked over her shoulder. "Let's head back to the car. We need to call this in."

"Yeah, I reckon." Rocking back and forth, his heels sinking into river glop, Sullivan assessed Maggie.

Though her face was the gray-blue white of Lladro porcelain, she wasn't falling apart. Unwavering determination kept her small, delicately-shaped body glued to the horrifying scene.

Over and over she'd told him she was a good cop.

Now, standing in the pitch-black night stinking of rot and chemicals, he believed her.

She was a good cop.

Even at Taggart's, fighting the betrayal of her body, she hadn't given up. He believed that if he hadn't stepped up behind her, she would have figured a way out of her dilemma. He hadn't had a defense, though, against the sheer grit of her effort.

She would make herself do whatever she had to.

Maggie had gumption.

"Look," he hesitated, wondering if he was making a mistake, "I want to find the dumping site. That's what I came for. We can't help him—" he gestured to the ground "—and I want to see for myself what's been happening out here."

"The dumping site?" Swatting at a cloud of mosquitoes buzzing in front of her, she slapped her face by mistake. Then she cast a quick glance at the body. "Okay. Anyway, maybe it isn't a good idea right now to go back to the car. Someone might have spotted it. Or us." The pale square of her face and the light pink of her T-shirt wavered like swamp light with her every movement in the murky dark. The notepad popped as she clenched it.

One by one he unwrapped the fingers clamped around her notepad and pen. "Shh, easy does it," he whispered, needing to let her know she didn't have to fight her demons alone. He stuffed the pad and pen, her version of a security blanket, in his T-shirt pocket and then placed her cold fingers under his shirt, snug against his belly. "Maggie, I promise you. No matter what you think about my indifference to my own life or death, I won't let you be harmed tonight. I will keep you safe."

Knowing what it cost him, he made the pledge. He didn't want the burden of her life in his hands, had never again wanted the weight of responsibility for someone else's wellbeing. But he was responsible for Maggie Webster this night.

No matter that she insisted she was accountable for her own decision, he'd dragged her to this hellish place. And even though she'd argue to the bitter end, he knew she was scared.

Her soft mouth firmed in stubborn denial of whatever fears chittered in her mind. Brave Maggie in her new pink shirt, her hair every-which-way around her pale cheeks and strained eyes.

Shaken by unwanted self-knowledge, Sullivan pulled her closer, fastening her arms around his waist and holding them there tightly against the small of his back. The cool circle of her arms around him chained him to her, toe to toe, male to female, strength to strength.

Truth to tell, he'd wanted her here with him.

But not now with danger hanging like a miasma, tainting the night.

"Maggie, I swear to God I'll keep you safe." His voice was raspy with the intensity of his vow.

"I know." She'd locked her arms around him and her breasts were a soft swell flattening against his belly.

So much shorter than he and fragile despite all her courage. As she rested her face against his chest, one of his legs slipped between hers, and the juncture of her thighs lay against him, burning through denim to him. He stirred restlessly as she stood on tiptoe and murmured, "I know, Sullivan. I know."

There was no reason for her to trust him, no reason for her to think that he could protect her against whatever monsters ranged in this place, but in this moment in the desolate environment of Seth's Landing, a drifting current of illusory happiness moved in him, lightly, lightly, as though a window in the basement of his soul had cracked open.

For a long moment he drank in the fragrance of her, let the illusion move through him and push back the shadows clouding his heart.

Then he unlocked her grip and stepped back.

Air moved between them, leaving him chilled, missing the warmth of her against him as she said, "Where would the dump be? Your contact was going to lead you to it."

"Follow our noses, Detective Maggie." He pinched the designated organ.

"Hey! You made another joke," she said, taking a deep breath, then shaking with stifled coughing. "One of these days you might break out laughing."

"Don't count on it." Looking left toward the east bend of the Palma, Sullivan watched the water move past them. "Maggie, I don't know of any other road coming in here except for the one we entered on. Do you?"

"This is the first time I've been here, but when I was studying the county maps for patrol duty, I don't remember seeing other roads marked for this area."

"The river flows west. Right now we're east of where we parked the car, but I don't know how the road twists and turns back here." He raked his hands through his hair. "If it were daylight, this would be a piece of cake." Adrenaline surged through him, reminding him of all the night maneuvers he'd done with the SEALs. His mouth twitched with pleasure as he said, "Just for the hell of it, Maggie-my-girl, what do you think? Want to head east and go inland for a short distance?"

"Or toss a coin," she suggested, looking toward the thick brush they'd have to trudge through. "Either way, we'll have the same chance of finding the dump. Zero."

"O ye of little faith," he said, shaking his head woefully. "Actually, I did have an idea. I think the old docks of the landing are east of where we are. They're nothing but a pile of rubble, but they should still be accessible by boat. They would make a good landing spot if stuff isn't being hauled in by truck, and I didn't see any signs that large vehicles had used that road. Did you?" He scooted her in close behind him.

"No. Maybe you do have an idea after all, Sullivan," she rejoined with some of her usual sass. Grabbing his waistband, she sighed, "And since you had the idea, you get to be the scout. Lead on, Tin Man." Her finger hooked over the band, and her short fingernail scraped his spine.

Everything south of that light graze tightened and leapt to attention.

Following the glimmer of the flowing river, he moved through the dark, Maggie's knuckle a constant at his back. Not knowing what they might find, he'd had no intention of letting her go first, but he was glad she hadn't made an issue of it. Agile, she moved easily with him despite not being able to see and having to follow his lead. Stumbling over a decaying pine branch, she said only, "Oh good. Not an alligator out for an evening stroll."

The rotten-egg smell of a chemical stew grew overwhelming the farther east they walked. Curiosity kept his boots moving. And Maggie wouldn't cry uncle until she fell in a heap at his feet. Not even then, most likely. Stopping, he glanced over his shoulder. "Okay?"

"Dandy, thank you. I love the scenic tour." Forcing circulation back into her hand, she shook her fingers.

As soon as he stepped forward, though, she latched onto him, her knuckle firmly back in the home it had made for itself against the pit of his back.

Pushing aside the large, flat leaves of a sea grape, Sullivan saw the flash of lights before she did. He froze in position, Maggie slammed right into his butt, then didn't move.

He'd figured right.

They were at the old docks.

A river barge had come in close, its running lights doused. A ramp led from the end of the barge to the shore. On the barge, four men wrestled several containers into position and down the ramp. At the edge of water lapping against five tipped-over 55-gallon drums, one man marked out locations under the docks with orange flares that flickered luridly in the dark.

"Jeez Louise, man. Get a move on, will ya? I don't wanna spend the night here, you mope." Even muffled, the voice carried over the water.

A drum rolled crookedly down the ramp and splashed into the water. "Hell," the man said, spitting over the side of the barge.

"I'm not going in after that drum," said a short, squat man. "Not in this water. Don't think I will, Tolly, 'cause I'm tellin' you. No way."

"You'll dive in and drink the stinking crud if I tell you to, Gil." Tolly's casually issued threat held real menace. "But I won't. Not this time." He slapped Gil on the back. "Call it an early Christmas present, buddy." Glancing at the shore, Tolly called out, his voice low, "Leon! What the hell's taking you so long?"

"Watching where I walk, that's all, boss." An orange light wavered under the far end of the dock. "Sheesh, this is a nasty place. You didn't tell me it was this bad."

"Stuff it. You're getting paid."

"Not enough. Not by a long shot, Tolly. You couldn't pay me enough to do this again."

Leon's subdued assertion raised the hair on Maggie's arms as she edged around Sullivan's shoulders so that she could see.

Sullivan's outstretched forearm stopped her. Slanted over her breasts, his palm facing her, his arm was an immovable barricade. She frowned and started to mutter something scathing to him, but then she looked at him.

In the flickering light, his face was grim. Motionless, he didn't turn his head to look at her. The only sign of life he'd made since stopping so abruptly was to thrust his arm out, braking her.

Maggie didn't move, not even to shrug off the weight of his arm across her chest. She didn't breathe until Sullivan slid his arm down her, an excruciatingly slow, controlled stroke that had her quivering in a long rolling wave of pleasure and fear.

Watching the men unload the barge and roll the drums under the docks, where the containers half sank out of sight, apparently into the muck, Maggie felt the tension radiating from Sullivan.

He was enjoying himself.

Unmoving, watching the operation with narrowed eyes, he was coiled for action.

They would have stayed there all night, but Leon returned along the high shoreline, his flares planted behind him. Swearing steadily, he shielded the beam of a powerful flashlight from the river as he swept it in short arcs at the edge of the shore.

He would pass right by them.

So stealthily he might have been a shadow moving through the night, Sullivan edged backward, Maggie with him. She knew what he was doing.

Movement always caught the hunter's eye.

And they were prey.

Two feet from their hiding spot, Leon swore. "What the—" He flashed the light toward the sea grape. "Tolly!" he yelled, and Sullivan whipped around, grabbing her around the waist, lifting her off her feet in his rush to get away from the shore.

He didn't let her feet touch the ground until they were several yards from the river, Leon and his piercing light now joined by Gil and Tolly flashing similar high-beam lights.

"Maggie, he spotted our T-shirts. Try to keep up. Don't worry. They won't catch us. I won't lose you." Taking her hand, he yanked her forward, his urgent roughness speeding her feet as she heard crashing behind her.

She knew they couldn't use her flashlight, and without light, they were running blind, low branches slapping her face. Taking one long stride to three of hers, his legs eating up the ground, Sullivan plunged in a zigzag route through cabbage palms and dying pines. A twig jabbed the corner of her eye and her eye watered, blurring the little vision she had.

Urging her to move faster, Sullivan burrowed through the brush like a swamp creature heading home. She didn't know how he could see three inches in front of his nose, but his progress was so sure that he apparently had a plan.

She hoped.

"Come on, Maggie. I won't let you fall." Looping his arm around her waist once more, he hauled her to his side and zigged once more, the white glare sweeping after them.

Hugging Sullivan's lean waist, Maggie tried to match his steps. She didn't want to be caught in that bright spotlight. Tolly wouldn't buy any excuse they gave for being at the docks. She had no desire to test his forbearance.

An enormous cypress loomed in front of them. With a wind-up swing, Sullivan pitched the flashlight far to the left of the tree. It crashed into the brush. A high-pitched squeal followed the crash. Branches snapped and popped.

The arcing light flashed left.

With a swift, sideways step, Sullivan pulled them behind the rough bark of the tree. His fingers dug into her ribs as he thrust her up into the lowest branch. Low though it was, she wouldn't have been able to swing herself up into the sanctuary of the cypress. Noiselessly, he swung up behind her, a lopsided grin lifting his mouth as he poked his head up through the leaves, a brilliant gleam in his eyes.

Her blood roaring in her ears, she grinned back at him.

Safe.

Watching his glittering eyes, Maggie knew she'd been right. Sullivan had loved the mad scramble through the night, the zing of danger.

To their left and below them, lights shafted in and out of the darkness for long minutes. "Damn you, Leon, how'd you lose sight of 'em?"

Leon wisely kept his mouth shut.

"He's gonna be real ticked off with you, Leon. He's not going to be a happy camper at all, Leon. You better damn well keep your distance for a while if you got any brains left in that damned skull."

Then, with a last broad sweep of lights, their hunters ringed the area back from the river, headed down to the shore and were gone.

With its running lights off, the barge couldn't be seen.

Sullivan squeezed her hand and wound his fingers between hers, a comforting celebration of their escape.

Waiting, her head against cypress bark, Maggie gulped in air and felt her pulse drop back to a reasonable level as she heard the start-up rumble of the engine, its faster whine as it headed west, downstream.

Cocking his head toward the river, Sullivan listened in silence, shaking his head and touching her lips once when she started to speak.

They waited in the dark for a long time like that, his finger pressed against her mouth, his hand wound into hers, joined by touch and darkness. When he traced his thumb down her neck, letting it rest in the hollow of her throat, she felt the rough caress in a rippling shiver running all the way down to her toes and curling them inside her boots. Acrid with its poison, the night breeze off the river ruffled her hair, but Maggie stayed mute, in thrall to the gentle tide of pleasure lapping through her.

"They're gone," he said eventually, his voice harsh and low, his thumb moving in a slow circle around her throat. "I thought they might be smart enough to leave someone behind, but they didn't. Not to say they won't stop somewhere downriver closer to the road and send Leon and Gil on a search party, though."

"Think we can find the flashlight?" she whispered, "And the car?"

"Yeah." He cupped her neck. "But not in the dark. We were lucky I found the cypress. I didn't think they'd look up." Satisfaction shone with the flash of his teeth. "Most people forget to do that. Especially when they hear clumsy people making lots of noise off in another direction." His lopsided grin quirked and vanished. "Well, here we are, birds of a feather, sitting in a tree—"

"K-i-s-s-i-n-g." She finished the old grade-school taunt with a smirk.

"Waiting for the sunrise," he said, with a cryptic glance at her mouth that made her breath hitch in her chest.

Maggie leaned over and stared at the jagged shapes of bushes and vines below. She'd blurted out the rhyme, teasing, not thinking. "At least most of the snakes are on the ground."

"I wasn't going to bring that up. That snakes climb." He shuddered. "God. Creepy, crawly, damned things. I hate snakes."

Maggie snickered. She couldn't help it. "Poor baby," she cooed, patting his arm in commiseration. "Me, too."

"You mean you're not going to rush to my rescue?" He outlined the curve of her ear, trailing his fingers down the back of her neck.

She brushed her chin against the edge of his palm. "Not if snakes are involved."

"Are you going to rescue me, sweet Maggie?" Layers of meaning shaded his measured syllables.

"Of course. That's my job." She answered the only way she could.

"Yeah. For a minute I forgot." Releasing her, he reached for the branch above him and pulled himself up. Parting the leaves, he gazed out at the river before pulling her up beside him. "I don't see anyone waiting for us. Do you?"

Maggie squinted into the distance, watching for movement. "No."

The shimmer of the river flowing past them and the night wind lifting the leaves of the trees in shades of gray stretched in front of her. High overhead, wings flapped and the lonely *tu-whoo* of an owl signaled its evening hunt.

If it weren't for the stench burning her nose, the scene would have had a desolate, brutal beauty. Without the cloak of night, she knew she would see rusting drums, rotting fish, the oily rainbow that made the river shimmer.

"Well, Detective. My vote is to aim in the general direction of the car. I can't see the compass, but I can head us the right way. Then we'll see what morning brings." He yawned, the ligaments of his jaw popping.

"You want us to walk around all night? I'd rather stay here. Cozy pillows—" she patted the cypress bark "—and deluxe sleeping arrangements." Wiggling into the crotch of trunk and branch, she smiled up at him.

His returning smile was a brief twitch of the lips.

"Not all bad, Sullivan. Much better," she said, "than playing hide-and-seek with snakes and Tolly." Leaning against the trunk, she faked her own yawn as she slid to a sitting position. "You don't have to be a hero and prove you see through steel. It'll be okay to let down, enjoy the easy life for a change. Come on, Tin Man, the road back to Kansas will be much easier to see in daylight," she coaxed.

"You're something, Maggie Webster." His lips twitched again in what she was learning to recognize as next-best-thing to a smile.

One of these days, she promised herself, she was going to cajole a by-heaven-for-real smile from Sullivan Barnett. Chasing the always-present darkness from his blue eyes, that smile would curl a girl's toes.

And generate a major meltdown in a woman.

"Of course I am," she said smugly, wriggling her toes at him. "We're staying at the Cypress Inn, right? Right, Sullivan?" she said as she sat up, alarmed by the time he was taking to answer her.

"No."

"Darn you." She thumped the toe of his boot. "I've already unpacked and picked my side of the bed." She couldn't see any reason for leaving the safety of the cypress branch. It wasn't the most comfortable seat she'd ever had, but she was becoming attached to it. "Listen, Sullivan, I really, really, don't want to cavort through Seth's Landing anymore tonight." She scowled and blew hair out of her eyes, trying to assume as formidable an expression as Alicia would have. "I mean, I *really* don't want to."

"I know."

She didn't know how to act with him when he was being so agreeable. A good argument would disperse the treacherous yearning she felt for him, blast away the cobwebs in her sleepy brain and put the starch back in her spine.

Sullivan didn't like the situation they were in. When he'd been in country by himself, dug in for observation, he'd never cut off his bolt hole. His instincts had brought him home safe, had allowed him those months with Lizzie, the best time of his life. "Maggie," he repeated, "we can't stay here."

Her head drooped. But then she was looking him right in the eye, no quarter asked.

The weary shine of her face might have weakened his resolve, but he'd ignored that screeching inner alarm earlier when they'd left the car. He shouldn't have, and once upon a time, in another life, he would have listened to that insistent clanging. This time, though, Maggie had almost been killed.

He wouldn't make any more mistakes, not after he'd pledged to protect her.

"Maggie, our friendly dumpers may not be the guys who murdered the clerk." She'd been so brave, cracking jokes and teasing him. He dreaded dragging her through the night without being able to see anything. "I don't want to stay here and be trapped if a killer comes back for any reason. In the tree, our options for action are limited. I'd rather have a back door available."

"Okay." There was defeat in her exhausted acceptance.

Dropping to the ground, Sullivan held out his arms for her. "Won't be so bad, Maggie. Tomorrow you'll look back on this and laugh."

"Think so?" She lowered herself over the edge and dropped into his waiting arms.

"Maybe not," he conceded, staring into her dark eyes and not feeling a bit like laughing himself. She slid down his body, saying "oof" when her knees buckled. He held her upright with his arms still around her, wishing they were anywhere but Seth's Landing, wishing they were somewhere he could lay her down across cool, clean sheets and stroke her softly, endlessly, until she whimpered, her eyes widening with need for him.

And then, in that bright, clean place, he would burn in her, finding peace.

"Maggie..." He started to tell her how it would be in that sunlit room, tell her how he would touch her, what they would do, but the fantasy held him in its grip with such power that his throat closed.

He wanted her, wanted to see her in sunshine, wanted to see her the way he'd fantasized ever since she'd strolled into the office, the sway of her hips provoking wild, primitive impulses.

Finally, he understood. If he stayed around her, he would eventually give in to those impulses. Not because he couldn't control them, but because, ultimately, he wouldn't want to. He would no longer care what happened afterward.

And there would be consequences.

There always were.

"Let's go," he said, not liking what this night was teaching him about himself.

He headed west, taking his initial bearing from the river and establishing landmarks to use once they were out of sight of the Palma. Silently, Maggie worked her hand into his, trudging by his side as they forced a path through the growth snatching at their clothes, hair, faces.

Despite his own exhaustion, he forced himself to stay alert, watching for anything, everything, listening.

Sometime around midnight, by his best estimate, they found the chickee.

Its thatched roof rose out of the dark beside a shallow, meandering bayou that branched off from the Palma. Open on all sides, the hut's pond-cypress support logs rose to the cabbage-palm thatching.

"It's not the Cypress Inn," he said, tilting Maggie's face up to him, "but it has a bolt hole." He pointed to the dugout made from bald cypress and to the larger, creaky-looking wooden rowboat at the bayou's edge. "Want to see if there's a vacancy?"

Maggie walked stoically ahead and collapsed on a wooden bench by a rickety table at the far end of the hut. "You can't make me move again tonight, Sullivan." She glanced up at the thatching and dropped her head to the table. It wobbled beneath her. "Tell me there aren't any snakes in that." With an upraised arm, she waved apathetically at the fronds.

"There are no snakes in this thatching," he repeated obediently, knowing there were.

"Oh, Sullivan," she lamented. "You lie so good, and I don't even care that I know you're lying."

"Maybe I'm not," he said, stroking her bent head. "Since I don't see snakes, there aren't any." It wouldn't matter anyway.

Ever since Vietnam he'd hated snakes with a ferocity usually reserved for much more personal enemies. On reconnaissance in very unfriendly country toward the end of his enlistment, he'd stayed silent and paralyzed, not daring to move as a large snake slithered lazily across his camouflaged body. If he'd moved, he would have been spotted and killed by the ten-man squad huddled together yards in front of him.

"Sounds like a reasonable proposition to me." Mechanically, she lifted her head. "Do you want the table or the bench?"

"I hate to break the news to you, but we don't take either one. It's the rowboat for us, brown eyes."

She didn't even bother arguing. Helping him strip palm fiber from the thatching close to the ground, she worked steadily with him as they plaited the fiber into trip wires.

Dragging the rowboat into the shelter of a stand of palmettos, Sullivan bent branches over the boat, forming a cave. Around the clearing and near the palmetto stand, he bent other branches and fastened them with the palm fiber. The snapping swoosh of the trips would alert him if anyone approached.

Kicking loose brush from the rowboat and ripping out one of the seat boards so that he and Maggie wouldn't be twisted into corkscrews trying to get comfortable, he finished his preparations. They would be hidden; they had an alarm system and shelter. He'd done what he could.

He moved the last branch aside, pointing out the entrance to Maggie. Following her, he fastened the concealing branch around them. In the private cocoon fashioned of branches, they lay down in the rowboat, its sides screening them.

"Here." Sullivan turned to his side and shifted Maggie so that her head was cushioned on his shoulder as they lay face-to-face, her nose mashed against his chin.

At a sudden rustling and shrieking outside their cave, Maggie stiffened.

He lowered his head. She lifted her chin. His mouth found hers, soft and open in surprise.

He meant to reassure her, to tell her the sounds were nothing. He didn't mean to kiss her, not when he was strung-out with adrenaline still pumping through him, not when his guard was down and his hunger so powerful.

But he did.

And she kissed him back with an answering hunger that had him driving her fast into passion, yet not fast enough for the hunger spiraling him into sensation.

Slanting his mouth across hers, he tugged at her lower lip, opening her mouth and deepening the kiss, tongue to tongue, stroking the innermost recesses of her mouth.

She opened for him, her mouth warm and welcoming, inviting the sweep of his tongue.

He'd thought he wanted her to whimper with need.

Instead, her touch spoke for her as she twisted restlessly against him, one knee sliding over his thigh, and he cupped her, pulling her into his rhythm, pulse to pulse in urgent, tearing need in the night.

And he found that this, after all, was what he wanted.

Her, against him, pushing him higher with each light touch of her hand. Her, sliding her fingers recklessly under his waistband and working the metal button free as she brushed her knuckles against him, taking him into mindless, dangerous sensation.

Chapter 9

Maggie clung to him as if the world ended and began with Sullivan Barnett, exploded and recreated itself in his touch on her, hers on him. Somewhere in the dim corridors of memory, where time walked in a measured pace, she must have known this rapture of pounding hearts and a man's whiskered face against hers, this surrender to the honeyed flow rushing through her.

Must have known, and couldn't have, because once experienced, how could she ever have walked away from the electrical buzz along her skin, the craving to get closer than the barrier of skin allowed?

It was as if she had plunged into the sun and whirled in its brilliance, transformed.

She sighed in delight as Sullivan impatiently pushed her shirt up. Holding her with one arm wrapped around her waist, and half rising, he stripped her shirt over her head and flung it into the boat in one smooth motion, the pale flutter a butterfly floating to earth.

Still half sitting, he lifted her onto his lap, cradling her in the V of legs and groin. Sliding his arms under hers and back toward him over her shoulders, he rocked them slowly back and forth. With each rocking, she slid over him, that sliding push of his maleness against her a salutation to her feminine core. And he made her ache to have his touch on her, in her. Where he thrust, she yielded; where she retreated, he followed in a dance as old as time, as new as innocence.

Running her hands along his thin, well-defined ribs, she worked his shirt off. He buried his groan in the curve of her ear, his breath hot against her as he nipped the lobe and held it between his teeth, the delicate pain trembling through her in an unending wave of shivers.

"Oh, God, Maggie," he muttered against her breast, pulling her tight against him, taking her shivers and blending them with his shuddering response to the scrabble of her fingers against his back. "I want you." He raised his knees until they supported her back, and buried his face against her breasts. "God help me, but I want you so much it's killing me. And I hate myself for not being able to resist. Every time I touch you . . ."

And he touched her where she wanted most to be touched.

Wrenched from him, his admission affected the most vulnerable part of her soul, the part that had wandered sad and confused for months.

His lips closed hot and hard around her, the damp flick of his tongue against her nipple arching her to him with a longing she'd never imagined. Here in this private place, they were dependent on each other, and she needed him, needed the forgetfulness his urgent touch promised he would give her.

The back of his hand brushed her stomach as he popped the snap of her jeans. His palm was warm, sweeping across her, agitating her. "Lift," he whispered, cupping her fanny and tugging her jeans down.

She never noticed the downward slide of her zipper, but he encouraged her to give him access. Lifting onto her knees, she let him peel her jeans down to her ankles, leaving her clad only in her panties. The tips of her breasts brushed against the smooth planes of his chest, hardening into aching points. She twisted against him, wordlessly telling him where she hurt.

Gripping her hips, he slid her up and down his sleek chest in an agonizing delay until she lost all sense of anything except the drumming of her body against his, or his against hers—she no longer knew which. His flesh, hers, intertwined, humming with shared energy, both of them captive to that strumming beat.

But she knew she wanted to touch him and so she ran her open palms down the corded muscles of his belly, slipping her hands under the opened button. Spreading the worn fabric, she freed him from the thin cotton restricting him. A leap and throbbing against her palm as she touched him, a male force that urged her closer, tantalized her with the notion that she had created this power, that *she* had called it forth.

Untying the scarf, he released her hair. Crushing strands of it in one fist, he buried his face in it, trailed tendrils across his chest, his mouth. "So sweet," he groaned.

He brushed the silky scarf against her in a subtle teasing that tickled her stomach and the sides of her breasts, her nipples, her mouth, all her bare skin until each drift of the scarf merged into a cataclysmic rolling deep inside her that she couldn't stop, didn't want to stop, couldn't stop, and then he kissed her again, taking the deep tremors into his mouth, devouring her.

And when she lay limp and spent against him, he began to move again, a slow slide of his palms over her naked back, down to the dimples of her fanny, dipping his finger into them and drawing it up her sides and over her breasts, lightly circling her nipples before beginning again.

Underneath her, his satiny length pushed and pressed against her belly, asserted his intention with an aggression that should have frightened her, but Sullivan had shown her that she was the magician and that strength hers to command or deny.

His face was tight with the control he exerted, his mouth thinned in a grimace, and she marveled at his strength, exulted in it because he shared it with her. Taking his face between her palms, she touched the seam of his lips with her tongue. His tongue met hers in a kiss that stopped her breathing with its tenderness. So sweet, that mingling of breath.

Delicately she touched his flat nipples with the tip of her tongue and felt him shudder. Against the silk of her panties, he was hard and pulsing, a powerful statement of purpose. Shy, surprised by her delight in touching him, and not quite sure what she was doing, she lowered her head, slowly sweeping his chest with her hair, and kissed his navel.

He bucked under her touch and then lay still, his muscles straining beneath her with the effort it took to lie motionless. "Take, Maggie, whatever you want," he invited. His heart thundered under her right nipple and it blossomed to the rhythm of his life force.

Back at the river, the clerk stared unseeing at the night, but she and Sullivan were alive, alive, her heart beating over him, his under her, closing a circuit.

And yet...

Sullivan, vulnerable and aching, lay tensed beneath her, his hunger as great as hers and unsatisfied. He had eased the ugly memories for her, denied himself.

Enclosed in their small cave, they were wholly dependent on one another. "Oh, Tin Man," she breathed, "not rusty at all. All heart." And she bent and kissed him where his body throbbed to the rhythm of hers.

"Maggie," he said, his voice rough as he lifted her away from him, "are you sure?" He held her absolutely still. "Do you understand what this would be?"

"Yes," she murmured, "heaven."

"No. Nothing more than two bodies coming together, nothing else. Not love, not friendship. Lust, sex, call it what you want, but that's all this—" he pointed to where they still touched "—will be. Don't kid yourself. We won't be 'making love.' We'll be screwing." He spat the word out, making it as ugly as it could sound.

Maggie knew what he was doing, even if he didn't seem to. Smiling, she stroked his cheek. "So cynical. Making sure the boundaries are laid out. Are you afraid I'll take advantage of you, Sullivan, if you don't keep me at a distance?" She leaned forward. "I won't, you know."

He tightened his hands on her waist, forcing her to keep her distance. Through gritted teeth he said, "I can give you pleasure, Maggie. I can do that for you. I can even make you forget for an hour or two that all I'm offering is technique. Not my heart. Not my soul. They're gone."

Listening to him, Maggie wondered if he knew how hard he was working to dissuade her, how much his actions contradicted his words.

But she wouldn't tell him. Not yet.

"There's nothing left for you, sweet Maggie. Will you settle for technique? For skill?" His hard grip on her waist conveyed his anger. "Is anonymous, wild sex good enough for you?"

"Is that all you think it will be? Who are you working so hard to convince, Sullivan? Me or yourself?" She arched over him, giving him the gift of herself. "Are you sure, Sullivan?" she sighed into his ear. "Anonymous? I know you, Sullivan Barnett. I know you." She opened her arms to him. "And I want this moment for me, no matter what it means to you. Don't worry, Sullivan," she jeered gently, moved by his constraint, "I'll still respect you in the morning. And more importantly, I'll still respect myself. I won't regret this moment."

"Are you certain?" he repeated. "Be sure, because there's no going back."

She eased over him. "Do you promise it will be wild?"

"Aw, Maggie, what am I going to do with you?" he groaned, pulling her down and kissing her with a ferocity that rattled her bones.

"You know what you're going to do with me. You just finished telling me." Leaning her elbows on his chest, Maggie smiled down at his grim face. Poor Sullivan, trying so hard to convince her that he was conscienceless. "Or was it all talk, no action," she murmured, skimming her face over his abdomen, letting her hair trail over him.

So fast she wasn't prepared, he flipped her onto her back and he was over her, his face dark and determined. "You don't want this, Maggie, believe me."

"Believe me, I do," she insisted softly, rising to wrap her arms around his waist. "You don't know how much I want this," and she repeated his earlier gesture, looking down where their bodies touched, him heavy against the silk of her panties. "The question is, how much do you want me?"

His harsh laugh was filled with self-derision. "I can't hide what I feel, Maggie, but it's not love."

"I know," she whispered, kissing the taut cords of his throat. "But it will do."

He cupped her in the softest, most yearning part of her body, and his stroke wasn't anonymous at all, it was familiar and very personal. Whether he admitted it or not, more than his masculine drive was involved.

His movements were urgent now, all constraint suddenly gone, only him, Sullivan, driving toward her. His callused fingertips snagged on the silk of her panties, rough prickles against the skin of her thigh as he slid his fingers under the bottom of her panties, twisting the silky fabric against her as he kissed her inner thigh, his mouth hungry on her skin, hot.

And, as he'd promised, a killing pleasure speared through her, piercing and devastatingly sweet.

A pleasure to die for, to live for.

She longed for him, every cell in her body flowing toward him.

When she reached down for him, to urge him to her, he clamped her wrists above her head, holding her captive and still with his hands and thighs, cruelly letting the deep, internal shaking subside to flutters, twinges and tiny cramps dying away, leaving her stranded in a barren land.

"Maggie—" his mouth was a slash of white "—I promised you—"

"I know what you promised," she said wearily, struggling to free herself.

"I promised that you wouldn't be hurt tonight. Aw, Maggie," he said, taking her into his arms, his words slow and awkward, hesitant, "I didn't plan..." He pressed her against his heart which still boomed in his chest. "I can't protect..."

Not understanding him, she lifted her throbbing head. "But you did."

"No. I mean now. I can't protect you now from us, from me. I don't carry safeguards around in my wallet."

Maggie curled her arm around his neck, tenderness filling her. So Sullivan thought he only wanted anonymous, wild sex. He had made two promises to her. He'd sworn to keep her safe and he'd promised to give her pleasure. He'd kept both promises. In his own way.

Regardless of what he said he wanted, it wasn't anonymous sex. Caring in some fashion for her, he'd pulled back. He'd stopped when some men would have complained that they'd gone too far to quit. How Sullivan had controlled that rocket rush, she couldn't imagine.

Because, lost where he'd taken her, she would never have stopped him.

"Thank you." She kissed the base of his throat. His pulse pounded against her lips. His restraint was costing him dearly.

Resting her head under his chin, her arm still around his neck, curling to that slowing pulse, held against Sullivan's heart, she watched the starless sky turn toward morning.

Sometime in the night, Sullivan slept. In a half sleep, tuned to the twang of a trip wire, he was restless, his dreams muddled and disturbing, his unfulfilled body aching. In those dreams he wandered through a moonlit arctic waste where ice burned the soles of his feet and his mouth grew dry with thirst. Fire and ice and the world destroyed.

Then, just before morning, his dreams changed. In the distance, shifting, changing, Maggie and Lizzie opened their arms to him and he was running, running to them—

He jerked awake, his heart juddering. Wiping his mouth, he swallowed. God, he hated dreams. Treacherous, deceptive.

Maggie was still in his arms, her cloudy hair spread across his chest and clinging to his skin. Her mouth was slightly parted in sleep, a faint *b-b-b* pursing her mouth with each breath. Above her ear, a butterfly hovered, its wings catching in the wisps of her hair with each flutter.

Someone had discovered he was meeting the clerk. How, he had no idea. But he would find out. That someone was going to pay. He would see to it.

By raking him over the coals, Maggie had done him a favor. He was involved. He was responsible for incidents unwinding around him. He'd set events in motion. He would follow them to the end.

As for Maggie—

He brushed the butterfly free of her hair. No matter what she'd insisted, she deserved more than he could give her. After Taggart's he'd known how vulnerable she was. But he'd forgotten that underneath her sweet spunk she was fighting to bring her life together. He'd taken advantage of her. Oh, not meaning to—he'd give himself that, at least—but he'd stormed her senses. She'd been tired, keyed-up from the incident on the river and defenseless.

He'd used that vulnerability and turned her senses against her, made her betray herself.

He grimaced. His own behavior didn't bear examining in the bright sun of Seth's Landing shining through the palmetto branches over them.

Not liking the possibility that she had gotten under his skin, he stirred, stretching his legs and flexing them in the cramped space. In spite of the way he couldn't seem to keep his hands and mouth off her delectable self, he nurtured that residual caution that warned him against trusting her.

And yet he had. During everything that had happened on the river, he'd never doubted her. In the daylight, though, he remembered her friendship with Royal, remembered the seeming coincidence of her investigating his case. That question kept pecking away at his brain. Why had she, a brand-new detective just back on duty after a long convalescence, been turned loose on an old case?

None of it added up.

If she were an innocent pawn, as he began to suspect she might be, she was in over her head, and he'd be stupid to trust her, not knowing what she might reveal.

And foolhardy on his part to yield again to the pull of her sweetness.

As for Maggie... His thoughts came full circle in conclusion, resolving his doubts.

Not comprehending he had nothing to give her, she would be hurt by any involvement with him. Emotionally, at this point in her life. Physically, because involvement with him could put her, innocent pawn or not, into danger.

The thick rim of lashes lifted, lifted again, and she was looking at him. His heart, that shriveled kernel, turned over in his chest.

She yawned, her pink mouth parting. Her smile was tentative. He wasn't surprised. He'd told her she'd regret making— having sex, rather— In the morning with her uncertain smile facing him, he didn't know which to label what they'd shared. What they'd not shared. He took the easy way out. "Good morning, Detective."

She wrinkled her nose. "Okay." She stretched and looked down at herself in surprise. "Oh." She snapped her jeans, the sound a metal punctuation to her discomfort.

Sullivan had sensed that she would feel that way when she awoke, so he'd dressed her while she slept. It had seemed important to him at the time that she not wake up embarrassed by her nakedness.

"Thanks." She went bright red.

He flushed, too, remembering the moment when he'd broken apart from her, his aching unsatisfied.

She scooted to the end of the rowboat and retrieved her scarf, blushing again. "Don't suppose you have a comb?"

Shaking his head, Sullivan raked his fingers through his own hair, sweeping it free of his face.

"Any visitors during the night?"

"Nope." He rummaged for his wallet, which had worked itself free of his jeans pocket; handed her her notepad which had fallen out of his shirt.

He ignored the spark that leapt from his hand to hers. He'd made his decision. He would take care of her. He wouldn't get involved with her. He should feel relieved that he'd finally worked through his conflicting emotions and reached a sensible, rational decision. A decision that was best for her. For him.

He should feel relieved.

He felt, instead, ticked off and irritable. And frustrated.

He would get over it.

"Are we going to the car now?" Her face was wistfully hopeful. "We have Lala's cookies and peanut-butter sandwiches in the back. I'm hungry, Sullivan," she moaned, her stomach gurgling in proof.

"Yeah."

"And we're going to the police?" She was turning the notepad over and over.

"Maggie. You're the police. We've officially reported it to you." He didn't want to stroll into the police station with Maggie in tow.

"You're going to go in with me." Her tone was firm.

"What? If I don't, you'll arrest me?" He stepped out of the rowboat and peered through the brush to the clearing and the chickee.

"Hey, I might. Don't tempt me." She climbed out right behind him.

In the interest of his own sanity, he let her comment pass
without the easy jab, *Do I tempt you, sweet Maggie?* He ignored the voice in his head and pulled the palmetto cave apart.

"Yeah, I'll go with you." He reached back into the boat for
his compass. "Come on." He stared up at the glare of the sun
shining through the dank air, estimating the hour. "It'll take us
over an hour to drive into town. You'll want to shower first,"
he said, looking at her wrinkled pink shirt. No longer spank-
ing fresh and new, it was smeared with mud and glop from the
boat. Twig bits decorated her hair, and the scratch on her cheek
was a dried red line.

"People in glass houses shouldn't throw stones," she said,
reading his inadvertent grin. "Take a look at yourself."

His shirt and jeans were in worse shape than hers.

"Hmm. Wonder what this is?" he said, scrubbing at a large
greasy stain on his shirt.

"If you find out, don't tell me," she answered with a shudder. "But we're not going to stop to clean up. I want the evidence techs out here as soon as they can gear up. Too much
time has already passed. We disturbed the crime scene. Ani-
mals will mess it up more, and while I don't think anyone's
going to come back to check on him, I'm worried. Too much
time has passed."

"You realize the only chance you have of discovering who
killed him is finding out how someone knew he was coming
here," he said conversationally. "Two people knew originally
about the meeting plans. Me." He held up a finger. "The
clerk." He held up a second finger. "I told you." He unfolded
the third finger. "You were with me from the time I told you,
so I know you didn't pass on the meeting place."

She dropped her notepad and floundered for it on the damp
ground as he continued.

"We don't know who the clerk might have told, but having
talked with him, having seen the care with which he set up this
meeting place, not giving me any more information than I had
to know, I don't believe he blabbed. He struck me as an extremely careful man." Holding his fingers up, he concluded,
"Three people we know of. But someone, somehow, found

out." He scooped the notepad out of the mud and wiped it on his jeans before returning it to her. "And when we know how the killer found out, we'll know who he is."

"Maybe," she said, her tone unconvinced.

"Not maybe. Definitely."

The trek to the car and the ride to town passed in silence. Sullivan didn't feel like talking. He was having enough trouble staying reasonably human with irritation chomping at his gut, and Maggie, apparently, had her own thoughts.

Obviously spent, she drove at the speed limit, nibbling cookies from Lala's stash. When a sprinkle of crumbs dusted her small chest, she flapped her T-shirt with one hand, and Sullivan looked away from the winking flash of smooth stomach, satisfying himself with a stale peanut-butter sandwich.

Maggie pulled into her parking lot at the station shortly before ten.

Roaring with laughter, a group of uniformed cops stopped and stared as Sullivan climbed out of Maggie's car.

"Whooee, Mags, rough night?"

"Shut up, Clancy." Her glare frosted Clancy where he stood.

"Don't get mad, Mags, get even!" yelled a blue-uniformed woman with frizzed yellow hair sprouting under her hat. "Clancy's due for some *in*tense," she emphasized, "consciousness raising."

As Maggie pushed open the glass doors, preceding him to the front-desk area, Sullivan saw Royal's head jerk as he saw her. Looking up from a form he held casually in his hand, he watched her approach, his green gaze tracking her. Until he saw Sullivan at her heels. Then shutters slammed over his alert eyes and he slouched against the duty sergeant's desk, his lizard-skin boots crossed at the ankle, waiting. But he still watched Maggie, cataloging the rumpled pink shirt, her slim legs in the filthy jeans, his green-eyed gaze lingering on her curling, out-of-control hair as she approached.

Sullivan had never liked Royal, liked him less as he stared at the arm the detective slung possessively around Maggie.

"What's up, Mags?" Keeping Maggie at his side, Royal turned sideways to Sullivan, asserting territoriality. "Who's your... friend?"

"I'll explain later. We have to see the chief. Is he in?"

"Johnny's always available." Royal laughed. "You know Johnny. Afraid the building will fall down in a cloud of plaster dust if he's not here to see personally that every *i* is dotted, every *t* crossed."

Sullivan didn't like Maggie's wide smile, the crinkling of her nose at Royal. In his pressed jeans, the expensive cotton shirt gloving his health-club-defined chest, Royal was too perfect, too golden. Even his hair had every barbered strand sleekly in place.

Rumpling his own hair, Sullivan closed in, invading Royal's space. He knew Royal recognized him. They'd seen each other around town. He'd bet good green dollars Royal had read the series he'd written on corruption. Sullivan stuck out his hand, forcing Royal to drop his arm from around Maggie or ignore the extended appendage. "Sullivan Barnett."

A glint in Royal's eyes acknowledged his appreciation of Sullivan's tactic. Acknowledged it and countered, "Nice meetin' you, Barnett. Good series awhile back. Stirred up a hornet's nest, didn't it? Haven't seen anything lately. You been busy?" he asked, his blandly courteous question concealing the knife.

"You should know," Sullivan said, putting a spin on his words and deriving mean pleasure at the man's quick glance at Maggie. "Lots of cute little scams to keep us reporter types busy. You know how it is," he wound up, enjoying the flicker of confusion in Royal's eyes. Either Royal knew something or he was thrown off balance by seeing Maggie with him and wondering about them. Didn't matter. Let him wonder. Sullivan liked sneaking in a knife jab of his own, but a second later he wasn't sure which had given him the most gratification, the hint that Royal was hiding something or Royal's uncertainty about what he and Maggie had been doing.

The score even, Sullivan turned to Maggie. "Get Jackson, why don't you?" His irritation was turning into a full-bore acid stomach. "I'd like to get home."

He was afraid Maggie read him too well when she turned, a tiny grin tucking in the corners of her full mouth. Her eyes slid to Royal and back to Sullivan, but she didn't say anything. The quiver of her bottom lip, however, spoke volumes.

"Right. Sullivan's in a hurry," she explained to Royal, that smile spreading like cream over coffee. "He's impatient for his bath."

Jamming his hands in his back pockets, Sullivan managed not to snarl. "Yeah," he said, "cleanliness is next to godliness, I hear." He surveyed Royal's pristine appearance. "Personally, I've always had my doubts."

Not giving Royal time to retort, Sullivan took Maggie's elbow and stepped toward Jackson's office. "Do we need an appointment?" he asked, his question heavy with sarcasm.

"Easy does it, Sullivan," Maggie said, patting his arm. "I know you don't like cops, but you don't have to be so obvious about it. Especially on my turf."

She'd missed the point of the whole byplay. She'd thought Sullivan was being generally hostile toward cops, Royal responding in kind. The way Royal had staked out his claim to her had sailed right over her head.

Or maybe she'd liked the way he draped his arm over her, his hand dangling all too close to her breast for Sullivan's comfort.

Jackson's secretary rang them through, Sullivan by now in the grip of a raging stomach burn.

"Hey, y'all." The chief's smile was friendly. "What can I do you for, Mr. Barnett?"

Sullivan had always hated that stupid line. He leaned against the wall and let Maggie run with the ball. Anyway, he was curious. Be interesting to see how Maggie explained the events of the previous night.

"Chief, we have a problem."

"That's what I'm here for, Webster. This guy giving you trouble?" He waved expansively toward Sullivan, winking.

"No. We have a corpse at Seth's Landing."

"Hell's bells." Jackson's chair squeaked as he leaned back. "Son of a gun."

And Sullivan listened in grudging admiration as she detailed the night's events in clear, concise order, telling what was necessary, omitting extraneous detail. She included Tolly, the dumping, the ensuing pursuit. She explained the delay and made it credible.

She was impressive as hell.

"Shoot, Webster, you know how that riffraff out in the county lives. Y'all were in the wrong place at the wrong time." He shot a shrewd glance at Sullivan. "What makes you think this guy was your contact, anyway?"

Jackson squeaked back and forth in his chair, friendly as a crocodile, his cheeks creased in a sunburned smile, and Sullivan wasn't about to tell him anything.

When Sullivan didn't answer, Maggie reviewed the main points, emphasizing that the man would have had no other reason for being in the waste that Seth's Landing had become.

"I dunno, Webster. Sounds like a back-country drug buy that went sour. The county sheriff's office has been making a bunch of busts out in that neck of the woods. Y'all broke up a drug buy, that's what." He looked sincerely regretful. "'Course, the department could use a good murder investigation." With a crafty look at Sullivan, he added, "We been gettin' such bad press and all, lately."

Sullivan had to grin. The old fool had a certain charm.

It had kept people electing him until the rules had changed. Now the city council, in its infinite wisdom, was in charge of hiring and firing the chief of police. Jackson's likability—along with his charm and his willingness to make himself available to cook hush puppies from his sainted mother's recipe for every fund-raising fish fry in the county—had helped him there, too.

Hard to think bad of a man slapping steaming hot hush puppies on your plate and heaping piles of coleslaw next to them.

But Sullivan didn't trust him any farther than he could throw him.

Patiently Maggie explained the sequence that had led them to the man's body. "Chief, he was right where he was supposed to meet us."

"No-o-o, Webster. Seems to me you said he was down at the river's edge, and Mr. Barnett was going to rendezvous with him back in the woods?"

Clever old coot. He hadn't missed a trick. Rendezvousing in the woods had been the original plan. Sullivan had only thrown that out in a brief aside to Maggie during the long night, but she'd included it in her notes, and Jackson had picked it up without writing one word down.

"Yes. That was the original plan, Chief, but you can't write off his being at the river as only a coincidence."

Jackson swung his chair back and forth. "You real serious about this, Webster?"

"I believe it's all connected to Mr. Barnett's articles. The bombing. This murder. All of it."

She hadn't slipped and referred to him by his first name. The woman was remarkable.

"We'll have to send the crime-scene boys out no matter if this joker's some drug scum or Barnett's source." Jackson looked thoughtfully at Sullivan. "You the one insisting this guy's your contact?"

"Seems reasonable," Sullivan said, still keeping his own counsel. Jackson was a mixture of country shrewd and city slick, and he could be lethal.

"All right, then." Jackson's eyes flicked to the door and back to them. "Have Gaines take the report on this, Webster, and you go home and get some rest." Swiveling so that his back was to Sullivan, he added, "How you doing, Mags? Is returning too much of a strain? We can arrange more time off, you know."

"Everything is fine, Chief. I'll give Royal my report. In the meantime, I'm continuing with my investigation." The clickety-click of her pen revealed her nervousness.

Sullivan felt pity stirring in him as she waited for the chief's reply. Cynically, he considered the undertones in Jackson's affable manner. Seemed as if Jackson had issued a threat in his genial way. Or perhaps it was genuine concern for Maggie, and Sullivan was being too suspicious. Hard to tell with Jackson. He could have a soft spot for her. But he'd made her his protégé, too, just as he had Royal Gaines.

"Sure. You find out who's sending this fine young man such nasty letters. The federal boys are going to be involved, too, since it's the mail, but see what you can do." Jackson beamed. "Be a credit to Palmaflora's police department if you can find anything out."

And that was the end of it.

Sullivan knew the clerk's death would disappear in paperwork. Anger and stomach acid erupted.

As he and Maggie walked outside, he rounded on her. "Jackson's not going to do diddly about this, you know. And you're going to hand over your report all neatly typed up to Gaines, who'll sit on it. That guy out in the wood is dead, and no one's going to do anything more than make nice-nice.''

White-faced, Maggie stood there, letting his attack roll over her.

"They're too damned cozy with each other for my comfort, and you seem to be thick as thieves with both of them. You and I are the only ones who knew about the meeting. I don't see how you could have said anything to either one of them, since you were with me every minute, but I'm asking you right out, Detective, did you tell anybody? *Anybody?*''

She should be defending herself, telling him he was a jerk for even thinking she had. Her white-faced silence lit the match to his fury.

Gripping her shoulders, he shook her. Her bones were fragile under his hands, reminding him of the feel of her in his arms during the night, and he was consumed with a sense of betrayal and buried rage. "Did you, Maggie—did you somehow tell someone?" He shook her again, her white face haunting him.

Chapter 10

Maggie wanted to throw up.

Instead she listened, not believing the torrent of accusations pouring forth from Sullivan.

"Thick as thieves?" she finally said. "You think Chief Jackson and Royal are involved in some conspiracy?"

"You left out one other person." Slashing red across his cheekbones, anger left its mark.

"Me." She nodded. "How could I have forgotten? You're accusing me of being involved in that clerk's death, aren't you?"

"I want to know if you told anyone about the meeting," he insisted stubbornly. "That's all."

"It isn't all there is to it." She was shaking inside with a sick fury at her foolishness. "You're accusing me of being crooked. You've implied as much about Chief Jackson before, but you don't ever give me any proof. And now you accuse Royal, my friend—they're both my friends!" she cried.

"I think they're involved in a lot of under-the-table crooked deals going on in this town." Scowling, he'd folded his arms, an unsubtle message.

"You expect me to believe you? And you don't offer any proof? How can you? I've known them for years. They spent time at my side when I was in the hospital. Royal has taken care of me on the job in ways you'd never understand. He and I are *friends,* and you're asking me to doubt him? Who in heaven's name do you think you are to accuse these people I know better than you do? The next best thing to family I have?"

"Why are you so willing to give them a pass?" he argued.

"Because I know them. I care about them, and so I trust them. Why can't you trust me?"

He laughed, and it was the bitterest sound she'd ever heard. "Because a man died last night. Because you're the only one besides me who knew."

"You keep insisting that no one else could have known. What if the contact *did* tell someone? What makes you so sure he didn't?" She could never tell Sullivan now that she'd called Royal and talked with him.

"I don't know what I think," he finally said, rubbing his head and lifting the dusty strands of brown into spikes. "I want to trust you."

Maggie didn't believe him.

"No. You don't. You don't trust me, and no matter what I said, no matter what I told you, you wouldn't believe me."

"I might, Maggie. If you told me the truth."

"You wouldn't know the truth about me if it slapped you in the face. You made up your mind the first time we met and you've had this mental checklist of transgressions. Every time I do something that seems suspicious to you in your seat of judgment—Sullivan Barnett versus the Rest of the Whole Wide World—you mark another tick against me."

"I don't sit in judgment."

"Don't lie, Sullivan. Face it, you look around you and you see conspiracies, betrayal, evil. I don't."

"You're too trusting. Especially for a cop. Cops and reporters don't trust people."

"The difference, though, is that you like not trusting people, Sullivan, don't kid yourself. You hold your mistrust of people, your cynicism to you like a heating pad. Does it keep you warm at night? All that passionate cynicism? You think everyone is lying to you unless you have proof they're not."

"That's why I'm a damned good reporter. People lie. I show them for what they are. Liars. Thieves." He paused, looking at er for a long minute, fury in his gaze before he concluded, "Crooks. But I don't want you to be a crook, Maggie."

"I think you do." Wounded, hurting in ways she couldn't have dreamed, she went for the jugular. "Who did I kiss last night, Sullivan? You? Or a reporter? Tell me, because I'd like to know what kind of fool I almost made of myself."

His lips thinned and he turned away from her.

"Let me know if you figure it out, will you?" she called after his rigid back.

If she were a weeper, she'd be bawling. Had she and Sullivan been in the same room together? Hadn't he heard every word she'd said? Her insistence that the matter was important?

She rubbed her nose. Sullivan had said it wouldn't be making love, and maybe it wouldn't have been. But she'd come perilously close to surrendering herself body and soul to him during those drawn-out, isolated hours.

He'd held her and protected her.

She'd trusted him.

In his arms she'd felt whole for the first time since the shooting. She'd felt none of the disorienting shifts that frightened her, none of the confusion that kept her doubting her actions and judgments. With Sullivan, her actions had seemed to have the clarity of crystal ringing in her mind, her body, everything meshing in a delirium of joy, pealing like chimes in harmony.

She'd been a fool. Was a fool. And all that wonderful clarity she'd felt last night had shattered like crystal into sharp pieces that were cutting her to ribbons. Judgment? She had none. She would have given herself as completely as she knew how with Sullivan.

But he didn't trust her.

And she couldn't trust her judgment, only her instincts at the deepest level of her truest self. There, and only there, did she experience certainty in all the muddle.

With that thought speeding her feet, she did an about-face and stormed back into the station, pushing past Clancy, who was smart enough to let her pass with no comment.

Royal was huddled over Jackson's desk, the two of them conferring in low voices when she stepped into his office without knocking.

She'd never gone into the chief's office unannounced.

"Webster?" The chief looked worried. "What's up?"

"I need to talk with you. With Royal. If you have the time."

"Sure, have a seat. Gaines, we'll discuss that other situation after the three of us finish. That okay, Maggie?"

He was speaking to her in a soothing voice that rubbed her the wrong way. She didn't want to be soothed. She wanted that pinging clarity again, not this muddy, out-of-tune clanging inside her all the time. "Whatever you say, Chief."

"Spit it out, Mags." Royal was off to her side. She could see him, but she couldn't keep both of them in view at the same time. She'd used the same technique herself, but it irked her that they were using it on her.

"Okay. Here it is in a nutshell. Barnett believes that he has proof that several politicians and cops are involved in a conspiracy that covers several areas."

"What areas?" Jackson walked behind her and shut the door. "Tell me, Maggie. Every word will stay inside this room."

"He doesn't know how it all ties together, but this conspiracy involves real-estate holdings, payoffs to politicians for rezoning votes—"

"Most of that has been in his articles, Mags." Royal's voice was calm. "What's the problem?"

"He believes the man killed was a contact who intended to provide him with records documenting the way the conspiracy had manipulated deeds and dummy corporations so that they could buy up land around the county and develop it, making fortunes several times over for everyone involved."

"Neither of you said anything about these records. You didn't say he was going to have them with him."

"It would have been in my written report."

"Did the man have them with him?" Jackson paced in front of her, his quick glances making her uneasy after Sullivan's attack.

"No. I didn't see any papers lying around him. We looked." She couldn't recall why she'd omitted the fact about the records. She should have included that information. It was in her notes and she'd skipped past it. Maybe because Sullivan was standing in the corner watching her every move. That, and Jackson himself had made her nervous.

"Why was Barnett so sure the dead man was his contact, Mags? Did Barnett recognize him?" Royal was kneeling in front of her, his incredible smile beguiling her.

Trust.

She had called him and told him where she was heading. She'd explained the purpose of the meeting.

Loyalty.

An essential compact between people.

She'd trusted Royal last night and a man had been killed. She'd trusted her instincts about Sullivan and had seen the result in his furious attack on her in the station parking lot.

"Hello, Mags. Come back, babe." Royal's green eyes were open, guileless, unlike Sullivan's hooded blue eyes that judged everything and everyone.

If she were to trust anyone, it would be Royal. She knew him. *And she knew Sullivan, too; had instinctively trusted herself with him in the most elemental way. He hadn't failed her.*

"Sorry, Royal. Tired, I guess. A long night and I'm short on sleep. No, he'd never seen him before." It was the truth.

"But did he know who the man was? Where he'd gotten the records?" Jackson was still in his soothing mode, and maybe that caused her to lie. Maybe not.

"He had no idea. Or he didn't tell me if he did." There. She'd lied to her friends, betrayed their trust. No wonder Sullivan had doubts about her. She had her own wagonload of misgivings at this point.

"Thanks for filling us in, Maggie, but I don't know how this will help." Jackson was heading for the door.

"One more item, Chief. Barnett indicated that the records also included proof the illegal dumping was tied in with the financing of the real-estate deals and kickbacks. The same people were involved." She owed Royal and Jackson that much loyalty.

"Sheesh." Turning to Royal, Jackson asked, "You heard anything about illegal dumping?"

"Rumors. That's all. Supposedly some of the paper-and-pulp industries aren't thrilled about the cost of complying with the EPA regulations. There's always been a problem with pesticide disposal. Some of the farmers and big agricultural-pesticide companies make noise all the time about the nuisance. The cost of high-temperature incineration.''

Jackson sat on the edge of his desk. ''Anybody in particular?''

''None that I know of, anyway. But you know me, Chief, I don't hang around with the cow crowd.'' Royal rose and included them both in the genial warmth of his smile. ''Biggest problem I have is keeping my boots clean.''

''Maggie's the one with the problem. You know you haven't been yourself since November, Maggie. Now, I don't want to insult you, but you look real stressed to me. You should think seriously about going back on sick leave. For a while. I didn't want to bring it up in front of Barnett—might see it in the paper if I did—'' he laughed ''—but I'm real worried about you, girl.''

Woman, Maggie thought, gritting her teeth. Had Jackson always made her edgy like this or had Sullivan colored all of her reactions?

''Chief Jackson—'' she rose and faced him ''—I appreciate your concern. I always have. You've been a friend to me when I needed one. You've helped me make my way through some of the hassles of being a female cop. But don't worry about me. I can take care of myself. I'm tired, not stressed, and I can handle Barnett.''

Jackson raised his shoulders. ''If you're sure. I don't want anything happening to you, Webster. You gave us all some bad hours. We want you well and back to your old self again.''

''I'll do my best. I came back because it seemed an opportune time to make my position clear if I hadn't, and to get some clothes out of my locker. I apologize if I intruded.''

''You're never an intrusion, Maggie. Don't even think it.'' He shook her hand. ''Royal, why don't you keep Maggie company and help her carry her things to her car?''

Royal stood next to her, a shade too close at the moment, and she moved away as he opened the door. ''I'll touch base with you later, Johnny.''

''Do that, Gaines. But take care of Maggie first.'' In Jackson's gravelly drawl it came out sounding like a threat.

Maggie wanted to go home, escape this place that had been like a second home to her for years. No. It had *been* her home. She hadn't had time for anything else except her work, and now that had turned against her. She didn't know if she would ever truly feel comfortable around Jackson and Royal again.

Once she'd clarified her thinking about what was happening to her, then she'd see how she felt about Jackson. The situation with Royal would take more thought. They had too much history between them for her to sort through it easily.

She had too many secrets.

Royal opened her car door and hung her uniform on the garment hook in back.

"Thanks. Look, Royal, I feel terrible about the other night, but you've been wonderful. I'm relieved nothing has changed between us. That we can be friends."

"Things have changed, babe, you know that." He shut the door behind her as she slid into the hot driver's seat. "But we'll get through this. So long as you don't make a good friend out of Barnett." His smile was teasing, but his green gaze stayed on her a beat too long for teasing.

At that moment, Maggie wanted nothing more than to run away from her best friend and cry herself to sleep.

In her rearview mirror, she saw Royal standing with his legs apart, his boots gleaming in the sun as he watched her leave.

Sullivan rang the doorbell of the modest concrete-stucco house. The house seemed empty in the late-afternoon heat, the doorbell echoing for a long time in the silence. He felt like a heel for showing up at Paul Reid's house, but he had to talk with the man's widow.

Paul would have made copies of the records he'd taken to Seth's Landing.

Stalking away from Maggie at the police station, Sullivan had started hiking, too furious to do anything under the circumstances except walk his rage off. The walk had burned off his anger and left him able to think.

Stomping down the hot highway, his boots beginning to pinch after three miles, he'd realized he had one chance of salvaging the story. One chance to recover the information. Notes. Records.

He'd gone into a local liquor store and called a taxi. He'd gone straight from there to the courthouse, where nobody had yet spread the news about the death. Pretending to interview a secretary in the Recorder of Deeds office, he'd brought the conversation around to courthouse staff, letting her think he was going to do a sidebar on the people who waded through the mountains of records and papers. She'd supplied Paul's name. His address.

Sullivan had thought he might have problems, because he hadn't bothered to change in his hurry to find the clerk's identity and address before it was too late. The secretary obviously thought reporters were a seedy bunch. She hadn't reacted to his Seth's Landing garments. The press was clearly in trouble with its image.

Sullivan had made a couple of stops before he went to the clerk's house. He'd bought a remote starter for his car, and he'd gone home and cleaned up, embarrassed by the indifference to his appearance the secretary had shown. On the way to Reid's, he'd driven in a circuitous, random pattern, watching to see if he was being followed. He hadn't parked his car in front of the Reids' home. He'd left it a block away.

As the door opened, Sullivan hoped he wouldn't have to break the news to Reid's widow.

He didn't think he could bring himself to face the first moments of her grief.

The door opened slowly.

"Yes?" A tall, slightly chubby young woman scarcely out of her teens opened the door. A suntanned blonde, she was pretty in the way girls are, their youth lending a bloom of its own. Her red-rimmed eyes, though, were old with early grief.

She might age well. Her face, though still unformed by life, had possibilities. It held strength. A strength that would be tested in the coming months, he thought, as an infant wailed drearily in the back of the house, distracting her.

"Mrs. Reid? I'm Sullivan Barnett. Your husband and I had a project we were working on together. I'm more sorry than I can tell you about his death."

She nodded. She looked as though speech were too great an effort. He wondered what she'd been told about her husband's death. Sullivan wasn't going to fill in any blanks for her.

He didn't have the courage to make this girl-woman face any more reality today.

"I wish I didn't have to bother you, but I need to talk with you, if you don't mind?" He stood waiting in the heat, glad he'd taken the time to clean up and put on his one pair of good pants and a shirt with a tie. He owed this child the formal trappings of respect. Life was going to be hard for her.

"I have time." Tears welled in her light blue eyes, pooling at the sides and dripping down her round cheeks. She wiped them away with the back of her hands. "Come on in, Mr. Barnett." The tears started again and she hiccuped.

"Look, Mrs. Reid, if you want to wait, I can come back. If this is a bad time?"

"It's a bad time, for sure." Her voice was high and girlish. She would be a giggler in happier days. "But I can talk. I can't sleep, so you might as well come on in. I'd be glad of the company."

"You don't have anyone with you right now?" Poor kid.

"My ma and pa are coming down from Atlanta this evening, but they couldn't get here any sooner. I called them right after the police came and told me about Paul. Wait here. I want to check on Paulie." She shut the door and walked down a short corridor to the baby's room. Humming in a tear-shaky voice, she patted the boy until his wails tapered to snuffles, much like his mother's.

Sullivan wanted to turn around and walk out of the clean little house with its carefully framed photos and pots of geraniums along the window ledges. He couldn't do this.

But she returned before he could call out that he was leaving, and he was trapped.

She sank onto a burgundy-and-blue love seat. "What did you want to talk about, Mr. Barnett? Did Paul owe you money or something?"

"Nothing like that." Of all the interviews he'd ever done, this one was turning out to be the most difficult. The child-mother, the baby weeping the way the mother wanted to, and the memory of Paul Reid's sightless eyes locked the words in Sullivan's throat.

"Were you a friend of his?" She wiped her eyes again, this time with a tissue she'd stuffed in the pocket of her skirt.

"No, not exactly." He cleared his throat uncomfortably. Impossible. What had he been thinking of to intrude on this child's tragedy? A tragedy he held himself partially responsible for.

"I think I remember Paul mentioning you."

"Did he say anything about the project, Mrs. Reid?" Sullivan hoped Reid had, hoped he hadn't. One way got Maggie off the hook, the other—

"Oh, no, Paul seldom talked about work. He said it wouldn't be ethical to reveal anything about the records he saw. They were private. He was real conscientious about that." Pride colored her girlish voice.

"I'm sure he was." Looking around, Sullivan didn't see a desk in the tidy living room. "He had some material for me. Records of the project he intended me to have, but, unfortunately, couldn't give me. Would he have left copies of those reports here? In your home?"

"Paul was real thorough. We even keep receipts from the grocery store." Her smile was watery. "I could show you where Paul keeps all his records. If that would help?"

"It would be an enormous help, Mrs. Reid. You have no idea."

In the room designated as Paul's study, his wife pointed out the computer and neatly arranged shelves, the file drawers with their computer-generated labels. "Go ahead and look through them. The detective who came went through them, too. He took some folders with him."

"What?" That had been fast work on somebody's part.

"He gave me a receipt. Was that right?" she asked in a worried voice. "Paul always took care of things like that. He liked to. And I liked fixing the house and gardening. He said it balanced out for now, but he wanted me to learn how to take care of the business end of our lives, too." A full sob broke loose. "I'll have to learn now. Excuse me, Mr. Barnett. I'll be right back." Sobbing, she left the room.

Quickly, not expecting to find anything after the detective had beaten him to the punch, Sullivan thumbed through the remaining files, looking for anything relating to the material Reid had been holding. The eye of the computer stared silently at him, a stack of disks beside it.

He turned on the computer and worked his way through its hard-disk directory, seeing nothing that set off a buzz in his brain. He would know what he was looking for when he saw it. Changing directories, he checked the five-and-a-half-inch floppies.

Nothing on them except household records. As he stared at the stack, he realized suddenly that, though most of them were black, some were coded by color—red, blue, green, yellow. He was so used to using the utilitarian black ones himself, he'd missed registering the colors the first time through.

Thoughtfully, he picked up the blue stack. One bore a smiley face on its label: Paulie.

Paul Reid didn't seem like the happy-face type. Or the type to be drawn to an array of colorful disks. Possibly Mrs. Reid had been. And possibly not.

He inserted the happy-face disk. He'd only check its directory, not pulling up any files. Now that he thought about it some more, the label and the directory puzzled him.

Why did Paulie's disk have a directory of grocery stores and pharmacies? What would a proud new father keep records of? Surely the disk should contain records of Paulie's weight, his feeding schedule, his visits to the doctor? That might be in the pharmacy file. But it seemed too vague in contrast to the carefully indexed and labeled folders in the file cabinet. His wife had made it clear that she hadn't handled their records, so she hadn't created the haphazard, cutesy disk in an excess of motherly pride.

Calling up the directory again, Sullivan entered the first file. Bingo. He didn't need to enter the others.

He'd been right about Paul Reid—a careful, conscientious, cautious man who'd wanted to make the world a better place for his new son. And so he'd fed Sullivan the information on Paulie's disk, bit by bit.

The information would be in the pharmacy file. Sullivan knew now how Reid's mind had worked. He'd been a good man, and he'd deserved to see his son in that better world.

Sullivan exited and turned off the computer.

He found Reid's wife curled up on her side on a twin bed in the baby's room, the child tucked inside the shelter of her arm and facing toward the wall. Both were asleep. A hissing static came from the baby monitor on the wall.

As much as he hated to wake her, he had to. "Mrs. Reid?" he said, pitching his voice low so as not to waken Paulie, who was sucking wetly on the minute thumb of one starfish hand.

"Oh, Mr. Barnett, I'm so sorry." Her voice was groggy and her eyes puffy as she struggled to wake up. "I lay down for a minute with Paulie and forgot all about you."

"Don't get up. You need your sleep. So does the baby. May I take this?" He held up the Paulie disk. "I'll write out a receipt for it and let myself out."

"Is it the project records?"

"Yes."

"Good. Paul would feel real bad if he let you down." Her head slumped back on the pillow next to the fuzzy yellow of her small son's downy hair.

"Don't worry, Mrs. Reid, I don't imagine Paul ever let anyone down in his entire life."

Closing the door of the house softly and checking to make sure it locked behind him, Sullivan looked back at the purple hydrangeas and the trailing vines growing on a trellis next to the fence. Paul Reid and his wife had made a good life for themselves. They should have had more time to play with their son in this shady, well-tended yard.

They should have had all those years that had been stolen from them in the mud at Palma River.

He couldn't give Paul Reid's son a father, but he could give him a hero to look up to. By the time he finished his series, Paulie Reid would know what his father had tried to do for him.

It was dark by the time Sullivan returned to the cottage. He hadn't gotten into his car until he'd searched under it, and then he'd started it with the remote control. Now, in the dark, he slipped as silently as a cat around the beach house, checking for lurking intruders. He didn't enter the house until he'd examined the perimeters again with his flashlight, looking this time for signs of tampering.

When he was finally inside, he switched on all the outside lights and double bolted the doors. Stripping out of his shirt and tie, he showered the kinks and knots out of his body, letting the water pound into him for the second time today. Then, bare-chested, he pulled on an old pair of gym shorts over his naked body and poured himself a stiff drink.

It was going to be a long night.

Taking the drink and a plate full of cheese, he settled himself in front of his computer in the bedroom. Regardless of what he found in Reid's records, he was going to need additional documentation before the paper would run the story. Reid had had copies of the original deeds, transfers, work orders and checks, but those were gone.

The originals might or might not be in their respective files. If he were involved in a plot of this size, he'd leave as small a paper trail as possible, considering the current mania for faxing and copying. And he'd make damned sure he didn't leave any original papers around once they'd been copied and perhaps handed over to some investigator.

But crooks weren't always smart, no matter how bright they were. They might assume they had all the copies. They might be arrogant enough to leave the originals, figuring no one would be persistent enough to wade through all the documentation again.

Going in armed with dates, numbers and names, he would be able to find documentation because he would know where to look, where to imply he had facts when he was still searching for them, where to exert pressure on someone already jittery with guilt. Thanks to the material Reid had collected, he would find the proof.

He had the patience.

And now he had the motivation.

He would carry with him forever the sight of Paul Reid's wife and son curled up together in that blue-and-yellow baby's room that they'd furnished with such love.

The cursor blinked its command, and Sullivan inserted the disk, pulling up the file he'd skimmed earlier. Grocery Receipts. Reid had had a sense of humor. The file was a listing of land purchases with the original owner, the buyer, the sale price, the broker and the history of the parcel. Each purchase was indexed under the name of a local grocery store. Sullivan sipped his whiskey and scrolled through the detailed lists, looking for patterns, repeating names, names he'd seen before in other contexts.

And he found them, as he'd known he would.

Working his way steadily file-by-file, he was fascinated by the complexity of the manipulations. He could see how the situation had snowballed. So much easy money to be made. So easy to give in to the opportunity of a lifetime.

The doorbell rang at the front door. He exited from the file, but left the computer booted up, its green cursor insistent on the monitor. Standing to the side of the door, he looked outside.

Maggie Webster was the last person he would have expected to find on his doorstep. Wearing a green T-shirt dress that ended above her knees, she looked as delicious as lime sherbet.

"Hello, Maggie." He barricaded the doorway with his arm. "I told you I don't like surprises." He looked both ways down the dark road. "Where's your car?"

"Two streets over. I cut through the backyards."

"Very smart. If I were you, I wouldn't leave my car parked in front of my house, either. I'm high on the list of really unpopular people."

"May I come in?" Her hair was piled up on top of her head, and huge gold hoops swung from her delicate earlobes. She was wearing lipstick.

Sullivan blinked as he realized it was the first time he'd seen her wearing makeup. "I don't think that would be a good idea."

"I want to talk to you." One pale green shoe edged forward.

He blocked it with his bare toe. "Well, Detective, I don't want to talk to you."

"We need to clear the air, Sullivan."

"Oh, I don't think so," he said, watching her gold hoop earrings sway as she shook her head.

"Please." Her hands at her side, she waited. "I need to talk to you. I'll leave after I've said what I have to."

"You know, I can't think of one damned thing that you could say that would interest me right now."

"After you left the station, I went back to see Chief Jackson and Royal."

"What?"

"You had made such terrible accusations. I was confused. I had to see if what you'd said made sense when I was with them. We'd been friends for so long. I don't make friends easily, Sullivan. I don't treat friendship lightly. It's important to me. You were asking me to betray my loyalty to them, to trust you. But you wouldn't return that trust. It was all one-sided." A gulf breeze played with the hair curling around her face.

"One-sided?"

"I had to do the trusting. You got to decide if I passed the tests. Trusting goes both ways, Sullivan, or it leads nowhere. It's a dead end. All you have to do is listen. Is that too much to ask?"

He thought under the circumstances it was, but she kept looking at him with her eyes big and pleading, sapping his resolve. "Maybe I'll listen, or maybe I'll just look at you, all gussied up in your pretty green dress. Is the dress for my benefit?" He gripped the edge of the doorjamb so that he wouldn't trace the V neck of the dress.

"Actually, for mine. After Seth's Landing, I felt as if I'd never get rid of that smell."

He wouldn't let her in. She'd had her say at the police station and again on his stoop. Maybe she had a point, but he didn't have to invite her inside in her skinny green almost-a-dress. "Did you think dressing up would help get you through my door?"

"Couldn't hurt, is what I thought."

She was so tempting to him, the energy in her small body feminine and mysterious. She looked so determined and earnest, so intent.

And underneath her lipstick and the brave banner of her green dress, underneath all that purpose burning in her, she looked weary and lost.

It was the vulnerability that once again got to him, shoving aside any good sense he still laid claim to. "What the hell, Maggie. Come on in."

Chapter 11

She ducked under his arm, glancing at him. "I didn't think you were going to let me in." Her skinny dress flowed with her movements, a clean, cool river over gentle curves.

"I wasn't." Already regretting the impulse that had guided him, he shut the door with a snap. All she had to do was get three feet away from him and his willpower turned to jelly. He was drawn to her in spite of his every effort, and he didn't like it one damned bit.

Her arms upraised, she jabbed tendrils of hair back into the mass at the top. "Why did you change your mind?"

"I don't have one damned idea."

Her underarms were pale and smooth. He wanted to run his mouth over that smoothness, see for himself if it was as silky as he'd thought.

"But you let me in. You changed your mind. Why?"

"Curiosity again—I don't know. Pass it off to delayed adolescence, if you want to. And, no, I'm not drunk," he ground out. "I just had a few sips. Smell." He leaned toward her and exhaled. "But I'm beginning to wish I were." He followed her down the hall. "Why don't you turn that sweet butt of yours around and leave? That's what would make me happiest."

Looking over her shoulder, she didn't say anything. In the kitchen, she glanced once at the newspaper clipping and then at the closed door to the beach. "Taking better care of yourself, Barnett?"

Give the woman an inch, and she had all her sass back. "I'm working, Maggie. Say your piece." He leaned against the sink, stretching his legs out. He was exhausted. Not up to a battle with Maggie. She looked fresh and cool, a curve of green drifting around his kitchen, stopping here, there, not staying in one spot.

"I said most of what I had to on your step."

"Oh, good. You're leaving, then?" He straightened quickly. "I'll walk you to your car." He wanted her to leave. He wanted her to stay. He still wanted her.

Even though he'd seen how close she, Jackson and Gaines were, he wanted her.

"No, not yet." She passed by him to the bare counter, touched it and passed him again, the breeze generated by her movement bringing her scent to him. "Sullivan." She stopped in front of him.

"What?" Her scent was driving him wild.

"When I returned, to talk with Royal and the chief?" She fiddled—there was no other word for it—with the flap of her dark green leather purse, lifting it and snapping, lifting and snapping.

He almost reached for a pen to give her. He missed the authoritative *click-click* he was used to. This indecisive Maggie made him very nervous.

How could she turn him inside out like this? All that sweet fragrance and her delicate curves. More than that, though. Her essence—that was what pulled him. Something in her nature that sang to him like a siren song, pulling him off course, pulling him to her and the knife-sharp rocks.

"They were head-to-head, talking."

Mrs. Reid had said a detective had talked to her. Sullivan should have asked her which one, but he'd been uncomfortable with her grief. He'd wanted to exit as fast as possible after he'd retrieved whatever files Reid might have left. "They're buddies."

"Not really." She smoothed the leather flap shut. "Although Royal likes the chief, well, we *all* do. He's behind his cops all the way. And we give him our loyalty in return." Now she fiddled again with her hair, not with her usual purposeful efforts to control the mass of curls, but in troubled distraction.

"Good for you. I'm sure Johnny's real glad you're all behind him."

"Listen to me for a minute, will you?" Exasperated, she reached out to hold his arm.

But he turned, and her square palm with its short nails slid in a light scratch down his bare chest.

"Maggie. You listen to me." He jerked out a chair and gestured to it. "Sit. Don't move until you've finished. You're making me nuts with all your hither-and-thithering." He leaned over her. "I'm listening. Talk." He glared down at her.

"This was different. There was . . . an atmosphere. Do you know what I mean?"

He did.

"I felt like a stranger, an outsider. As though I'd interrupted something. Jackson was so—" she stopped "—I had the strangest sense he was putting a spin on things for me. *Handling* me, like a hostile civilian." She slid the strap of her purse off her shoulder and tied knots in it, one after the other until a row of them shortened the strap to a tennis-ball-size loop.

"You've never felt that way before?" His curiosity caught for real, Sullivan was listening. "This was different?"

She buried her face in her purse. "Very." The topknot of her hair wobbled, threatening to surrender to gravity.

"How?"

She lifted her head and her eyes were shiny with tears, but she wouldn't cry. Not Maggie. "You're going to think I'm insane."

"Probably. But tell me." He craved to touch her. Once more. That was all. One touch would be enough.

"I haven't told anyone this. I've been too frightened to talk about it."

He couldn't imagine Maggie frightened. She had a born-in-the-soul courage. "Talk to me." He gentled his voice. She was holding herself together by sheer will. He'd believed she couldn't affect him anymore, but her effort moved him in spite of himself. Her courage had always gotten to him, right from the beginning, creating a reluctant and unwanted admiration for her. "I won't tell anyone."

"You wouldn't. I know that. That's part of what's weird. Royal and Jackson are my friends, but I can't tell them. Somehow, in spite of anything that makes sense, I trust you." She shook her head. "I don't know why I do, but I figured it out when I realized that I didn't want to tell them everything, couldn't."

"Like what, Maggie?" He reached out to her and stopped. Not smart, Sullivan. Stick to business. "Go ahead."

"While I was in the hospital and doped up for pain, sometimes I'd open my eyes and not recognize anything, anyone. I was so scared. I'd drowse and wake, feeling lost, as though I were looking for something." She laughed shakily. "I know it was the medication, the loss of blood, the operation—all those things. But I was so different when I finally surfaced through that drug fog and stayed conscious for longer periods. I felt as if I'd been reborn and had a second chance at life."

"That's not uncommon, Maggie." He wished Lizzie had had one more chance. That would have been enough. He would have bullied her into marriage, never let her push him out the door even for those brief hours. "People who've gone through similar experiences report the same feelings. You're okay." He wanted to sit down and pull her onto his lap, comfort her.

"Don't you start handling me, too. Once today was enough to last me for a lifetime." She grimaced. "The problem was that I didn't see people quite the same way I had." Her words gushed in a torrent. "Everything is off center. Skewed. I'm not sure of myself about anything. Like at Taggart's. I don't know what happened to me."

"Stress trauma..."

Her fingers were twisting and twisting in the loop of the purse strap. "No. Different. It's like the gun doesn't belong to me anymore. I wasn't scared at Seth's Landing. Not even when Tolly and his troops were chasing us. Certain parts of my life don't mesh anymore." She took a deep breath, the green knit shifting and flowing with her, and looked out at the gulf, obscured by the outside lights and the blinds he'd closed. "So when I saw Royal and Jackson huddled together, it was as if I didn't know them. I did, once upon a time. But I don't now.'' She shivered.

"I told you I went back to see if your accusations made sense to me when I saw them face-to-face. I wanted to explain more of what had happened at Seth's Landing, too."

"I figured you would tell them everything."

"Sullivan, when I opened the door and they looked at me, I wanted to run. I was scared."

He'd worried earlier that she might be in danger, and he'd turned his back on her and left her with them. Sullivan knelt on the floor and grabbed the chair back, enclosing her in the harbor of his arms. "Shh, Maggie. Don't be scared. I'll take care of you."

"Sullivan, I didn't tell them you knew the clerk."

Mrs. Reid's detective had gotten to her awfully fast.

"Royal asked. I lied." She dropped her head. "I don't know why, but I lied to a man I've trusted with my life. And now he's a stranger to me, and I'm telling you things I couldn't trust him with. Couldn't trust the chief not to make me take sick leave or force me to go on early retirement if I tried to explain how confused everything was." She rubbed her nose with the leather strap and dropped it, her hands quiescent.

"Aw, Maggie. Don't torture yourself like this." He bent forward and laid his forehead against hers. "I don't understand what you're talking about, but you're okay. I've seen you in action, remember? You're gutsy as hell. And I heard your report to Jackson. Your mind works fine. The accident didn't change you. Made you see what your life meant to you, that's all. You don't have any reason to doubt yourself."

"No?" The shine of tears lingered in her eyes and her mouth was pink and full, her lipstick chewed off as she'd tried to explain her story. "Want to hear the really goofy part?"

"Sure." He lifted her out of the chair and settled her in his lap, wrapping his arms around her and rocking her like a child.

"In spite of everything, I'd be partners with Royal again. He wouldn't hurt me. I don't know how someone found out about your meeting, but I can't believe in my heart Royal was involved in that clerk's death."

"A man—Paul Reid. A man with a wife and child."

She nodded. "Paul Reid. He shouldn't have died there in the mud. Someone found him out there, but it wasn't Royal. I know that in the deepest part of my being. Royal might cut a few corners, but he's not a dirty cop. Can you give my judgment that much trust?"

"I don't know." He'd only given one other person in his life that kind of trust. "You're asking me to be someone I'm not."

"No, only to recognize that some things in life have to be taken on faith. Some things can't be documented in black and white. I can't see the moon some nights, but I know it's up there behind the clouds. I haven't seen atoms whirling in a table, but I know they're there. I accept as facts things I can't see or touch. Things I can't verify with my senses." She curled her fingers against his neck. "Oh, Sullivan, there's more to life than what we can smell or taste—or feel."

He pulled her closer. "That's not my style. I don't take anything on faith. You know that."

"I know it doesn't make sense to you, but I'd trust Royal with my life."

Sullivan felt her fingers skim over his neck as she wound them into his hair.

"With my life. But not with what I've told you. There's the kind of faith I have in Royal—and the no-holds-barred faith I gave you when I rang your doorbell. I *knew* you wouldn't let me down, no matter how angry you'd been when you left. I knew I could tell you what it's been like for me these last months and you wouldn't *handle* me. I knew you would listen and not think I was crazy."

She rubbed her face against his bare chest and he trembled with the need to give her what she asked.

"I didn't ask you to trust me." The curve of her against him was seduction, persuasion, reason enough. But it was the memory of her at Taggart's, at Seth's Landing; the memory of her standing so bravely in her green shoes and dress on his front step—those memories threatened to conquer him.

He'd tried to convince himself that her only appeal was physical. He'd told her that the bond humming between them was nothing more than sexual. But the Maggie of those memories seduced him with her courage, her vulnerability, her spirit.

That spirit lured him, spoke to him in a language he heard distantly and longed to understand.

"Trust me. A little. Please." She lifted her face to his, her eyes unguarded and warm, daring him to leap into the unknown with her.

She left him defenseless.

A tendril of her hair tickled his nose, brought with it her scent, her sweetness. With her in his arms and her scent lingering near his mouth like a voice calling him, he couldn't fight her, couldn't fight himself. No longer wanted to.

She'd come to him tonight out of the dark in her leaf-green dress like a promise of spring, tender and vulnerable.

She asked him for trust.

She asked him to slash the bonds of earth and soar beyond the horizon.

He didn't know if he could.

Didn't know if he had it in him to forget the lessons he'd made himself learn through the years. To depend only on himself. To look before he leapt. To lower his barriers and trust her when logic, the ruling principle of his life, argued against it.

But logic, ah, logic was a weak soldier against the lure of Maggie's spirit.

"I'll try," he muttered into the curls tempting his mouth. "It's not the answer you want, Maggie. It's the best I can do."

"That's all I want, Tin Man," she whispered. "I never wanted to live in Oz, just find my way home to Kansas."

Straightening in one motion with her in his arms, Sullivan covered the distance to the bedroom, where the green cursor, the only light, blinked its silent command as he laid her on the bed among the rumpled sheets and lowered himself on one knee beside her.

Dim, the room was filled with memory and possibility, shadows and substance, the quiet ticking of the clock echoing the slow beating of his heart. There was more here than the pulse of desire. More than the craving of his body.

Something outside his comprehension, beyond his understanding.

Risk.

For her. For him.

Tantalizing.

And terrifying.

In that strange light, as he knelt on the bed, his right knee close to the curve of her waist, wonder moved in a deep tide through him.

"It won't be only anonymous sex, will it?" There was wonder, too, in her eyes.

"No," he murmured, touching her face, pushing away a stubborn brown tendril near her cheek. "Something else entirely." He twined his fingers in her hair, loosening the topknot, letting the rich mass of her curls spill free. "Did you come to chase away my phantoms, Maggie-the-Cop?" He lifted one long curl and separated the strands, spreading them across his pillow in a cloudy fan.

"How could I? I have my own. They comfort me in the night when I'm frightened and lonely." She stroked her fingertips across his mouth, and he caught one gently with his teeth, tasting her. She turned toward him, one knee raised, her dress sliding up her thigh.

Shadows and shadows.

"What do you want?" He raised her hand to his mouth and turned it over, kissing the palm of her hand.

"Whatever you want," she whispered, the honeyed sunshine of her voice glowing inside him, blending with the tide swelling in him, pushing back the phantoms.

Her voice offered entry to paradise when he'd thought to linger forever at the gates, locked outside.

With the backs of his knuckles, he edged the ribbon of green higher, letting his hand span her waist where the delicate flare of her hips began. Thumb and little finger resting on the points of her hipbones, he pressed the heel of his palm softly across her, smoothing the silky slide of her panties against her skin, his, as he rotated his hand.

As he trailed his thumb under the lace border at her waist, he felt the flutters in her abdomen, felt them inside himself as she walked the fingers of both hands up his ribs to the underside of his arms and down his back, circling the sagging waistband of his gym shorts. Easing himself beside her, he lay facing her, watching her eyes change, darken, as he slipped his forefinger inside the bottom edge of her panties, brushing against her in minute sweeps closer to her intimate heat.

"Do you want to go up in flames?" he whispered, letting his breath caress her stomach.

"But not alone." With her fingernails, she stroked the cleft at the bottom of his spine and over his haunch to the front of his thigh. "I don't want technique, Sullivan. I want you. With me, burning together."

He slid his thigh over her restlessly moving legs, holding her still as he reached into the nightstand quickly for a silver packet, its crinkle as he unwrapped it a counterpoint to the slow ticking of the clock in the background. "Sweetheart, I can make you burn so hot you won't care about anything except what we're doing here tonight. I want to see you like that, blazing for me. Let me do that for you, for me. Let me watch you explode into cinders and burn again like the sun, again and again until you swear nothing else exists."

With his free hand, he slid the sleeves of her knit dress down her arms, imprisoning her. "Then, when you're sure you have nothing left, I'll make you burn again," he promised gruffly, moving his mouth across the rim of her breasts where the green knit flattened them, the taste of her exquisite. "And I'll be there with you. All the way, burning as hot as you."

With the flat of his hand he rolled her panties down her hips, grazing her with his fingers, stroking her until she sighed, such a tiny, feminine sound in the quiet. Her dress covered her breasts and the tops of her arms, and she was bare to his touch everywhere except where that cool green band hid her. Sliding over her, he nudged her legs open with his ankles and made a space for himself in the haven of her body, rocking slowly against her, his gym shorts riding lower with each rocking thrust.

She twisted and turned under him, raising her knees to his sides, half sitting up, her arms restricted by the binding of her dress. Slipping beneath him, she ran her hands under his shorts to his bare skin, sliding his shorts down until they tangled around his feet.

Barbaric, that green binding across the curving sweep of her. He watched the pink flush rise from his stroking hand up across her stomach, vanish under the band and reappear in a slow ascent up her slender throat as she arched beneath him, her mouth fastened to the pulse in his throat, drinking from him, her hands grasping his hips and holding him to her.

"Open, sweetheart." He nudged her thighs wider and sank into her, pressing against her, waiting for her invitation as he traced the green ribbon around her, lingering in the vulnerable tenderness of her underarm. When she hooked her legs over him, a sweet, trusting move that left her infinitely accessible, he swept the ribbon up and away, tugging the hot bud of her nipple into the dark cave of his mouth. He touched the very tip with his tongue. She arched wildly beneath him, shuddering and silent as he slipped inside her, impaling her on the moment of her pleasure and then driving her higher as he wrapped her legs tightly around his waist and slid his hands under her thighs, lifting her to each deep thrust.

He wanted to make the moment last forever, wanted to stay with her in that burning darkness, consumed.

But his hunger for her betrayed him. Lonely, he'd hungered for her, wanted her to the point of pain. As he held on to the rails of the bed, driving himself toward that burning with an urgency he hadn't dreamed of, her whimper sent him tumbling over the edge into the sun.

He watched her flash and burn with him, her eyes wide and filled with him until that final moment when she arched, shuddering into him, her eyes closing, and he followed her into that heat, losing himself in her.

And in those nighttime, shifting shadows, he sent them soaring twice more into that brilliance where nothing existed except the exploding sun.

After the last time, he tucked Maggie against his side, where she drifted to sleep, a teasing smile on her lips as he traced them over and over with the pad of his thumb, her lips nibbling the end of his thumb lazily. Her mouth parted even in sleep with each stroke he made against its fullness.

The cursor wouldn't let him fall asleep beside her. It forced him out of the rumple of sheets and to the monitor, where he saw the pale reflection of Maggie as he called up the Paulie file. Drained of everything except the urge to find out Reid's well-kept secrets, he yawned and rolled his tired eyes, then was kept awake by the hunt through lists so detailed they boggled his mind. Paul had been incredibly thorough, and Sullivan owed him the attention his work demanded.

As he worked, the shadowy form of Maggie lay still in the monitor's glass. He wasn't surprised she slept so deeply. They had exhausted each other. Only his sense of lingering responsibility for Reid and an unflagging curiosity held him stationary.

In a subfile Reid had called Firsts, Sullivan found a collection of notes and observations, pieces of conversations Reid had overheard in the courthouse. There'd been no guesswork on Reid's part as he recorded the pieces—he'd been meticulously objective and factual—but Sullivan saw the same pattern Reid had seen. Saw how the puzzle pieces fell into place as each innocuous bit added up to a contemptible whole.

Illegally circumventing the Resource Conservation and Recovery Act, the conspirators had established a toxic-management company. Arriving in authentic-looking, sealed trucks, the disposal teams made the rounds of a number of pulp-and-paper industries and several pesticide companies. There they would collect the sludge that legitimate chemical companies burned at high incineration, 3000°—an expensive process required for safe disposal of the sludge by-product, which had once been buried underground.

Payoffs from the factories and companies to the so-called Toxic Management Corporation were funneled into the pockets of city and county officials, who had facilitated approval of the state permits required for toxic collection. The rest of the money, thousands and thousands of dollars, with the potential for much more, was deposited into banks, where it made its way into land purchases.

In his computer monitor, a ghostly presence behind the horrifying material he was reading, Sullivan saw Maggie's arm slide off the bed, her hand tangle in the pile of sheets and clothing. He wanted to return to her side and forget what he was reading, but he couldn't. The corruption and betrayal were worse than he'd thought. In his quiet, unobtrusive way, Reid had stumbled onto a situation so foul that reading about it scared the hell out of Sullivan.

The participating paper mills and pesticide-manufacturing companies saved money, even with the payoffs. Sullivan swallowed against the chill running up and down his spine as he recognized names. No wonder Reid had been killed. He'd been sitting on the proverbial keg of dynamite.

And it had detonated with him on top.

Sullivan shifted uneasily in his chair, feeling the keg under him now with Reid's material in front of him.

From Reid's notes he learned that the industrial process that bleached the pulp at the paper mills yielded dioxin, which also required high-temperature incineration to be disposed of safely. The chlorine from the pulp-bleaching process yielded dioxin when it came into contact with oxygen. The pesticide companies produced chlorinated pesticides that also produced dioxin as a by-product.

Sullivan had seen some reports of follow-up studies after the Love Canal disaster, which had indicated dioxin wasn't as dangerous as originally thought. But the majority of the scientific community disagreed, still considering it the most potentially toxic waste disposed of in ground because of its mutagenic and carcinogenic properties.

At Love Canal, the dioxin had been stored in pits lined with eighteen inches of impervious clay, through which water couldn't pass. Later, when the land was developed, the weight of the constructed houses had pressed the fifty-five-gallon drums to the surface, where they'd leaked.

The desolate area around Seth's Landing had been used for the last three years as a dump by the Toxic Management Corporation. Seth's Landing was a Love Canal in the making. The county owned the land, and, according to Reid's notes, the long-range plan was to sell the Landing cheaply to developers who intended to put up expensive retirement condos. A vile circle of money, influence and greed was destroying the land and callously endangering lives.

Reading on, Sullivan was sickened by the nastiness of what had been planned. And done.

Reid wouldn't have been allowed to live once he'd started his careful note taking, not even if he'd never fed Sullivan any of the information. There was too much money, too many reputations and lives at stake. Killing Reid had been a blip on a radar screen to these people.

Shoving back his chair, Sullivan turned to Maggie. He'd endangered her by keeping her at his side. Every time he tried to dismiss her from his life, she floated back in. Because of her loyalty to Royal, she was the wild card in the deck, regardless of her plea for trust, despite her growing discomfort with Jackson.

The dumping at Seth's Landing couldn't have continued for three years without protection, not in a state where drug deals occurred routinely in the bayous and isolated back areas. The conspirators had paid off officials all down the line. Sullivan hadn't found all the names yet. But he would if he continued reading. Somewhere among Reid's details he expected to find the names *Royal Gaines* and *Johnny Jackson*.

Maggie's trust had been misplaced. He was convinced of it.

Stretching his aching muscles, he went into the bathroom and ran cold water over his eyes. In the mirror, he stared at his bristled, shaggy-haired reflection, his eye sockets black with a fatigue that had gone beyond tired. He wondered how he'd ever sleep again with what he knew.

In the kitchen he emptied the glass of whiskey down the sink, its smell nauseating him. Rinsing the glass, he filled it with clear faucet water. Looking at the water, Sullivan wondered for the first time where that drinking water originated. He set the glass down and looked toward the gulf, which was driving shoreward beyond his shuttered windows.

Where else was dumping going on?

No wonder the bomb had been set in his car. Ignorantly, he'd been closing in on evil.

And evil, as always, had responded. Quickly and impersonally.

No. Not impersonal in his case. Someone wearing boots had found it amusing to try to kill him.

Eventually, he would have succeeded.

Sullivan returned to the bedroom. Maggie's knees were drawn up to her chest as she slept on her side, facing him. He covered her with the sheet and turned back to the computer.

Long after Reid's words and notes made sense, Sullivan saw several lines that had been left uncompleted. He'd read past them three times already, his tired brain not registering the words, when he read them once again.

Several of the conspirators had agreed to meet at the River-front Pier during the fireworks at tomorrow's festival celebrating the landing of the Spanish Conquistadors and their discovery of the area that had become Florapalma.

Reid had been interrupted before he'd been able to list the names of the people who were to meet.

Sullivan knew he had to stop. Reid's notes might as well be hieroglyphics for all the meaning they had at this point. His brain was numb and he was making stupid mistakes on simple tasks like entering and exiting the files. If he didn't watch out, he was going to delete the whole cotton-picking disk.

Blearily, he stumbled into bed beside Maggie, sliding his arms around her, curling into her warmth to dispel the chill deep in his bones.

Everything was blurred and surreal to him. Through the closed window he thought he heard the muted roar of the distant gulf. The ticking clock marked off the minutes in a rhythm as familiar to him as his own breathing, and in the corners of the room, shadows drifted. The moment was filled with possibility.

As he looked at Maggie's square face, soft and pillow creased, she opened her eyes and smiled, her face sleepy and unguarded. Caught in the undertow of sleep, she would reveal the last of her secrets. He would know for sure if he could trust her.

He would have proof.

Looking into her defenseless, drowsy eyes, he intended to ask her two questions. What can you tell me, Maggie, about Royal? What will you tell me?

He meant to. Every instinct he possessed urged him to ask her those questions.

But he didn't. Instead, surrounded by the flowery fragrance of her hair and the scent of her, of them, he touched her cheek.

In the quiet moments before morning, he touched her, and she returned his touch in a silent reaching out that surmounted the barriers of rationality and distrust. Her murmured "Mmm" as he entered her was filled with contentment.

Holding her carefully in his arms, he let his body speak for him, let it speak to hers. To the slow ticking of the clock mea-

suring the strokes of their coming together, he took her on a
journey into the world of the senses.

His soul, lost somewhere in darkness, reached out at last,
seeking, yearning, and led him down pathways of pleasure with
Maggie Webster.

And there was magic in the night.

In the morning when he turned again to her, the bed was
empty, the sheet where she'd lain cool. Maggie nowhere to be
found in the cottage or on the beach, though he searched until
he was convinced she was gone.

When he returned to the cottage, his feet tracking sand into
the bedroom, he stared at the computer. On the last word of
Paul Reid's file, which he'd forgotten in his exhaustion, the
cursor flashed steadily, mocking him.

Chapter 12

Following Maggie, Sullivan went to the police station. He arrived just in time to see her climb into Royal's car and drive off.

Turning into traffic, he followed them, staying several car lengths behind and watching the traffic lights in case Royal decided to speed through on a yellow.

Or not stop at all. He grimaced as he watched Gaines take a red light with his siren wailing, steering into the oncoming traffic to pass and back into his lane again, while Sullivan remained stuck behind a van full of kids, surfboards and inner tubes.

Finally through the light, Sullivan checked each intersecting street, his head turning left and right as he tried to catch a glimpse of Royal's car.

Gaines had lost him.

On purpose? With what he knew about Maggie's partner, he suspected that the arrogant running of the traffic light had been for his benefit, Gaines taunting him and letting him know he'd been spotted.

He headed to the newspaper office. He wanted to let Walker know what was going on. Walker would need to contact the lawyers and start discussing the legal implications for the paper once Sullivan had finished the story and the paper ran it.

Walker liked to be prepared. He'd have the lawyers in by to-morrow, and he'd be discreet about it.

Should he tell Walker about the meeting scheduled for the pier? Walker had called in the police about the threatening notes. Accustomed to using his own judgment, Walker would make his decisions based on what he considered best for the paper. He wasn't careless, but...

Sullivan decided to leave a sealed note for Walker after they'd talked. He didn't want anyone unexpected showing up at the meeting.

Later, he headed to Paul Reid's. He wanted to ask Mrs. Reid again which detective had showed up.

This time when he rang the doorbell an older version of Paul Reid's wife answered the door. "I'll go get Suzy," she said. "You can talk to her. She's doing better today, but I think it hasn't all sunk in yet."

Like a little girl dressed in her best clothes, Suzy came to the door, Paulie riding her hip. "Hi, Mr. Barnett. Thanks for let-ting me sleep yesterday. I was plumb tuckered out." Her smile was wobbly but there, along with tear tracks.

"Mrs. Reid, I could have called, but I wanted to stop by to thank you for letting me take the disk yesterday. It was a big help, but I had a couple of additional questions, if you don't mind?"

"Of course not. I'm glad to help."

"Do you remember, by any chance, which detective stopped by yesterday before I arrived?" Sullivan waited while she thought, her face wrinkling in her concentration.

"No, I'm sorry, I sure don't. All I remember is how much Paulie liked his hair. Kinda gold with red in it, you know?"

He did.

"You missed him again today. He came by to ask me some questions about Paul's work—who he knew, who he got phone calls from. But I couldn't tell him much. Paul and I didn't have time for socializing, with the house and the baby." She shifted Paulie to her other hip.

"Did the detective have anyone else with him?" Had Mag-gie led Royal straight here?

"Gosh, I don't know. Mama opened the door. I was in the baby's room and she led him back there. We only talked for a few minutes. He said he was real sorry about Paul." One fat tear hung at the end of an eyelash.

"Well, thanks, Mrs. Reid." He'd dunked one, blown one.

"Sorry I wasn't any help," Suzy Reid said, holding Paulie's hand up to wave bye-bye.

"You were a lot of help. Thanks again."

Climbing into his car, Sullivan tried to decide what to do next. He could chase around all afternoon looking for Maggie, or he could come up with a plan. The best he could think of was to watch for her tonight when she went to the pier.

A lousy plan, but the only one that wouldn't have him choking on Royal Gaines's dust all day.

A bearded conquistador seized Maggie around the waist and swung her in a circle, lifting her feet off the ground. Her heavy purse swung with her, flying out with centrifugal force. She grabbed for it before it beaned someone, preferably the bearded celebrator holding her high.

"*Bella señorita,* come run away with me where the nightingales sing and the sun shines all day. We'll eat coconuts on the shore, sip rum straight from the bottle and swim naked in the clear Caribbean."

"Put me down or I'll send you to the pokey." Maggie motioned to the steel cages off to one side of the street. Several clean-shaven men clutched the bars, captive until they could coax or threaten a merrymaker into paying their fine for not wearing a beard during Palmaflora Days.

Lifting the visor of his silver helmet, Charlie Callahan said, "What say, Mags? Does that mean I can't talk you into running off with me?"

"Maybe some other time, Callahan. I don't have time to fool around right now."

"When will you fool around with me? I'll make it worth your while, honey." He winked. Sweat beaded his forehead.

"Not this week. My schedule's full."

"Don't be a spoilsport." He swept her up in his arms and walked down the street with her, his red cape flapping with each step, the crowd around them cheering his capture of her.

His elaborate velvet outfit was trimmed in gold and multicolored ribbons. His dark red tights were smooth against his

thighs and calves, and the pouf of the pants should have mad
him look ridiculous, but didn't. He was gaudy and magnifi
cent, the heavy rings on his fingers flashing and glittering in th
night as the torchbearers in the parade danced by them.

Maggie was annoyed. She didn't have time to waste witl
Charlie, even though he sometimes made her laugh until sh
cried with his silliness.

But not in the last few months. He'd become increasingl
obnoxious. When had his antics quit amusing her? She hadn'
laughed much at all these last months. Maybe the fault wa
hers. Charlie hadn't changed, she had.

The first day she'd arrived in Palmaflora to start her job
she'd heard what a wild and crazy guy Charlie Callahan was—
the life of any party. Everybody loved Charlie.

"I've had enough. Put me down now." She was genuinel
angry. She didn't like being the center of attention, and sh
didn't like playing captive maiden to Charlie's conqueror.

"Whatever you want, Mags, but you're ruining the fun.
don't like spoilsports."

"And I don't give a damn if you do or not. I'm fed up witl
this charade." She was furious.

He swung her to the ground with a flourish, his cape whip
ping behind him. "Pay your forfeit, fair maiden." His eye
twinkled as he flipped up the visor once again. Bending he
backward, he held her in a passionate embrace that had every
body laughing.

Arching so far that her hair trailed on the brick street, Mag
gie saw the crowd pushing nearer, egging Charlie on to mis
chief. Lights and color whirling her to dizziness as Charlie'
mock kiss edged into an aggression that had her raising he
knee to the pouf of his skirt. Her mouth was tender from th
night she'd spent in Sullivan's arms, her body imprinted witl
his. She despised Charlie's taunting kiss.

A float rumbled into view—the queen's court perched o
tiered risers covered with roses and gardenias, the floral scent
filling the air and mixing with the smells of sweat and beer. Th
white-gloved women of the court waved to the cheering crowd
while their escorts strode beside the float, tossing net bags o
gold-coin chocolates and hard candies to the children.

The streetlights along the route to the pier glowed yellow, their old-fashioned electric bulbs casting long shadows on the road and the revelers thronging the grassy verges and weaving into the street.

"Don't do it, Mags. You'll regret it." His beard scratchy against her chin, Charlie wasn't smiling. "Don't make me look like a fool." In the helmet, he looked threatening looming over her, one more stranger in her life. Goose bumps shivered over her skin as he kissed her once more before whirling away as the crowd cheered.

"Don't lose your sense of humor, Mags," he called back, swinging his visor closed. "Life's too short."

She shivered again. Tonight everything seemed threatening to her, even Charlie's offhand jokes.

Shoved and jostled by the crowd, she worked her way through the costumed mob, using her elbows to clear her way. Sullivan would have cleared a way with a look.

She missed him. She wanted him by her side, the way he'd been during the night—all barriers down, as he'd taken her to heaven and back, their lovemaking an exquisite blending beyond the limitations of the senses.

She slipped on a brick, her foot skidding out from under her, but caught herself. If she fell, this crowd would never see her— would walk right over her. Looking down, she saw she'd stepped in a gooey chocolate melting in the heat. Scraping her sneakers on the sidewalk, she wished she were back with Sullivan.

Waking with him curled spoonlike at her back, she'd crawled over him, touching his bristly face in a brief caress. Following her as she moved, he turned over, sprawling on his back as she left the bed. His hard, bare chest in the early light was beautiful, spare and defined, his ribs outlined by his skin in concave hollows that captured the gleam of the early morning sun.

Lingering, drawn by the sculpture of his body, she'd brushed her mouth across the muscled ridges of his abdomen. He'd muttered and turned again, toward her. He'd had black circles under his eyes and his face was drawn with fatigue. She'd slept through part of the night, but he'd been awake for most of it, obviously. She'd let him sleep.

She needed to think through the next steps of her investigation, too, but she'd wanted to see first what had been done about Paul Reid's murder.

Jackson had had the previous afternoon and evening to set some kind of investigation in place. Even with the added pressure of Palmaflora Days, surely he wouldn't let the murder slide.

He'd told her to finish her own investigation, and she intended to.

Scooping up her clothes, she'd headed for the bathroom, casting a sideways glance at the monitor Sullivan had left on. She didn't intend to violate his privacy, would never have read the screen without his permission, but two phrases leapt out at her and she stopped, the clothes falling in a heap at her toes.

This was what Sullivan was working on? She skimmed the file, scrolling through to get the gist of it after she'd seen the note about the meeting at the pier. When she'd read enough to grasp the general concept, she picked up her clothes, sick at heart.

She recognized some of the names, Sullivan would, too. But at least she hadn't seen Royal's. Or Jackson's. Nobody she knew personally. Of course, she'd only raced through a small part of the material, while Sullivan had worked on it all night.

And there would be names not yet known, names Reid—the files had to have come from him—hadn't discovered.

She dragged her clothes on, hurrying. If she stayed, Sullivan would confront her with this material, would think she'd covered up for Royal. She had. But not in the way he thought. During their slow, sweet lovemaking just before dawn, she'd felt as though she'd finally come home after a long, terrifying journey. In the aftermath of that tenderness, she couldn't bear to see him retreat behind his cynicism.

She couldn't bear to see him look at her with judgment and doubt in his eyes. Not now.

Worse than his suspicions, though, would be the consequences if any of the conspirators knew he'd found this material. His life wouldn't be worth any more than Paul Reid's had been. Maybe less, since Sullivan had the paper as a potential loudspeaker for whatever he discovered.

She sent a silent prayer of thanks into the vastness of space that she hadn't revealed the fact that Sullivan knew the clerk's identity. She'd bought him time. And now she needed to find out more than ever what Jackson was doing about Paul Reid's murder.

The more she'd thought about Jackson's behavior during her conversation with him, the more uncomfortable she became. Telling Sullivan about her reactions had clarified for her why she was uncomfortable.

Jackson's eyes had said one thing, his mouth and body language another. Had he been her friend? He'd acted like it.

"Acted" was the key. She'd always known Jackson was an actor, the way good politicians are, knowing the right thing to say, the way to smooth over unpleasant moments and always knowing how they looked to people observing them.

Jackson had always been a performer.

Sullivan was in danger. She saw the message as clearly as if it had been written in enormous white letters across the bright blue of the morning sky. Sullivan was in danger.

It would be her fault if anything happened to him.

She would do anything to keep him safe.

Her heart pumped with sick dread as she shut the door of the cottage behind her and raced across the lots between the beach and the bay toward where she'd left her car. Her hands shook as she stuck the keys into the ignition, and the first time she tried she couldn't start her car.

Urgency filled her.

In the pounding of her heart, she heard the echoing tick of a clock measuring out the moments of Sullivan's life.

In the dark, and surrounded by revelers hurrying to find the best seat for the waterfront fireworks, she scraped her shoe free of candy and felt even more acutely that sense of time accelerating.

All day long she'd hurried. And discovered nothing. The clerk had been identified. An autopsy was being done. She hadn't seen Sullivan all day. She'd gone with Royal to the coroner's office. Jackson had absented himself to check personally the parade route and police assignments. She'd been frustrated at every turn, not knowing where to search, whom to trust, knowing only that Sullivan was in danger and she could save him if . . . She frowned, a vague idea stirring in her mind.

If she hurried.

Darting through a break between the floats, she raced to the opposite side of the route, which looked less crowded.

It wasn't.

Driven now by the need to get to the place, she wove her way through the conquistadors striding down the street, dodging their outstretched arms. Ahead of her she saw the pier where everyone would gather to watch the fireworks explode over the water.

The bridge was south of the pier. The meeting mentioned in Paul Reid's notes would probably take place at the pilings on the far side of the pier. That made the most sense to her. Isolated, it afforded the advantage of providing a reasonable explanation for anyone being found there.

Looking over her shoulder, she thought she glimpsed Sullivan like a specter at her back, but then, surrounded by the crowd, the black-clad figure merged into the dark.

Running flat out now, her feet slipping on the grass, Maggie veered to the left. She would go around the back and through the roped-off area set aside for the fireworks. Police barricades would be up there, preventing the crowd from surging into the zone.

She patted her pocket for her badge in case she needed to identify herself. She pulled her Smith and Wesson free of her purse and stuck it in the back of her jeans. Her hands were slippery with sweat, fear urging her forward.

The metal barrel against her back was uncomfortable and she was too aware of it. She didn't want to use it. It had become alien to her, and she'd thought briefly about leaving it at home.

But the oppressive sense of danger had been too great, and she'd stuffed the semiautomatic into an old purse. Empty now except for an extra clip, which she slid into her left pocket, the purse dropped at her feet as she ran.

The fireworks would begin within minutes.

Sullivan had spotted Maggie as Callahan swung her into the air. He'd wanted to punch out Callahan's lights. Would have if he could have gotten to him through the marching band that came around the corner, majorettes twirling, cartwheeling and tumbling in every spare inch of space on the road.

When Callahan kissed her, Sullivan had taken a running jump over two garbage cans stacked with plastic cups and paper plates, sending garbage spilling behind him. But he'd missed her. Ahead of him, he saw the red swing of Callahan's cape.

Torn, Sullivan hesitated.

Maggie had escaped.

He saw her dash across the street between two floats, narrowly missed by a group of buccaneers wearing eyepatches, all swinging their swords in a precision routine. The metal glinted menacingly as the pirates wove in and out between the floats, throwing their swords high in the air to the delight of the crowd.

When she veered off, he wasn't sure what her plan was, but he knew her ultimate destination. She would go to the bridge pilings away from the pier. He could catch her before she got there. He was faster than she was.

And when he did, he was going to kill her. With his bare hands. Slowly.

How dare she spout off to him about trust, and then take off in the morning, leaving him behind like some gigolo? What had she been thinking of? He'd find out before he killed her. He didn't want to believe she'd run to Gaines and Jackson, but the thought, once lodged in his brain, had taken root and grown steadily with each passing hour of the day.

With the fragrance of her clinging to him like a gentle promise, he'd rooted out the idea like a maniacal gardener, but the poisonous roots spread and sprouted, appealing to every rational cell in him.

She was still hiding something from him. With his instinct for detecting lies, he'd heard her evasions. She was keeping something from him. How could he trust her without proof that she hadn't slipped up somewhere?

Unlike her, he figured trust required some kind of proof. And all she'd given him was her sweetly whispered plea. "Trust me," she'd said. But where was she today? And why hadn't she left him a note?

But he'd catch up with her and make her tell him everything this time. Damned if he'd be as weak as he'd been last night. He pushed down the memory of her curled trustingly against him, tried to forget the reflection of her in his monitor as he'd worked for long hours.

A beefy arm grabbed him from behind, stopping him. "What ho, me bucko! No beard?" The pirate sported his own thick black beard and an eyepatch. "Off to jail with you," he blustered.

"Don't even try it," Sullivan grunted, losing sight of Maggie once more.

"Hey, no offense, buddy. The money's for charity, you know."

Throwing bills at the pirate, Sullivan took off once more, dodging the onslaught of a squad of men on small tricycles.

He couldn't see Maggie at all. He'd been so sure he could stop her before she arrived at the pier. Whether she was a pawn or not, she was in danger.

He was terrified for her. She had no idea what she was dealing with. If she'd read the monitor screen and passed on the tidbit that he had Reid's files, she'd be in even more danger. She didn't know how far evil had cast its sticky web.

And she trusted Royal with her life.

Sullivan had roamed around town all day, one step behind her, missing her at every stop. He couldn't let her go to that meeting.

If she did, she was dead.

They wouldn't let her walk away.

Something twisted inside him at the thought of Maggie dead. It wasn't possible that fate would deal him the same cards over again in life. He'd sworn to protect her. And he would.

With his own life.

Whether he trusted her or not, he would protect her.

Hurrying toward the bridge, he saw the first of the fireworks light the velvet southern sky, exploding in a shower of red and green sparks that faded to gold even as the next series detonated behind them.

Clapping and whistling, the crowd oohed and ahhed after each booming explosion. One rocket, shrieking as it detonated into a pinwheel of yellow whirls, sent sparks to the river's edge, where they hissed and died.

Approaching silently in the intermittent darkness, Sullivan heard the muted voices before he saw the men.

Reid's information was accurate.

Only one of the men grouped together under the bridge surprised him, the rest he'd expected. One was missing.

And he couldn't see Maggie anywhere.

Stepping around the barnacled pilings, he edged closer, the voices growing louder in argument as he closed in. Shrieks and cheers muffled the next words, but he heard Reid's name. White-and-yellow sparks lit up the sky as he moved to the shelter of the next piling. He had to get closer, find Maggie and get her away from here before they were spotted.

Where the hell could she be?

River mud squished under his boots and a fiddler crab skittered away in front of him. He stopped at the last piling, carefully swiveling his head, looking for Maggie.

He was three feet away from Johnny Jackson when Ryder Thompson, Palmaflora's mayor, said something that was muted by a rocket flare. Charlie Callahan, who'd been Lizzie's childhood friend, threw back his head and laughed, his beard backlit by fireworks, his cape twirling behind him. Jackson scuffed at the mud, chuckling, and picked up a shell, pitching it out into the water.

As he flung the shell, Jackson turned toward shore, and in the red flare of a series of explosions, saw Sullivan stepping out from behind the piling.

"What the—" Jackson's mouth dropped open. Red-faced in the reflected light, he took a step forward.

"Barnett?" Jackson turned to Callahan and Ryder. "Charlie? This your idea?"

"Not mine. But opportunity knocks, Johnny."

His right hand moving downward to his pistol, Jackson turned back to Sullivan.

In that red-tinged moment, hearing a scrape of shoes against shells, Sullivan glanced to his right. His heart stopped, paralyzed by fear. And then it raced, leaving him drenched in sweat and mind-numbing terror.

Unseen by Jackson or Callahan, Maggie was slipping between the pilings, coming closer by the second, her small, determined face concentrating on him. Behind her, Royal Gaines stalked her like a cheetah on the scent of prey. Not yet near enough to leap, he was a red-gold flash in the exploding night, closing in on her.

In a moment of clarity like none he'd ever experienced in his life, he knew she had nothing to do with what had happened. She had never betrayed him—not with these men, not with anyone. Loyal and honest, she had followed her best instincts.

The terror he hadn't felt for himself when Jackson turned to him, his gun in hand, exploded inside Sullivan like fireworks. But he couldn't call to her, alert her, or Jackson would swing and fire at her instead of him.

Distracting the police chief, Sullivan bent sideways even as he saw the man slide his gun free. Knowing it wouldn't be enough to save him, Sullivan flipped a handful of river mud thick with shells and weeds in Jackson's direction. Sprinting left, away from Maggie, Sullivan leapt for the river, giving her a chance.

Hugging the safety of the pilings, Maggie saw Chief Jackson fling the shell into the river and turn toward Sullivan, saw her boss's hand reaching for his gun.

Time accelerated, slowed and stretched in front of her, distorting voices, images, memories. Fumbling at her waistband, Maggie freed her Smith and Wesson.

It was like watching the video tape of the Quik-Deli shooting. But in the video, her fingers hadn't been trembling, and the gun hadn't slipped in her hand.

She gripped the gun hard with both hands and raised it.

"Freeze! Police!" she shouted.

At her words, Jackson turned, *step one,* turned, *step two.* His gun swung back and forth between her and Sullivan, who was racing for the river. The chief shouted, his words muted by the thunder of her heart.

Sullivan pivoted toward her, his mouth opening soundlessly, saying something she couldn't hear in her desperate rush to reach him. The dull crump of fireworks in back of her reverberated through her, fading in the distance until she was surrounded by silence as she raced over an endless expanse of earth, Sullivan's harsh face filling her vision.

In that space where time elongated and distorted, she heard the roar of the gulf through her open window, the quiet ticking of her bedroom clock, and as the veil lifted, fluttered for those moments in time, she remembered, at last, everything.

She needed to tell Sullivan he was right, and she'd been wrong, so wrong.

As she moved toward him, joy flooded her. Somehow, she'd been given a chance to make everything right, to tell him how much she had loved him all along but had never said so, afraid to take that risk. She should have believed his love for her would survive in spite of her illness. She should have had the courage to believe in him, in herself, in the deepest instincts of her heart.

Jackson was swinging his gun at her, at Sullivan. From an incalculable distance, shouts floated to her. Her boss pointed his gun one last time, raising it toward Sullivan.

Danger. She'd known that, had known she'd left something else unsaid. The gun was rising so slowly she counted infinite heartbeats as Jackson leveled the gun at Sullivan.

Racing, racing, she reached out for him, reached and understood at last why she'd been given a second chance, as the veil between worlds parted for an instant.

Like a blinding white light, bliss suffused her as she stretched her hand out to him, her fingers closing around his as she stepped in front of the small cylinder moving toward him, her fingers gripping his as she smiled into his bright blue eyes, taking the bullet meant for him.

"Oh, Sullivan," she whispered as darkness rushed in on her, "I love you. And I never told you, but I've loved you for so long, forever."

Her words echoing meaninglessly in his ears, Sullivan lifted Maggie, trying to put his body between her and Jackson, knowing he was too late.

She jerked in his arms as the bullet slammed into her back and she sighed, her breath warm against him. Her smile lit her face with radiance as her eyes closed, her blood spilling into his hands.

Stooping over Maggie as she slid to the ground, Sullivan ripped at the bottom of his T-shirt with such fury that the fabric split like oil separating from water. He lifted her gently, pressing the cotton against the wound in a vain attempt to stanch the dark blood pumping from her. Working feverishly over her, he refused to think about anything.

She would not die. He wouldn't let her.

He tightened the fabric, binding it to her with another strip he tore free. Squatting next to her, he checked the pad he'd made. It wouldn't last long. Blood was seeping at its edges. He pressed harder. He would keep her alive. She wasn't going to die. Couldn't.

Not possible.

In a flash of dying fireworks, he saw Jackson lying wounded. With his gun drawn, Royal stood over the chief and pulled out a walkie-talkie. Callahan and the mayor were cuffed back-to-back around a piling, ankle deep in muddy river water.

Royal? Later. He would think about Royal later.

"Oh, God, Maggie," he muttered as he changed the pad for a fresh one and watched it, too, grow dark with her blood.

In the background, tires whining as it rounded the curve and came down to the river, an ambulance squealed to a halt, its flashing red lights piercing him with an overwhelming sense of loss.

All around him rain was falling, falling into his eyes. Huddled over Maggie, he covered her from the cold rain drowning him.

A stretcher slid into view and two paramedics lifted Maggie out of his arms. He helped them carry her to the white vehicle, steadying the stretcher as they ran over the slick mud. He never let go of her cold fingers, which were gripping his.

Strength there in those small fingers. His Maggie had strength. Feel how tightly she held him. She wouldn't die. All that sass and spunk couldn't end like this.

Willing her to fight, he tightened his grip.

"Sorry, man, but you can't—" A black-haired paramedic shook his head as Sullivan climbed into the ambulance with Maggie. The paramedic grabbed his arm.

With one hand Sullivan pinched his neck. "Don't. Don't try to stop me." He pinched harder and the paramedic's face went white.

The second paramedic rushed up. "We got a problem here?" He looked at Sullivan, who stared at him, something in his face silencing both men.

The attendant shrugged. "Whatever, man. No skin off my nose. But don't sue the county if we crash."

Meaningless, the words Sullivan heard as he held Maggie's hand during the endless ride to the hospital.

"We got a code—"

A static-filled message returned over the radio. Sullivan braced himself against the side of the ambulance as it rounded a corner, siren wailing as it raced through red lights blurred by rain.

Maggie's face seemed to blur before him. Sullivan brushed her hair off her forehead.

The black-haired paramedic worked on her, hooking her up to the emergency equipment and trying to stabilize her irregular pulse.

Sullivan heard his murmured aside to the other attendant, "We're going to lose her. I can't—"

"No." Sullivan interrupted them, his voice flat and dangerous. "She is not dying. She is going to live." He grabbed the man's wrist. "And you're going to do whatever you have to to keep her alive, do you understand?"

His face filled with pity, the man nodded. "Sure. She'll make it." He glanced at the other paramedic and caught his eye. "Tell Terry to go turbo." The paramedic patted Sullivan on the shoulder. "She'll make it," he said and went back to work, his hands moving quickly.

Lights, malls, cars flashed by.

"Come on, sweetheart. Hang on. A little longer. Yeah, hang on." Over and over he spoke to her, his voice monotonous in the quiet ambulance, the voices of the attendants a low undertone in the background. "You're alive, sweetheart. I'm with you. Don't give up. I'm here. I'll take care of you."

And Maggie opened her eyes.

Their bottomless brown depths misted over, and, for an instant, luminously clear gray eyes stared back at him. "Hello to

you, too, Sullivan,'' she whispered, her fingers tightenin
around his. ''What took you so long? I thought you'd neve
come home.'' She smiled, sweetness curving her pale lips.

''Lizzie?'' Sullivan muttered, his whole world suddenly i
comprehensible. ''Maggie?'' he said, stunned and disbelievin
as the clear gray eyes yielded to warm brown before sinking int
unconsciousness.

''Maggie?'' Reeling, Sullivan clenched her hand. ''Talk t
me, sweetheart.''

''Back off, man, she's gotta have oxygen,'' a paramedic sai
as Sullivan leaned forward, staring at the pale woman belte
into the ambulance stretcher.

''What?'' He stared at the man speaking gibberish.

''I told you, man, oxygen.'' The paramedic brushed hi
back.

''Lizzie?'' Sullivan murmured as he watched Maggie's ur
conscious face disappear under the oxygen mask.

Chapter 13

Sullivan never let her go.

Would never let her go again.

Through the swinging doors of the emergency entrance, running beside her as hospital personnel surrounded her, he held on to her. He fought them all the way, not letting them separate him from her as they prepared her for surgery.

He knew he was crazy now. Accepted it. It no longer mattered. All that mattered was the woman being rushed down the hospital corridors and up the elevator to the operating theater. If she lived, craziness was immeasurably better than the cruel sanity he'd known. Crazy, he didn't care that nothing made sense, that he'd thought Lizzie had spoken to him.

Much, much better to stay crazy and remember those whispered words of love, that sense that she was here with him, her spirit, which had never lingered in the beach cottage, here now beside him again, filling the emptiness and making him whole.

He loved being crazy, desired it now with a passion.

So much simpler, life, when he was crazy. He didn't have to struggle to understand what had happened. He could have Lizzie, Maggie, the other half of himself back again.

Why had he struggled so long, trying to find reason and meaning?

The small woman under white sheets and blankets, her mas
of hair capped in surgical green, was the meaning in his life. Hi
everything. Heaven.

He would not let her die.

Over and over he chanted the words, clinging to her hand lik
a lifeline.

"Hey, we need a next-of-kin signature over here. You he
husband?" The white-capped woman trotting beside him hel
out her clipboard.

Of course he was her husband. Should always have been.

"Name?" When he didn't reply, she tapped his arm. "Yours
sir."

"Barnett, Sullivan."

"Good. You're doing fine. This'll take only one more sec
ond." She jotted down information. "Her name? The para
medics said 'Maggie.' That right?"

He nodded. Her name wasn't important. *She* mattered.

Sullivan signed the form and the nurse veered off to the right

The elevator buttons lit up at each floor, chiming as the meta
cubicle rose steadily upward. Its doors swooshed open, and sh
was rolled down another corridor, the operating-room door
now straight ahead under the red neon No Admittance sign a
the end of the hall.

The nurses and attendants who had taken over from th
paramedic peeled away, two remaining, others hurrying to re
place them. The white-suited male nurse turned to him, sym
pathy coating his words. "I gotta stop you here, Mr. Barnett
This is as far as I can let you go." *Conrad Tinker* was the nam
on his badge.

Shaking his head, Sullivan gripped the metal side of the gur
ney with his free hand. "I go where she goes."

He would tear them apart if they tried to take her away from
him.

Tinker loped over to the nurses' station and picked up
phone, speaking quickly into it before returning to Sullivan.

"Mr. Barnett. You can't go through those doors. That's th
bottom line. We don't have time to argue. If you want her t
live, she goes in. You stay here."

Two uniformed security men jogged toward Sullivan.

In a remote part of his brain, he heard Tinker's order and it ltered through to him. "What?" He shook his head. What?''

"We're out of time, Mr. Barnett. Let her go." Tinker's face as pained. "She's dying. Let her go now or she has no chance. Jone. Zip. Got it?"

Blinking at Tinker and gulping air, Sullivan unwound his ngers from Maggie's. "She's not dying," he said again, his rms hanging by his side as they sped her through the doors and ut of his sight.

He stood in the hall looking after her, hearing her voice in his ead, seeing her eyes turn gray and back to brown. He was asping; there was no air in the overheated corridor as he leaned gainst the wall, his head still turned to his last sight of her.

If she didn't come back to him and he'd left her alone again, rick by brick, pipe by pipe he would dismantle this damned lace until not a stone was left standing.

On his haunches, he watched the surgery doors, standing very time they swung wide and sinking back as they closed gain.

She had stepped in front of him. On purpose, determina- on shining through her. She'd known what she was doing hen she ran between him and Jackson.

Gulping for air, Sullivan felt his head swim. She'd saved him, nd he'd never wanted anything in his entire life except for her live. He inhaled again, his chest heaving. Hospitals were uffy, airless places where the sounds and smells were all the ame.

God, he couldn't breathe.

The doors thunked open. Tinker was walking back to him. Sullivan snapped to attention.

"It's going to be a while, Mr. Barnett," Tinker said. "Take easy." He stood in front of Sullivan, making sure not to block is view of the doors.

"How long?" The words were grating and harsh, as if he'd st the power of speech.

Tinker shook his head. "No idea. The surgeon will come out nd talk with you when they've finished. I'm a gofer. You now, I gofer the gurneys, the pans." He grinned. "The secu- ty guards."

Indifferent to anything except information about Maggi
Sullivan looked at him, waiting stolidly.

Reaching into his pocket, Tinker pulled out a plastic ba
"Here are her things. She didn't have much with her. No purs
The cops took her gun with them. Evidence, I guess. Her badg
is in here. Earrings." The gold balls were bumps under th
plastic as he handed the bag to Sullivan.

She'd worn these at Seth's Landing. The smooth gold seeme
to hum against his finger as he touched one earring.

"Mr. Barnett, I came back because I felt like a dog makin
you leave her. I want to apologize. I know how it is to los
someone you love, and you have to deal with impersonal hos
pitals."

"What?" Sullivan looked up from the earrings. He'd swea
they were warm from her skin. Couldn't be, of course, b
when you were crazy, details like that didn't matter.

Tinker shrugged. "I just wanted to tell you I'm sorry. I hop
she makes it."

"She will." Sullivan slid down the wall to his haunches agai

"Why don't you go to the family waiting room? You'll b
more comfortable. Like I said, it's going to be a long night. Th
chaplain can stop in." He raised his eyebrows in a question.

"I'm staying here." Sullivan cupped the plastic bag in h
hands.

"Fine. I'll pass the word to look for you here. I'm going f
a smoke. Want me to bring you coffee?"

"No. Thanks." He opened the plastic bag and stroked on
earring. "Thanks."

"Any time." The soles of his shoes squeaked against the til
floor as he ambled down the corridor, pausing at the nurse
station and motioning toward Sullivan.

Night into morning into night. Time losing all meaning u
der the fluorescent lights of the hospital corridor.

Sweetheart, he called. *I'm waiting. I won't leave you.
promise. I'll be here.*

Hours, days, seconds. All the same except for the waitin
the rumble of carts, the chime of the elevator doors interm
nably opening and closing. Sullivan dropped his head to h
knees at some point, then jerked awake to watch white scuffe

shoes in front of him, passing back and forth in constant motion.

He never looked at his watch.

Not once.

A slow wheeling of pictures in his mind. Lizzie, her fair hair streaming behind her. Maggie, laughing and sassing him, her thick brown curls fighting her every attempt at control. Lizzie, loving him. Maggie. Their faces overlapping, blending, in kaleidoscopic pinks and greens. Under the smells of the hospital was a faint flowery fragrance, teasing him.

And the constriction in his chest, growing tighter and tighter.

One pair of white shoes stopped. And stayed. Sullivan struggled to his feet, his knees snapping and popping.

White shoes. Green surgical scrubs. Surgical mask dangling under a tired face with kind eyes. Deep pouches under those eyes, dark and permanent. Clipboard in his hand. "Mr. Barnett?"

"Yeah."

"Some good news and some not so good." The surgeon leaned against the wall beside Sullivan. "I'm Connor Chapman. Let's go get a cup of coffee and I'll tell you what I know. I'm not sure about you, but I'm running flat out on empty. Come on." Not waiting for an answer, he took off down the hall.

On automatic, Sullivan followed. Good news. Maggie was alive. He would see her again. He wouldn't have to tear this nice man's hospital apart. Good news. His eyes weren't focusing clearly as he walked down the hall. Blurs passed in front of him, to his side as they went into a private sitting area. The surgeon motioned to an upholstered chair. "Have a seat. I'll be a minute." He shut the door behind him as he left.

Nice man. Nice pictures. Pastels. Very restful. Sullivan waited. Another eternity before the surgeon returned with steaming cups of coffee.

"I bypassed—"

Blinking stupidly, Sullivan said, "She needed a bypass?" This was the bad news?

"God, no. I meant the coffee."

Sullivan looked at the coffee and back to the surgeon.

"I bypassed the cafeteria. The coffee there isn't good for your health. I got this from my office. Freshly ground Columbian. Smell." He held out a cup.

Sullivan sniffed. And tasted. "Good."

"Life has its rewards. Coffee's one of them." The surgeon propped his feet on the sofa and leaned back in his chair, sipping coffee. "I didn't think she'd make it through the surgery. She did. That's the good news. Bad news. Lot of blood loss. Internal trauma and bleeding. Couldn't save her spleen." He drank down the rest of the coffee in one long swallow.

Following his lead like an automaton, Sullivan took a deep gulp.

"It was one of those damned bullets that rattles around inside on impact. They mess up the internal organs really swell. She's a mess inside with edema and bruising." Chapman sighed heavily and let his feet drop to the blue-carpeted floor. "I'll be honest. I hate like the very devil to say this, but I'm not optimistic. It doesn't look good for her."

Coffee splattered onto Sullivan's knee. He rubbed the stain. She'd survived the surgery. He couldn't follow the rest of what Chapman was saying. Chapman was wrong. Lizzie was going to make it. He shook his head. Maggie. Coffee slopped onto his knee again. His hand was shaking. He put the cup on a side table and sat on his hands. "She's going to get well," he said, pinning Chapman with his gaze. "You don't know what you're talking about."

Not taking offense, Chapman nodded, his face weary. "You're right. I don't. Every case is different. The one thing you learn in medical school that's worth the whole shebang is that sometimes science doesn't have all the answers. Sometimes it doesn't have any of them. I did my best, Mr. Barnett, and I'm pretty damned good in messy situations. I gave her the best chance I could. The rest..." He stood up and stuck out his hand. "Who knows? For damn sure I don't. We'll see."

"Thanks." Sullivan shook Chapman's hand. Long surgeon's fingers. He said he'd done the best he could. A deep shudder rolled through Sullivan. He sank to the chair. "Sorry."

Chapman started to pat his shoulder, let his hand fall, grimaced. "I wish I could do more."

"Yeah. I know." Sullivan did. Waiting in the hall, helpless, he'd wanted to butt his head against the wall.

"Wait here a while. Then head up to Intensive. They'll let you know the arrangements up there." Chapman stopped with his hand on the doorknob. "But if you want to stay with her, and you have any problems, have the head nurse call me."

"Yeah." Sullivan was able to get the one syllable past his grinding teeth.

"Anyway—" Chapman shrugged "—I don't see any harm in letting you be with her. Might even help. I'm a firm believer with Hamlet that there are more things in heaven and earth than are dreamed of. So, as the melancholy Dane said in a different context, leave her to heaven." He opened the door. "Go on up to Intensive, Mr. Barnett. I'll check in with you later." He shut the door softly behind him.

Leave her to heaven? He'd be damned if he would. Sullivan jerked to his feet and staggered to the door, caffeine jolting through him and purpose propelling him. If Maggie-the-Cop thought she was going anywhere without him, by damn he was going to tell her a thing or two that would scorch those shell-like ears.

Staggering like a drunken man on a two-day bender, he found his way to the Intensive Care ward.

She was still in recovery, but he'd wait. He was becoming expert at that occupation. He'd add it to his resume if Walker fired him.

Finding a vinyl chair, Sullivan stretched out in it, slouching down as far as his tailbone would bend. Damn Lizzie, anyway, to think she could pull a trick like getting herself shot on his account and backing out on the deal. She'd saved him and she was going to have to put up with him. That was all.

He shook his head. He had to get ready for Maggie. Lizzie. Ready for her.

When they eventually wheeled her through the doors, she looked so small and defenseless under the dripping tubes and flashing monitors that she broke his heart open in one cracking, rending upheaval.

She needed him.

He explained the situation very calmly to the nurses, letting them see what a restful person he was to have around their series of pastel prints. He'd fit in. They'd never know he was there. "Call Chapman," he said when nothing else had worked.

Chapman was a miracle worker, all right. The head nurse herself came down and explained what they were doing as they plugged in monitors and raised the metal bar of Maggie's bed.

Once the nurses finished and left him alone with her, Sullivan began talking, drawing on every reputed skill the Irish had ever had for blarney, talking, talking, giving her the river of his words to find her way back to him.

"Let's begin at the ending, sugar-buns. You hate that, I know. So? Sugar-buns. Getting mad, Maggie? Good. Get real ticked off with me, sweetheart. I want you to be so busy thinking of ways to tear a strip off my hide that you won't have time to do anything else. Hear me, Maggie?"

Floating in darkness where waves washed her gently back and forth between two shores, she waited for a signal.

And in that darkness, words wove in and out of her consciousness. Words washing her to and fro. Sometimes she floated with the tide, letting it carry her along to a bend in the river bright with sugary sand. Sometimes she struggled against that inexorable tide toward darkness and pain, and that voice tugged at the line holding her in the dark river's midpoint.

The voice was rough and harsh, dwindling sometimes to a whisper like wind turning the leaves, like rain pattering gently against the river, pocking its surface.

That voice caressed her, lulled her.

Pissed her off.

Agitated, she fought toward that irritating sound.

But the struggle exhausted her and left her content for a while to drift with the tide moving the river forward to that white shore.

She listened and waited, content to let the words wash over her, pain fading in the brilliance around the river's bend.

"Lizzie, did I tell you what Leesha's up to? She has this little dude, Tommy Lee by name, a real terror. Leesha's working on him. You know how she is. The squirt has stopped pushing the other kids around. For a while when he first started at Sunshine, Leesha couldn't understand why none of the kids had their quarters when they went to the ice-cream shop down the corner. You know she keeps that quart jar filled so every kid can buy a creamy—that's what Katie calls her ice cream now." Sullivan moistened Maggie's mouth with the damp washrag, slipping a bit of ice onto her tongue.

Her sweet mouth was dry and starting to crack at the corners. There had been one time when the monitors had indicated a change in her comatose state. The squiggles on the screen gave him hope.

"Remember Katie, sweetheart?" he continued, his throat raw after days and nights of talking hours on end. "She remembers you. She wants you to read to her again, that story about a nighttime kitchen? You know the one."

He dabbed lotion onto Maggie's lips.

"Anyway, sweetheart, Leesha found out Tommy Lee was putting the squeeze on the kids. After she passed out their money, Tommy Lee'd make them give it to him. Skipper blew the whistle. Beat the bejeebers out of Tommy Lee, first, though. Katie played peacemaker."

Sullivan poured water from the carafe into his glass. Ice tinkled to the bottom. "Lizzie, they need you. They miss you."

Stroking her arm, he whispered, "I miss you, too. I need you so much more than I ever let you know. Wherever you are, sweetheart, come back home where you belong. Please."

He took another sip of water, his throat aching and his eyes itching with unshed tears.

The river flowed faster, with her bobbing along in its current, the tether of that rough voice fraying with the power of the tide as it flowed toward the wide bend. She was fretful, wanting the voice to be silent and let her reach that bend where the river's sweep would snap the thin line holding her.

"Lizzie, you know I forgave you the minute I walked out the beach-house door. I had to. I love you too much to stay angry with you. You should have believed sooner. I told you I loved you. Why couldn't you believe that, Lizzie? I would never have let you down. No one in the universe has ever loved anyone the way I love you, sweetheart. Don't leave me in this darkness alone again. I'm begging you."

The bend was near, and the current strong, pushing her along in its grip. She yielded to that power as she watched the shore approaching, huge in all its shining whiteness.

Sullivan pressed his ear against her breast, listening to its thready beat as he continued his stream of words, his voice cracking. "Sweetheart, there's never been anyone in my life except you. You're the only person I've ever loved in my whole life. You know that. You're the only person I've ever trusted. After my mom walked out on the old man and me, he vanished, too, burying himself in work. That's why I joined the navy after the old man died. There wasn't anything else for me. Until you. Loving and trusting haven't been easy lessons for me to learn, sweetheart, but you've been a good teacher. How can you leave me now?"

Sullivan's voice broke and he rubbed his eyes. They were burning with fatigue. Swallowing, he buried his face against the edge of the bed, holding Maggie's thin, dry fingers.

She was so small and pale, slipping away from him day by day.

Her heavy brown hair was dull and matted against the pillow. He picked up the natural-bristle brush he'd bought for her the first week she'd been in the hospital. Pulling her hair back from her face with long, slow strokes, he ran the brush down the strands of her hair. Lifting her palm to his hand, he kissed its center.

The high-pitched shriek of the monitor startled him and he looked up, puzzled. To the left of Maggie's head, the monitor shrilled loudly as a straight green line pulsed across its screen.

"Maggie! Don't you dare...!" He leaned over her, one knee on the bed, and placed his palms one on top of the other flat on her chest, compressing five counts and breathing twice, compressing and breathing into her, breathing his life force into her.

As his breath passed into her, he swore at her, willing her to come back to him. "Live, damn you," he muttered fiercely, tears sliding down his cheeks, all the tears he'd never shed burning down his face, splattering the sheet over the small mound of her chest with their hot acid.

"Live, or I swear to God, I'll follow you. You'll never escape me," he said, breathing and compressing, as the medical team surged through the door with paddles and syringes, trays of life-saving supplies stacked on the metal cart rattling behind them.

Not stopping, Sullivan continued pressing and breathing, swearing at her. "You won't escape me, Maggie. Wherever you go, I'll be right behind you. Live, damn you!" he breathed into her.

Her eyes fluttered and she was looking at him, her eyes dazed and unfocused, not really seeing him.

Rushing to the bed, a doctor shoved him aside, yelling, "Clear!"

"Mr. Barnett, you must leave. We'll call you." One of the nurses grabbed his arm, urging him to the door.

"The hell you will," he said, yanking his arm free. To one side, away from the equipment and out of the way, he stayed as Maggie's body lifted with the force of the paddles. Lifted and dropped.

Tears running down his cheeks blurred the sight of her face, no matter how fast he blinked them away. Over and over he whispered, "Live, sweetheart. For me. For yourself. For the kids. Live, Maggie."

In the dimness she heard him, the power of his voice, his will fighting the swelling tide, pulling her with him when she was too weak to struggle by herself.

That strong voice wrestled her free of the wild sweep of the river rushing toward the bend, wrenched her back toward that pain and darkness that held the voice. The river filled her mouth as she was yanked backward against the tide. She swallowed and coughed, jerking up through the swelling waves and sinking under again as the voice towed her back, each pull jerking her up out of the river's grip.

In the place of shadows and phantoms where she had gone, Maggie heard Sullivan swearing at her in a long, unending stream, heard him muttering and cursing, calling to her, his voice filled with such pain that she ached for him.

She tried to tell him not to worry. She tried to tell him she'd be right back, that she knew the way home now, but she couldn't. Her body was at the mercy of a jolt of electricity roaring through her like a jet plane, throwing her to the ground.

The beeping of the monitor resumed. The green peaks pulsed steadily across its screen, the tidal rhythm of Maggie's heart translating into a series of tidy green hills marching forward.

Sinking into a chair at the end of Maggie's bed, Sullivan rested his face against the soles of her feet, holding on to her as the nurses and residents packed up. Rubbing her toes under the sheet softly with his bristly chin, he took a deep breath.

She'd flatlined.

But she'd opened her eyes.

Wrapping up the cords of the paddles, the nurse who'd tried to remove Sullivan breathed out in a long whoosh. "Close. We almost lost her that time, guys. Poor little thing." The nurse looked first at Maggie, then at Sullivan. "Anything I can get for you, Mr. Barnett? Flatlining's sure a scary thing."

"Yeah." He'd experienced his father's death, seen death on tour in the navy, held Maggie in his arms with her blood pumping over his hands.

This had been worse than anything he'd ever known.

"Dr. Chapman will be in later this evening. We've already called him. He's been real interested in how things are going." She put the paddles on the cart. "We've all been pulling for your wife, Mr. Barnett. She's been a real trouper, but she's not out of the woods yet."

She wheeled the cart past him and out the door.

Sagging at the end of Maggie's bed, Sullivan watched the rise and fall of the sheet over her chest. What a miracle of nature the beating heart was.

"Maggie, sweetheart? We've got a lot of talking to do. Any chance you could avoid more scenes like this one? I don't know if I'm up to another round with the paddles and that green line, sugar-buns. Do me a favor, huh? Stay steady on course."

Swaying among the weeds at the river's edge, she heard the voice again, recognized it this time, had known it many times in many forms. Young when she was old, old when she'd been young. Sometimes they'd found each other; other times they'd just missed touching, their outstretched arms brushing past and on down the tunnels of time.

But always they'd loved and been torn apart, always lost to each other as time ticked forward in endless rounds.

No matter how fiercely they loved, they destroyed their love. Over and over, they repeated the pattern they feared.

At the moment of decision, she would pull back, lacking the courage to risk everything with him, to risk loving him despite the fear that her love wouldn't be enough for him.

She'd lacked courage.

He'd lacked the ability to trust her, to know that she was always his, that he could be his truest self with her. Jealousy and betrayal, again and again.

Swaying there, she wondered if she had the courage to try again.

Perhaps it was time to forget the struggle and let the pattern end forever in this moment in time.

They had come so close this time, so close.

But they always destroyed each other, one way or another.

She recognized the voice.

But not herself.

Watching Maggie through the night, Sullivan finally slipped up beside her on the narrow hospital bed and held her, not moving her or disturbing her, but being there.

Just in case she opened her eyes again.

He would be there.

Chapter 14

Clattering in with her morning meds, the nurse woke him up. "Mr. Barnett, really. Not in bed with the patient. That's asking too much of us."

Opening one bleary eye, Sullivan surveyed the room. Light filtered through the closed blinds and hurt his eyes.

Maggie lay next to him, her lashes fanned across her pale cheeks. He thought her lashes fluttered for a moment. Yawning, he dropped his feet to the floor. "Yeah. I reckon it is."

He wondered why he felt so good and so lousy at the same time. Too much adrenaline spiking over an extended period, probably. He'd seen guys get slaphappy after a thorny maneuver into unknown waters. The body adjusted to stress eventually and in weird ways. "Camping out seemed like a good idea at the time, though."

"Perhaps." She frowned severely, her short nose tipping down with the force of her disapproval. "This is the Intensive Care unit of this hospital. We've already made an exception for you because Dr. Chapman requested it. We try to accommodate him."

"Of course you do." Over the three weeks he'd stayed, nights and most of the days, Sullivan had learned that Chapman was, indeed, a very good surgeon. In this hospital, he was one rung lower than God. But not by much.

"This isn't a hotel, as you very well know." Her nose wiggled at the tip like an extremely annoyed bunny.

"Yep. I caught on to that right off, and y'all have been jim-dandy about letting me park here." If Nurse Beatrice Bunny scolded him for one second longer, he wasn't going to be his usual charming self. "I'm going home to clean up, Beatrice. I'll be back, though."

"I'm sure you will be." Wiggle, wiggle, little pink tip quivering.

She was the only nurse on the unit who liked asserting her authority. She earned his forbearance because she was terrific with patients. Beatrice was a martinet with visitors, but he'd also seen her leaning face against the wall, sobbing her heart out at three a.m. after she'd lost a patient.

She made him so damned eager to break her rules and regulations that he couldn't stay around her more than ten minutes. He was afraid she would tempt his sarcastic tongue from where it had been hiding for the last weeks.

Grabbing his sneakers and shoving his feet into them, he looked at Maggie, the green peaks to the left of the head of her bed blipping across in a wonderful, monotonous rhythm. He bent down to tie his laces, not wanting Beatrice to see his expression.

While he was nose-to-tile with his shoe, she hesitated and said, "I wish I'd been here last night. I started my new rotation or I would have been here."

"Yeah, I know." He couldn't hold her gaze. "Well."

"Yes. Well." She flipped back her clipboard and began recording vital statistics. "However, I'm on duty until three-thirty."

Sullivan walked stiffly to the head of the bed. "I'll see you, Maggie. Don't go anywhere without me," he whispered out of Nurse Beatrice's hearing. Maggie's breathing seemed different to him this morning. He frowned. It was nothing he could pinpoint, but he'd lived with her for three weeks in this space and her rhythms were as familiar to him as his own. A different sound. That's what it was.

"Beatrice, what do you think? Come listen."

He waited while the nurse checked Maggie's respiration rate
"It's the same as it was yesterday, Mr. Barnett. I'll watch he
particularly closely and keep an eye out for anything that migh
not show up on our monitors."

"My imagination, I reckon." He was troubled. Something
had changed in her since the night, but he didn't see a damn
thing and neither did Nurse Beatrice.

If anything were different, she would notice. She noticed
everything, storing it in some mental file.

All the same, he figured he'd wait a few more minutes. He
would give Maggie as much time as she needed to come back to
him. The meeting with Walker and the lawyers could wait.

When Beatrice left, Sullivan leaned over and picked up
Maggie's thin wrist. "Hey, sugar-buns." He stroked the underside skin. Her pulse was a mockery of the strong beat he had
first touched, that pulse thrumming in sync with his own heart
He reached for an ice chip and tucked it into the corner of he
mouth, letting it melt over her tongue and down her throat.

"I know you're in there listening, Maggie. Can't fool me with
that butter-won't-melt-look. You don't have a guileless bone in
your whole sweet little body. And a very nice little body it is.'
He ran his thumb over the side of her neck and down to he
collarbone. She was all pale skin and bones.

And spirit. It was that spirit flickering inside her that propelled the green line of the monitor into peaks instead of a long
horizontal. It was that spirit that had delighted in sassing him
and not giving him an inch he hadn't earned.

His Maggie was no wuss.

He eased another ice chip down her throat. "Wouldn't you
like to wake up and see what a really swell hairstyle I've given
you? Not as sexy as the topknot with an insecurity complex you
create, though. Got to admit I like that topknot. I love the way
it reads my mind and falls apart, letting all that gorgeous hair
go wild around your face." He wanted to see her hair spread
again across his pillow, across his chest. Wanted to clothe
himself in its warm richness. "If you wake up, I'll go wild with
you, sweetheart. Remember?"

The monitor blipped and bleeped.

"I don't know what you're doing or where you are, but I
hope you're having a damned good time, because I'm not. I

case you're interested, Maggie, you look fetching as hell in your open-backed hospital gown, but don't turn over, sweetheart, or you'll moon that guy over there in the oxygen tent. He might not recover."

What was Sullivan talking about? Her nightgown? Maggie tried to tell him he was waking her up, and she wanted to sleep for another hour at least, and what was this stuff about her bare fanny? She tried, she really did, to tell him to shut up, but her mouth was dry and her tongue thick.

He was shouting too loud. How did he expect her to sleep?

"Beatrice! *Stat!*"

Maggie tried to lick her parched lips, but her mouth wouldn't work right. Who was poking her chest?

Not Sullivan. She knew his touch.

And she knew his voice. Remembered hearing it along a dark river somewhere.

Seth's Landing.

She opened her eyes and saw Sullivan looking down at her. "Hey, Sullivan," she croaked. "Don't you have something—" she managed to get her tongue working "—more interesting to do?" She thought that's what she said, but his face was so shocked she might have said aliens had landed on her chest and were tap-dancing on her nose.

"Maggie?"

The man looked as if he'd seen a ghost. The man looked like a ghost himself, burned to the bone. Somebody needed to tell him to take better care of himself. He needed a haircut and a shave.

"Can you hear me?"

He was shouting. Of course she could hear him. Why couldn't he hear her? And he'd brought all these people into her bedroom. They would have to leave. She told them very clearly to get out of her room, but they only stared at her. Heck with 'em. If they wouldn't answer her, she was going back to sleep.

She let her eyelids drift down. They'd gotten so heavy. Maybe aliens really were . . .

"Maggie!"

She reached out to him to tell him . . . something.

Sullivan saw the flick of her little finger as he yelled.

He rubbed the heels of his hands against his eye sockets scrubbing hard. Maggie had heard him. She'd pushed at th tube in her mouth until Beatrice removed it.

That series of gurgling sounds was so faint he wouldn't hav heard them if Chapman hadn't pulled him closer to her.

"Guess what, Mr. Barnett?" Chapman was thumping him on the shoulder. "Guess what?"

Beatrice grabbed him around the waist and squeezed him lik a squeaky toy. "Maggie's going to be all right, Sullivan." He nose was wiggling like all get out. Beatrice's eyes were damp a she hugged him. Finally realizing she had him wrapped in a bear hug, she stepped back, her face almost as pink as her nose

His knees buckled.

Chapman grabbed him and plunked him into the chair "That's right. We've been watching for infection, but she' fought off anything like that. We had to see if her body coul survive the massive insult to her systems. I didn't think she' come out of the coma, if you want to know the truth, Mr. Ba nett. She's one damned lucky lady, let me tell you."

Sullivan bowed his head in his shaking hands.

Maggie was going to live.

Once she started speaking, they couldn't get her to shut up She chatted about the weather, the hospital, Nurse Beatric Bunny, everything except what had happened to her.

He didn't understand what she was trying to do.

He wanted to ask her about that instant at the pier whe she'd stepped in front of him.

She wanted to talk about everything else.

He could wait until he took her home.

And if she thought she was going anyplace else except th cottage, she could go fly a kite. That's what he told her whe she argued with him, swearing on the illustrious names of a imaginary line of relatives that she would not go to the cot tage.

"You don't have a choice, Maggie, so shut up." He thumpe her pillow.

"Of course I have a choice. I'm not going. Period." Sh thumped her pillow back the way it had been.

Chapman himself told her she had to go with Sullivan or he wouldn't release her from the hospital, even though she'd been out of the Intensive Care unit for a week.

What Sullivan didn't want to tell her yet was that Jackson, Ryder Thompson and Callahan had all posted bond on their attempted murder charges. They'd been arrested, but Sullivan, Maggie and Royal were the only witnesses.

The wild card in the deck had turned out to be Royal instead of Maggie.

Callahan and Thompson had implicated Royal, swearing under oath that Gaines had shot Jackson before arresting them in an attempt to avoid charges himself. With Palmaflora's esteemed banker, mayor and police chief under indictment and on the loose, Sullivan didn't want Maggie anywhere he couldn't see her.

Federal agents from a drawerful of alphabet agencies were settling into Palmaflora. Indictments were papering the county like parking stickers. One supervisor at a pulp company had been indicted by the county grand jury on forgery and conspiracy charges.

A team of investigators from the Federal Department of Housing and Urban Development had upcoming subpoenas under preparation by the US Department of Justice for Callahan and three county officials, on the charge of receiving kickbacks for referrals in mortgage transactions.

As the result of a pending federal grand jury investigation into his activities while director of the savings and loan, Callahan was being charged with misuse of monies and with making false entries in the thrift's books.

Conspiracy charges under the Racketeering Influenced and Corrupt Organizations Law were run-of-the-mill. Everyone was being charged with conspiracy.

Convictions, however, in most of the cases, were going to be another matter, Sullivan kept hearing as he made phone calls and went on interviews. The complicated banking, real estate and toxic-dumping charges could drag on for years.

Reid's notes were a starting point, but the different agencies were all going to have a chance to stick their respective oars in very muddy waters that would only become muddier.

The chances were excellent that no one would ever be charged with Reid's murder. No witnesses. No evidence. *Nada*. Zip.

Sullivan was irate. He'd wanted Reid's murderer caught and executed. He believed he could pull the lever of the electric chair himself every time he thought of Baby Paulie and his mother.

But the charges of attempted murder involving Sullivan and Maggie were immediate and provable.

The witnesses were alive and kicking.

Sullivan intended to see that they kicked for many years to come.

Maggie had found out Royal had been indicted.

She'd been reading a newspaper article, Sullivan's name on the byline, when he'd walked in. She'd folded the paper inward, the large black headline sandwiched between the back page advertisements for a back-to-school sale. She'd looked up at Sullivan as he sat on the bed, the newspaper lying between them with its story of greed and betrayal. She'd touched the folded edge once as if she meant to speak, but she'd dropped the paper to the floor and said nothing.

The television stations carried nightly reports updating the progress of the different investigations. Sullivan refused to be interviewed on camera, his protest against a world that preferred its news in bits and bites.

Maggie had teased him about missing his opportunity to be a star.

Royal had been interviewed, though, his photogenic features playing well to the camera, his crisp suit, dark gray and elegant—even Sullivan recognized the style of it—showing up well on the seven o'clock news as, flashing a smile, he'd said first, "No comment, guys." As the local reporters persisted, he relented. He made a brief statement indicating that he'd known nothing of what had been happening. He had been at the meeting site because he'd been trying to catch up with his former partner to ask her a question about a meeting they'd had earlier.

When he'd seen Jackson threaten her and Barnett and fire on them, he'd shot Jackson and arrested the men with him. Everything sounded plausible. He stepped through the minefield of implications and questions perfectly, never setting a foot wrong.

Sullivan had seen the interview.

Maggie had seen it.

And they hadn't discussed it.

He waited for her to bring it up, reluctant to face her with the betrayal of her friend.

But he would face her with it once he had her safe at the cottage. He could wait until they had time to sort through the muddle of what had happened and straighten out things between them, wait until she talked to him about real things, not all the fol-de-rol she'd been using as a wall between them. He didn't know why she didn't want to talk about Royal, but since she didn't bring his name up, Sullivan wasn't about to.

There were issues between them they had to face. On his part. On hers.

He had to sort out his own thinking, too.

Maybe he had been crazy for a while and imagined those moments in the ambulance and at the pier.

His inability to forget them made him uneasy. The more time passed, though, the more he questioned whether they'd actually happened.

He wanted to believe in what he thought he'd seen, but was terrified to accept what his heart suggested with each beat.

Didn't dare believe in those moments.

And backed away from their meaning.

She'd saved him at the pier. He'd saved her during the days and nights at the hospital. Even Steven.

Why turn that simple equation into something it wasn't, couldn't be?

He let each ticking second move him further from the night he'd breathed his life into Maggie and believed her to be Lizzie, believed Lizzie had returned to him.

Every day he added to his list of arguments against those moments. Hallucinations. Exhaustion. Sleep deprivation. Depression. He'd been at a low point when Maggie had entered his life. The night she'd walked up onto his deck he had been drunk and confused, lonely. Sex. Oh, hell, yes, sex was the best reason of all for arguing against the otherworldliness of those seconds when he thought he'd seen Maggie's eyes mist into

Lizzie's gray ones and back again. The night he'd had sex with Maggie when she showed up at the cottage had been incredible.

He forced himself to forget that sense of homecoming when he'd entered her, when she'd welcomed him into her, turning with him in that sweetest, wildest moment.

Oh, yes. Sex could make you believe whatever you wanted to. Under the influence of hormones, a person might believe cows could fly to the moon.

In his mind he had pages of arguments against accepting what he remembered. And all of the arguments were rational. They all made sense of everything that had happened.

But.

That was the crux of the situation. He accepted every rational point. Believed them. Was comfortable with them.

But.

At the end of each argument he found himself, against all logic, adding that small conjunction.

What he remembered couldn't possibly have been real.

But.

His heart beat to a different truth.

And while he put in long hours with Walker, the lawyers and an assortment of gray-suited officials, Maggie talked a blue streak about nothing of importance to him.

The wall growing larger day-by-day between them was invisible and very real.

And time ticked on as he felt something precious slipping away from him with every day he added to his list of arguments.

The day Chapman released Maggie, Sullivan bundled her into his car while she ranted, raved and ripped into him. After fifteen minutes, she was too drained and too weak to continue her tirade. When he bribed her with a large, juicy hamburger on the way to the beach, she was too hungry for what she called real food to resist any longer.

He figured they could talk about Royal and the trials when he had her safely settled at the cottage.

"D'cious," she muttered, a pink stream of special sauce decorating her chin. She ate half of the burger before falling asleep in the car.

As had become his habit since Seth's Landing, he checked the house before he brought a sleeping Maggie inside and settled her into the clean sheets on his bed. He'd thought he would never see that mass of cloudy curls spread across his pillow again. He trailed his finger down one strand that curled under her stubborn chin.

What was Maggie to him?

He didn't know.

Oh, during those hallucinatory days and nights after the shooting, he'd believed she was his other half, his soul mate. As Lizzie had been. In the grip of his hallucination, he'd merged the two and thought he loved the one, the one lying in his bed, her pink mouth soft in sleep, the quiet *b-b-b* he'd become used to making her bottom lip tremble.

He cared for her. Lying on the bed with her in his arms, Sullivan admitted that. He had no problem now with admitting that he cared for her.

The emptiness he'd lived with after Lizzie's death had vanished, and in its place was...caring.

To believe what he felt was anything more would be...unthinkable.

He held her more closely, burying his face in the perfume of her hair, her skin. This was enough.

He didn't need love. Caring would be enough. So long as she stayed within arm's reach. He pulled her closer to him, curving himself around her. Facing the computer, he saw their images, tiny, caught in the empty blackness of the monitor screen.

As she recuperated during the days and nights at the beach with him, Maggie became a dance-away lover, the wall between them staying firmly in place, both of them growing increasingly afraid of disturbing the delicate equilibrium they'd established.

She slept with him, her body turning in sleep toward his. She slept with him.

That was all.

And he wanted more.

He wanted her the way she'd been with him at Seth's Landing, urgent and straining against him. He wanted her the way she'd come to him in the night, with that sense he'd had of something just out of his reach. He wanted her the way she'd been in that early morning, when their coming together had been exquisitely slow and dreamy, a homecoming.

He wanted.

But Maggie danced away from him to a distant beat he heard only faintly, the beat fading with each day.

Sometimes he saw her studying him, her brown eyes deep and mysterious, filled with his reflection. She studied him as if she were waiting for a signal from him, but he couldn't figure out what kind of signal that would be.

One morning as she curled up with him in a chaise longue on the deck to watch the sunrise, the sun coming up from behind them to gild the shimmering sand stretching down to the gulf, she said, "Sullivan, I love this cottage. But I'm going back to my apartment."

Contented, peace lying inside him like a blessing, he wasn't prepared for what she was telling him. He'd had no sense that this trap was lying in wait for him.

She stumbled over her next words. "I know you don't like surprises, but I didn't know how to prepare you for my decision."

"Damned right I don't like surprises. Why the hell would you go back to the apartment? Now after—"

"After what, Sullivan?" she interrupted gently. "That's what I've been waiting to hear from you. I know you, Sullivan Barnett." She brushed her hand over his hair, down its too-long locks. "I know what you've been thinking."

"Yeah?" Aggression bubbled in him. "So tell me what I'm thinking right now, sweetheart, okay?" He snagged her chin and looked deep into her brown eyes.

Her smile was sweet, her skin gilded like the beach, with rosy color creeping back steadily as she grew well. "You're turning everything that happened over in that cynical brain of yours, tidying up the loose ends until it all makes sense to you. Until all the sums balance. Until one and one are two." Her smile turned rueful. "Aren't you?"

"I don't know what you're talking about." He scowled at her.

"Don't you?" She curled her arm around his neck, her fingers resting inside the neck of his shirt.

"You're the one who hasn't wanted to talk."

"I know." She sighed. "I should have talked with you from the beginning, but each day I put it off, it became easier not to face some things. Easier, here, in this cottage with you, to let things go unsaid. But I watched you trying to work through all the knots of what's happened. I know where you're headed, Sullivan."

"You think you know where I'm headed, but I'm telling you right off, sweetheart, you're headed nowhere away from me." Panic skittered in his chest. "We'll talk now. And then we'll go for a walk down the beach and come back here and go to bed. And then, Maggie, we'll . . ." He stopped.

"See?" Her eyes were gently sad, luminous with knowledge as he gripped her chin tightly. "We'll what, Sullivan? Make love? You weren't going to say that, were you? Because that's not what it would be for you, would it?" She stroked his neck with her palm.

He couldn't answer. He'd let things slide too long. He'd let the wall between them grow too high, too thick, and now they were on opposite sides, and he had to find a way to break through to her or he might never have another chance.

Too late, too late.

The words echoed in his brain as if she'd spoken them to him. "Listen. I'm not letting you go. You can't. No way." He sought refuge in reasons. "Callahan or Jackson might come after you. I've been worried about that from the day they posted bond."

"I know you have." Her voice wrapped him in golden sunshine.

"And Royal might try to contact you, influence your testimony."

"Royal would never do that."

"He could try." Sullivan slid her forward, facing him, her legs parting around him.

He figured she meant that Royal couldn't affect what she would say, not that he wouldn't try. It was a sure bet Royal would try if he thought he could get away with it.

Sullivan wasn't going to give him a chance to get near Maggie, much less try to talk her into anything. "You're staying put, sweetheart. Right here where you belong." He'd settled it. That was that. "Whether we call what we do together making love or call it something else doesn't matter. They're only words." He'd settled that issue, too.

A fleeting thought of the time in the hospital when he'd thought names didn't matter, either, slashed across his mind, but Maggie's question chased the idea away.

"If they're only words, why can't you say them? Shh..." She placed her fingers gently against his lips. "Of course they matter. That's why you aren't saying them. You've tidied up the loose ends to your satisfaction. I watched you do it, Sullivan. In your mind we have a comfortable arrangement. As long as you see it like that, you can avoid the fear that it will be more than you want to risk." She leaned her head against his chest, rubbing her cheek across the fabric of his shirt.

"What's wrong with comfortable?" he said. "It's worked so far."

"Because I want more than that," she whispered against him. "I want your heart and soul, and you won't give them. I want your trust, unreservedly. I want the kind of no-holds-barred, Maggie, your-instincts-are-as-good-as-mine trust, and you can't give that. Can you?" she challenged.

He repeated what he'd said so long ago. "Trusting isn't easy for me, Maggie." Watching the sandpipers skitter across the sand, he sighed heavily.

"Nothing worthwhile is ever easy," she murmured.

"Isn't what we can have good enough for you?"

She slipped her arms under his shirt and around him. "No. Because without trust, we have nothing. A time will come when it will be important for you to believe in me and to trust me. I can't live waiting for the axe to fall, waiting for you to call court into session and judge me. People make mistakes, Sullivan, and without trust, they can't get past those mistakes. Without trust, there will always be a wall between us."

"I would never sit in judgment on you, sweetheart. How could I?" Sullivan shifted, settling her closer, sliding his thumb under her bathing suit and gently over the still-bandaged area of her back.

"Because you're what you are." She leaned into his touch, arching her spine, and then dropped her arms and took his hands and placed them at his sides. "What if I confessed to you that I had told Royal we were going to Seth's Landing? Before we went?"

"But you didn't," he said confidently. And felt doubts settle like dust on him. Tried, even now as he thought about Paul Reid's face, not to ask. Wouldn't.

"What if I did?" Maggie watched Sullivan's face carefully, seeing the telltale darkening of his eyes. "You would always have that in the back of your mind—the possibility that I had betrayed you—because that's how you would interpret it, wouldn't you?"

"How can I know what I'd think? It never happened."

"A large stone in the wall between us, and you'd add other stones, day by day, Sullivan."

"No, I wouldn't."

"Of course you would. You couldn't help it. And without the kind of proof you require, evidence that someone else might have revealed Reid's meeting with you, you would always hold me responsible for his death."

"Someone was responsible." His eyes were thoughtful, the blue deepening.

"I know. And I want that person punished as much as you do."

"Then I don't see a problem." He frowned at her, clearly struggling with the truth of what she'd said and yet not wanting to lose what they had.

"I couldn't live with your suspicion, the mistrust, your doubt around me all the time. We'd start leaving things unsaid. Haven't we already fallen into that pattern?"

"We can change." There was no conviction in his voice.

"Can we, Sullivan? I don't think so." Melancholy drifted through her like a hint of autumn. "I think maybe we doom ourselves to repeat the mistakes we've made before, over and over."

"We don't have to make the same mistakes."

He tried. She would always grant him that. He'd made an effort.

"But we would. Without utter, absolute trust in the other person. Can't you see how the poison would spread? It would be a Seth's Landing of the soul. I won't accept that. I won't let us destroy each other that way, the poison seeping into every look, every nuance of tone."

She leaned forward and kissed him, her lips a benediction and a farewell.

She felt his lips move against hers, and he was kissing her back as he hadn't kissed her since the morning she'd woken up in his arms and they'd made love, the blending of their bodies more than a coming together of skin and passion.

But that had been an illusion.

She slipped off his lap and stood up. His hair had grown so shaggy during the weeks she'd been in the hospital. She'd been meaning to trim it for him, but she'd put that off, too, wanting to keep things as they were for as long as possible.

The circles under his eyes had disappeared and the long grooves down his cheeks weren't as prominent. They would never completely disappear, though.

Sullivan Barnett would always have the look of a passionate ascetic, burning and intense.

But those bright eyes would no longer burn for her.

"I've learned what loving is, Sullivan. It isn't easy, it isn't just the lure of sex. But when love is right, when it's built on trust, it can survive anything. What you're offering is a living arrangement with wonderful sex, nothing more. I'm offering something special to you, Tin Man. Myself. Everything I have to give. But I want something back. I want you, your heart and soul. I want it all. Or nothing."

If she stayed, they would destroy each other.

And so she walked away from him, knowing she had no other choice.

Chapter 15

As Sullivan watched Maggie's curves in the satiny-smooth green swimsuit walk away from him, he didn't believe she would leave him. Not now. She was upset, not fully recuperated. Loss of blood was affecting her thinking. Anesthesia aftereffect.

He went on another list-making spree.

Confident that he could coerce her into staying with him if necessary, he followed her more out of curiosity than any real fear she was planning to leave him.

How could she? She wouldn't be safe. She had to know, he muttered to himself as he strolled after her back to the bedroom, that there was no way under the sun that he would let her leave while he thought she was in danger.

Sitting on the edge of the bed, she was folding the clothes he'd brought from her apartment. Yellow and red shirts, a pink one he'd bought to replace the Seth's Landing shirt, a green one he'd seen hanging in a store window and bought for her the day they'd driven to Tampa so that he could go through court records.

There was no hesitation in her capable hands as she stacked the shirts into a pile. Maggie at her most determined.

"All right. This charade has gone far enough, Maggie. You know I won't let you leave." He was calm. He'd had a lot of practice achieving calm during the days and nights at the hospital. He took the stack from her.

"I'll buy new clothes, you know," she said in a cool little voice he'd never heard her use before. Not with him, not with anybody.

His mouth dropped open.

It wasn't the tough-cookie voice she'd used with him the first time he'd seen her, nor was it the drop-dead-where-you-stand voice she'd thrown at the cop in the parking lot when she'd returned from Seth's Landing.

Resignation, when he'd grown accustomed to sass.

Oh, he didn't like this voice. It scared the hell out of him.

Wearing nothing but that sleek green suit and the skin he couldn't get enough of stroking, she just sat and looked at him, not moving, waiting for him to return her shirts.

Cut high on the legs, her suit—he'd bought it, too—went right up over her hipbones. Her legs were a long sweep of satin skin from those green cutouts down to ankles he could encircle with his thumb and forefinger, with room to spare.

Sitting on his unmade bed in a clutter of reds and greens and yellow, her face bright from the sun he'd made her sit in after coming to the cottage, she looked like a carnation in an English garden.

"Maggie," he began again in earnest, "you can't go back to your apartment. For your own good, you need to stay here where I can take care of you until you're fully recovered. You're not, you know." He stacked the shirts on the computer table.

Her chuckle barely made a dent in the grave repose of her face. "For my own good, Sullivan, I have to leave. It's not good for me to be here with you." She said it slowly, as if she needed to make sure that she remembered.

He leaned against the table and crossed his arms. "I made it good for you once, sweetheart. I can do that for you again. Anytime. And I will. It would be my pleasure." He looked at her steadily, let her see the intent in his eyes. "And yours."

Her face went a delicate shade pinker and she looked more like a sweet flower than ever. He knew she was remembering the things they'd done here, in this room, on this bed. "I know,"

e admitted in that cool little voice that slithered through his
ood. "You can. Because I want what you can make me feel
en you take me with you into the dark and beyond. But not
that's all there is."

"That's why..." He glanced at the bed and back at her.

"Yes, Sullivan," she said, the teasing he would have nor-
ally expected from her absent as she echoed him. "That's why
 haven't...haven't, whatever. The whatever would become
 thing more than...anonymous sex," she said finally, her cut
 ing right to his heart and slashing.

"It wasn't like that before. It wouldn't be like that now."

"For me it would be." Her sunshiny voice was muted.

"You know what you mean to me." He grabbed her arms,
 d shirts went bouncing off the bed as he kneeled next to her,
 anting his elbows on either side of her and caging her in his
 ms.

"Do I?"

Her voice was so quiet that it made the ice in his blood
icken like an ancient glacier, freezing him where he knelt.

"After all we've been through, how can you think of walk-
g out? You saved my life, Maggie. I saved yours. We belong
gether now. Remember?" He was shouting.

"Yes. But do you?" she whispered.

"Of course I do." He thumped the bed for emphasis. "For
 ur safety, I'm not letting you leave," he said furiously,
inking of her being vulnerable to Callahan and whoever he
 t to do his dirty work. "It's not safe for you out there."

"There's safety—and safety."

He remembered her similar assertion about trust.

"And it's not safe for me here." She held her hands palm up.
 'm not staying, Sullivan. There's no way you can make me."

"I'll handcuff you to this damned bed if I have to, before I'll
 you out there where they can get to you."

"Oh, right. I can see you doing that, Sullivan." She laughed,
 r amusement tinged with that resigned melancholy. "You
 uld never hurt me."

"Don't try me, Maggie," he said, as angry with her as he'd
 er been in his life.

Cool little Maggie in that strip of shiny fabric thought he
 uldn't lift a finger against her, when he outweighed her by

almost eighty pounds and was more than a foot taller than
foolhardy self. Well, Maggie wasn't going anywhere exce
right here.

"It wouldn't matter whether I pushed or not. You would
hurt me." Utter security rippled in her voice. "Not under a
circumstances. You wouldn't hurt me unless you had to in
der to save my life. You see," she said softly, "that's wha
mean by trust. I know you, and because I do, I give myself
you in trust that no matter what we do together, here in t
room or anywhere else, you will not harm me. I don't have
think it through and figure it out, run that trust against
checklist of your past behavior, my suspicions. And you ca
give me that kind of trust back. That's why I have to leave."

"It's Royal, isn't it? This is all about that slick-talking, fan
dressing cop, right?" he protested. "That's what this is rea
about. You're more loyal to him than you are to me. Even n
when he's indicted, and Callahan and Ryder are going to t
tify against him, you're giving him a pass. It's all about Roy
isn't it?" he said in cold fury, ice inside and out.

"No. It's about me and what I need. It's about you and wh
you have to figure out about yourself. I told you a long time a
that you'd be better off figuring out what's going on in yo
own head and not digging around in mine."

"I know what I want. You, here, in my bed where I can ke
my eye on you." Echoes from the past ran in dark red strea
through his brain, and he shook his head, driving them awa

She stood up and scooped the shirts up, dropping them i
a navy suitcase. Moving past him, the point of her hipbo
grazing his cheek as she passed, she went to the bathroom a
returned with her arms filled with the basket of lotions a
perfumes she'd had him bring from her apartment. All th
fragrances had tinged the cottage with her scent, so that
could follow her from room to room and know how recen
she'd been there.

She dropped the basket into the suitcase and clamped it sh
"Are you going to drive me back to town, or do I have to wa
I will, you know," she added softly. "You'll wake up and
be gone. It's that simple. I want to go. You have to let me, S
livan."

She was right.

Even though there was no way under the sun he'd let her go,
had to.

He was capable in the darkest part of his nature of keeping
r exactly where he wanted her. He could have done it. Her
nfident assumption that he would wake up and she would
ve escaped wasn't worth a hill of beans. She had no idea what
was capable of. What he could do.

He could have kept her captive.

But she made it impossible.

Because she knew he wouldn't use force against her. Be-
use, damn her wide brown eyes to hell, she trusted him. Even
keep her safe, he couldn't force her to stay where she didn't
nt to be. She was, after all, not an appendage or a posses-
n he could order at will.

She was Maggie, who'd always, her fears to the contrary,
own her own mind and heart.

He drove her back to town.

As she unlocked her door, he pushed past her. "Wait a
mned minute."

He wasn't letting her go into that place until he'd checked it
thoroughly as he could. She watched him, her eyes enor-
us in her face. The pink bloom in her cheeks had wilted be-
re they'd driven over the bridge and off the island.

When he'd checked every square inch, bolt, lock and pic-
re back, looking for anything, everything, he started over.
dden microphones, cameras—he didn't know. But he would
ve her the benefit of the only skills that she would accept from
n right now.

Finally, when there was nothing left to check and she stood
ate and determined at her door, waiting for him to leave, he
. He stood there, staring down at the top of her hair, where
e'd stuck a plastic comb. He memorized the shape and tex-
re, each curlicue in the plastic.

He stood there looking at the damned silly plastic froufrou
d couldn't leave, after all.

"Well, Maggie, I couldn't make you stay at the cottage. Let's
how successful you are at making me leave. I don't mind if
u handcuff me to your bed. I'll be your guest any time you
nt me. And you will, Maggie. You'll want me. And I'll want
u. But you'll be here and I'll be at the beach. There'll be all

this *wanting* between us. Think about how it will be lying
your narrow bed."

"Oh, Sullivan, don't. Besides, it's a double bed."

"It's going to feel like a single bed as the nights go on, Ma
gie. Will you dream about all that wanting between us going
waste? You in your double bed alone, me in mine?" He w
fighting with every weapon he was allowed to use, and he cou
tell, despite the catch in her voice, that he was losing.

"You know I'll think about . . . whatever." She was trying
make a joke, too, but her husky voice trembled on the la
word. She still stood at her front door with her hand on t
cheap wood, waiting for him to leave.

"Well, Maggie, when you want . . . whatever, let me know
He'd meant to make his comment a joke, to make her laugh
seeing how ridiculous the situation was. With everything
him, he tried to make her laugh so that she would lose that a
of resignation. So that, even at the last second, she would lau
and change her mind. So that she wouldn't turn her back
him and walk away.

He wanted to throw her over his shoulders and take her ho
with him where they both belonged, not standing here on h
balcony with her holding on to one side of her door and him t
other, both of them fastened to it like it was a life raft.

But he couldn't summon a smile.

And he hadn't made her smile. Not even a little.

So many memories of loss crowding him. Lizzie. Maggie.

His mother walking away and never coming back, leavi
him, her seven-year-old child, to pass on the news to her h
band, his father, who'd taken his own leave by disappeari
into his office and forgetting that he had a child.

They'd taught him well, those goodbyes.

He'd worked hard to make those lessons so much a part
him that he'd never again stand with his face pressed agains
window and watch someone he loved walk away from him.

His mother and father. Lizzie. They'd gone away from hi

"Sullivan, I have to shut the door," Maggie said, her f
gers lingering near his at the edge of the doorjamb.

She looked as stricken as he felt.

So why was she forcing him to leave? And all over a matt
of words.

Ie closed his fist around the edge of the door. Only a rem-
it of civilization kept him from ripping it off its hinges and
ging it to the courtyard below.

Demons growled inside him, rattling their cages and loos-
ng their bars.

"Maggie, I can't understand why you're doing this. I don't
w what you want from me." His fingers dug into the wood.
lake me understand. Tell me what I have to do so that you
I stay."

"I did tell you," she whispered. "But you can't give what
I don't have. The Tin Man didn't need to go to Oz for the
wers. They were inside himself. All he had to do was look
ide and find them." She pressed her face to the wood. "The
wer is inside you, Sullivan. You have to find it. No one can.
e you the answer." Silent tears ran down her face, and he'd
er seen her cry before, not his tough-cookie Maggie. "Oh,
livan, if I thought we could survive together, I wouldn't
ve."

Iis fingers dug into the wood, so hard that splinters ran un-
his fingernails.

"Maggie, give me one chance. Just one. I can change. I know
an. I can learn how to trust."

"Can you?" She covered his hand with hers. "I think you
I, Sullivan. But I don't know if you'll try to figure it out.
at's what's breaking my heart." She took his hand and
ssed it against her breast, where he believed he could feel her
rdy heart breaking. Or maybe it was his own.

Her tears splashed onto his hand, and he remembered his
rs falling on her, his breath going into her. Somewhere be-
en that moment and this, he'd taken a wrong path.

Maggie was leaving him.

All because he'd learned those early lessons too well. He'd
rned how to keep everyone at arm's length. He'd worked
rd to do that, thought himself happy, until Lizzie had opened
· door and taught him what happiness really was. Taught him
it he didn't have to be lonely, that there was someone in the
iverse who was his.

Taught him that poignant lesson and left him, taking all
ssibility of happiness with her.

Into that black emptiness Maggie had walked, lifting him
into the light.

"Sullivan, if you find the answer—" she was stumbling o
her words "—and if you still want me, come and get me.
wait for you, as you waited for me."

Sullivan knew he could turn her inside out with pleasure a
was tempted to use that as a weapon, but he couldn't. Th
too, would have been a kind of force against her, and
wouldn't use her sweet responses as a weapon against her.

Maggie was shutting her door, closing it gently against
flat of his palm that kept it ajar. He heard her sob and
dropped his hand.

The door shut in his face.

He howled, a primitive, animal sound that ripped his thro

But when no one came running, when no windows were flu
open, he realized it had been a silent howling in the arctic was
of his heart.

Three strikes and you were out.

He knew what he had to do.

She could walk away from him—that was her choice. But
couldn't leave her vulnerable to Callahan and Ryder.
wouldn't. That was his choice.

He made arrangements with her apartment manager to r
a vacant one-room apartment in the same building.

And he followed her. Sometimes she saw him, sometimes
didn't, but he was always there, watching over her.

And as he took care of her in the only way he could, he
as she had asked.

He looked deep inside himself, trying to find an answer t
question he didn't even understand.

Maggie was afraid she wouldn't have the courage to s
away from Sullivan. Everything in her turned to him, and
was terrified that she'd give in to the need to go running af
him, to settle for what he was offering.

She couldn't.

If they were to have any chance of happiness, Sullivan h
to have the same kind of trust in her that she had in hi
Without it, they had nothing.

As the days wore on and she caught glimpses of Sullivan
om time to time following her, her agony at being separated
om him only grew stronger.

His protectiveness touched her because she knew how his
nd worked. Taking care of her was his way of show-
, . . what? That's what he had to figure out.

She knew what she was missing, knew what they could have
gether.

But Sullivan would have to figure it out for himself. All or
thing, that's what she'd said—heart and soul. She wouldn't
tle for anything less.

She could have made it easy for him and told him that she'd
lled Royal. But the phone call had never been the real issue.
e real issue, from the beginning, had been whether or not he
uld trust her with himself. Or would he always keep a little
rt of himself separate, afraid to take the risk of letting down
last of his barriers and welcoming her into his heart as she
lcomed him into hers?

She didn't know what she would do if she were wrong in
mbling on what she hoped he would discover inside himself.
If he gave up on himself . . .

She waited while the federal officers unraveled some of the
reads of the conspiracy. She waited while Callahan, Ryder
d Jackson were brought to trial.

The charges against Royal were dropped for lack of evi-
nce.

She wondered if Sullivan would conclude that it was part of
cover-up.

Waiting for Sullivan, waiting until she could return to work,
e filled in her days at the Sunshine Center. Sometimes she
uld sit in the side courtyard area with Alicia and watch the
n go down, as she'd imagined doing before.

And it all seemed so familiar, as if she'd found her place at
t.

She didn't ask Alicia any questions about Sullivan. Alicia
dn't ask her any. By unspoken agreement, they skirted the
ue of what was going on with him. Once, though, Sullivan
d been going around the corner as she came into the center.
e'd stopped and looked at him, drinking in the sight of his
ng legs and broad shoulders, but he hadn't seen her.

He still hadn't cut his hair.

The longer she worked with the kids, the less she wanted leave them. She and Alicia talked, figuring out how they cou work out the financial arrangements if Maggie worked full tin at the center.

Maggie loved the idea.

Since the day at Taggart's when she'd been unable to fire h pistol, she'd known that it was only a matter of time until sl would have to leave active police work.

She remembered dropping her gun under the bridge at tl Riverfront Pier. She remembered the incident in bits and piec and was never quite sure if she would have fired at Jackson not.

She no longer wanted to carry a gun. That part of her n ture existed no longer. She hadn't known, however, what c rection to take until she began working with Alicia, and ther magically, it seemed, her life meshed.

Alicia worked through the financial red tape, making a ful time job at the center available. Maggie wanted to work ther very much. She found it more and more difficult each day leave the center and go back to her apartment. She wanted give Katie and all the other kids who found their way the some hope, some sense that, if they looked hard enough, the might find small, everyday miracles in their lives. She wante to make a difference and thought she could.

And every day, she longed for Sullivan.

And waited.

Sullivan sat hunkered under the poinciana tree with Katie la one afternoon toward the end of a hot and muggy Septembe Katie had a great deal to discuss with him these days and listened attentively, because strung like pearls on the thread her talking was information about Maggie. And Maggie w the reason he was waiting under the tree.

It hadn't been necessary for several weeks for him to follo her around protectively, but he'd grown used to the rhythm her days and had begun to make a game out of letting her mi him by seconds. He'd thought in that way to weaken her solve.

He only intensified his hunger for her.

Tearing poinciana blossoms into shreds to make snowflakes for Katie and her doll, he watched Maggie come out to the patio and sit down with her tea. She lifted her hair off the nape of her neck and leaned back against the chair, her hair trailing over the edge. She rested her feet on another table. She tilted her face to the sun, letting its afternoon rays fall upon her.

Watching her air of contentment, her look of utter rightness in being where Lizzie had always been, he felt all the questions that had been churning inside him for weeks finally settle.

He'd thought her insistence on trust a silly notion, but it hadn't been at all. Why hadn't he understood sooner?

"Katie, go tell Maggie to come here, will you please? And thank you." Sullivan waited, humming a tune as he watched Katie trudge toward Maggie, trailing pink-and-white blossoms behind her.

Maggie poked her head through the low branches. "Sullivan?"

He noted with a thrill the breathiness in her voice.

"Yes, Maggie, it's me. I have a question for you."

"Are we playing twenty questions, Sullivan?" Her lips were curved at the corners.

"Sort of. And it's not a game, Maggie. It's my whole life we're talking about here. Want to see if you can answer my question?"

"All right," she said, her eyes shining. "Go ahead."

"Why is it, Maggie, do you suppose—" he tossed blossoms her way "—that I identified myself as your husband when you were rushed into the emergency room at the hospital for surgery? Why do you think I stayed there day and night holding your hand, hmm, Maggie?" He pitched more blossoms toward her and they tangled in her hair.

"That's two questions." She sat cross-legged, with petals showering her golden skin and dark hair. "Why do you think you did such foolish things, Sullivan? Out of guilt, maybe, because I was trying to turn myself into a human pincushion on your behalf?"

"Could be. I've always been such a soft touch, you know. Might have been guilt." He nudged one of her toes.

Her grin was spreading across her face, her infinitely dear face.

"You know what I've been thinking about these last weeks, sweetheart?"

"Oh, tell me. Please," she said demurely, pursing her mouth. "I've been wondering a little bit about what might be going through your mind."

Leaning toward her, he stripped a branchful of blossoms onto her. They drifted down the front of her blouse, onto her legs, over her arms. "I think, sweetheart, I always saw you for who you are, even from the first. I think I recognized you from the beginning, and wouldn't let myself realize it. I think my heart did, though, and that's what I fought against—that conflict between what was in my heart and what was in my brain. My mind is, you know, a skeptical organ. Some things will never change."

"I didn't expect it to," she whispered in delight, her pink-frosted toes peeking up at him from bright green sandals. "What has changed?"

Standing up, he pulled her to her feet. Blossoms tumbled around her. "My eyesight."

"What?" She blinked at him.

"Yep. My eyesight. I was blind and now I see—through a glass darkly, but I see."

"Oh, Sullivan," she murmured, curling her fingers around his neck.

"It's not something I'm comfortable talking about, sweetheart, but I let myself think about that moment as you came running to me at the pier, and what I remember so vividly is that I would have died to save you. You beat me to the punch, that's all."

"I wasn't as confused. I knew what I was doing," she said smugly, her hair tickling his ear.

"Well, of course. You probably always have, being a member of the superior sex." He grinned at her, feeling so light inside he thought he could float right up to the sky on joy alone. "I thought about that moment a lot, Maggie, turning it over and over in my skeptical brain, and what I finally realized is that from the moment I saw you pop up from behind the piling, I knew you would risk your life for mine just as I would for you. I trusted you to do the best you could for me, just as I would for you."

"Well, of course."

"And I figured out that was the kind of trust you'd put in Royal. Now, I don't know if he betrayed your trust in him or not. I hope not, for your sake, but you trusted him to be a good cop, and you acted on that trust. You did the best you could, whatever it was, and I understand that now. I don't have to know whether or not you told him about the rendezvous. Although I can't imagine how, someone else may have revealed the information. But I know that you would have acted for the best, that you always will. You would never hurt me any more than I would hurt you."

"Do you remember the rest of that night, Sullivan?" she murmured against his neck.

"Oh, sweetheart, I've been fighting it all the way, but I think I've been handed a miracle on a silver platter. I think I needed time to grow used to the idea. I don't understand it anymore than I understand DNA, but I think we've been given a second chance. I know you, Maggie, my love. I think I always have. Your scent, your inner nature called to mine. It's just taken me a long time to figure out who I am."

"And who are you, Sullivan Barnett?" she whispered in his ear, as he carried her to his motorcycle and settled her behind him.

"Why, Maggie, I'm the man who loves you, heart and soul." He smiled at her. "Come home with me, sweetheart, and let me prove it to you?" He reached into his pocket, pulled out the silver barrette she'd dropped long ago and he'd saved without knowing why. He handed it to her.

She smiled at him, her eyes shining with excitement, shining all for him.

When they arrived at the beach cottage, though, Royal was parked outside in his red Mustang, waiting for them. Sullivan squeezed Maggie's hand and unlocked the cottage door.

"Come on in, Gaines. I'll get you a beer." Sullivan figured he'd always be a shade bristly with the man, but if Royal were important to Maggie, then Sullivan would cope.

"Thanks." Royal looked at Sullivan's arm around Maggie's waist and frowned, but he only squared his shoulders. "I won't stay long. I really came to talk with you, Maggie. I called Ms. Williams from the car and she told me you were headed back here. I came straight over. I hadn't wanted to contact you before everything was cleared up." Royal shrugged. "Not that it's completely clear yet, but my part is. I'm resigning from the department, Maggie."

"Why? I read that your lawyer had presented material before the grand jury showing that you weren't involved with any of the protection setup." Maggie's chin was headed skyward, and Sullivan knew she was ready to go to war on Royal's behalf.

"He did. But being under suspicion did something to me, Mags. When you came back into Johnny's office that day, I knew you were hiding something from me because for some reason you thought I'd gone dirty."

"I never believed that, Royal, not at all. Some people might have—" she cast a mischievous glance Sullivan's way "—people who have trouble understanding how friendship works, but I didn't. I know you better than that."

"Thanks, Mags. Under the circumstances that means a lot, I'll tell you. You're probably the only person in this whole damned town who feels that way. Even though I wasn't brought to trial, I see people looking at me and deciding that I must be guilty as hell. Where there's smoke, there's fire, and all that stuff. Anyway, thanks. You're a real friend, Mags. There aren't many people like you."

"What made you suspicious of me, Royal?" Maggie asked. She didn't have to be quite so sympathetic, Sullivan decided. He was tired of supporting the wall. And he was even more tired of how Royal looked at Maggie, as if she were the appetizer of the day.

"I listened to how you were answering our questions, and I knew something was up. I know you real well, Mags, and so I knew there was a real problem if you're weren't leveling with me. So, from that point on, I started asking questions of my own."

Seeing the glitter of pain in Royal's eye as he looked down at Maggie, Sullivan found room in his heart to feel a little sorry for the man. Royal's life had been golden up until now. But he'd lost Maggie, lost his reputation, and was losing his job, even though it was by his own choice.

Sullivan wouldn't agree with the golden-haired cop about many things, but he was damned straight when it came to Maggie. She was special. She would go to war for anybody she believed in and trusted. If you were Maggie's friend, she wouldn't let you down. Why had he been so slow to catch on to this trust thing? Well, life had lessons to teach, and it seemed as if he was facing a lot of lessons, lifetimes of them.

Maggie's hand was a little too comfortable on Royal's forearm, but Sullivan reckoned not throwing the guy out of the house ought to be his contribution to the trust issue for today.

"I wanted to tell you a couple of things, Mags, before you read them in the paper—" he shot a hostile glance toward Sullivan "—because what I'm going to tell you is going to turn this town upside down. Anyway, I thought you'd want to know."

Always curious, Sullivan made himself inconspicuous and listened.

"Of course. What's happened?" Maggie's hair seemed to turn electric, glowing with energy.

"Callahan was behind everything. Greedy as hell, and he started the ball rolling. He wanted the brass ring and couldn't get it legally. From what I've seen of Charlie, I think he got a bang out of the whole idea of getting away with something. And he did, for a long time." Royal glanced at Sullivan. "He's the one who set the explosive in your car. He wanted to see if he could do it."

"He almost did, Royal. And right in front of the Sunshine Center. I never liked Charlie." Maggie shuddered.

"He thought Barnett was getting too close to what was going on at the bank, with money shuffling back and forth to fund the real-estate deals, and he was afraid that Barnett's story would bring the Feds down on his neck, so he panicked. He's the one who sent you—" Royal nodded to Sullivan "—the threatening letters. He said he was glad he hadn't killed you, but he thought you looked real funny lying ass up on the sidewalk."

"Nice guy," Sullivan growled, remembering the laughter he'd heard. "I'd like to get my hands on him."

"Stand in line, Tin Man." Maggie was furious, Sullivan could tell. The children. He was getting the hang of how Maggie's loyalties ran.

"Jackson met Paul Reid at Seth's Landing. Jackson was supposed to bribe the man, but apparently Reid wasn't bribable, so Jackson killed him. None of the conspirators had bargained for murder, so the conspiracy started fraying at the edges after that. Anyway, Mags, Barnett, that's about it. I'll be sticking around for a while, and then I'm heading to greener pastures."

Royal stuck out his hand, and Sullivan shook it. Even if he hadn't wanted to, the glint in Maggie's eyes would have made him. She expected him to respect her turf.

Maggie stopped Royal at the door. "One last question, Royal. I know you didn't pass on the meeting location and time to the chief after I called you—"

"Hell, no, Mags, you asked me not to," Royal interrupted. "You know me better than that."

"I do. But I wanted to ask you how Jackson found out."

Suppressing a grin, Sullivan glared at Maggie. Give her an inch and she'd take the whole nine yards. Thought she was being sneaky, confessing like this. But he knew she would never have told him if he hadn't walked over the bridge separating them first. It had been her test of him.

And he'd almost failed it.

"Through the baby monitor. Can you believe it? Jackson had the police scanner on and picked up Reid's curbside cellular-phone call. Reid thought he was safe, but the monitor acted just like a bug."

Later, when Royal was gone, Maggie turned to Sullivan and said, "I wanted to tell you I'd called Royal, Sullivan, but you would have seen it as a betrayal."

"Yeah. You're right. I would have. Before I was enlightened." He grinned. "But you sure have one thing wrong about Gaines."

"What?" She tilted her head, and the silver clip caught the light as her hair slid to one side.

"You insisted you and Gaines were friends."

"We were. Are. Whatever."

"No *whatever* with Gaines, sweetheart. All the *whatevers* are mine." The jealousy slipped out, but he thought he'd controlled it.

Until Maggie grinned at him. "Go on. What were you saying about my friend Royal?"

"Well, sugar-buns, that's not a *friendly* glint in his eyes at all. Not unless you call the look the fox gets in the hen house friendly."

Maggie laughed and the topknot went flying. "Sullivan! You made another joke. That must be three by now, but I'm losing count." Her teasing smile seduced him completely.

"Come here, sweetheart, and I'll show you *friendly*," he said, reaching out for her.

And he did.

He was very friendly, Maggie told him much later.

"I'm learning, sweetheart," he murmured into her ear as the sound of the evening tide filled the room.

One morning Sullivan woke and found her gone. For a moment his heart pounded, all the old memories hovering. Pulling on a pair of old navy gym shorts, he walked out onto the deck. A line of footprints led from the deck into the bright gold-blue of the early morning gulf. In the brilliant blue, a shining brown dot swam out to the darker blue with strong, sure strokes.

Maggie.

Hurrying over the sand, Sullivan stripped his shorts off and dropped them near where hers lay in a sandy heap. Swimming after her, he circled around so that she saw him before he dived and grabbed her ankles, pulling her under.

Curving into him, her sleek body moved with his as he tilted to his back, sculling shoreward with one hand as he held Maggie with the other, sliding her wet, cool body over his, holding her close to his heart in that glittering morning as light filled the emptiness in his soul.

Maggie picked up her sandy shorts and turned to look as Sullivan followed her out of the sea. Water glinted in his hair, on the smooth, muscled length of his body. Casting him a mischievous glance, she dropped her shorts back to the ground, sinking with them as she reached out her hand toward his. Clasping his fingers, she pulled him to the cool sand, letting him turn her so that he took the gritty pressure of the grains against his back. The lopsided smile she loved to distraction finally reached his eyes and filled them.

With the radiance of the brilliant sun flooding her and Sullivan's bright blue eyes laughing back at her, Maggie made love to him, with him, the diamond earrings he'd given her for a wedding present gleaming like rainbows in the sun. "I love you, Sullivan Barnett," she whispered over and over. His echoing murmur filled her ears, until she no longer knew whether she whispered of love or he did, knew only that they loved, moving together in an old rhythm, their bodies blending bonelessly. Beyond flesh, endlessly, spirit to spirit, soul to soul as the shining light on the gulf moved to the farthest horizon, stretching forever.

*   *   *   *   *

HE'S AN

AMERICAN HERO

He's a cop, a fire fighter or even just a fearless drifter who gets the job done when ordinary men have given up. And you'll find one American Hero every month, only in Intimate Moments— created by some of your favorite authors. Look at what we've lined up for the last months of 1993:

October: GABLE'S LADY by Linda Turner—With a ranch to save and a teenage sister to protect, Gable Rawlings already has a handful of trouble...until hotheaded Josey O'Brian makes it an armful....

November: NIGHTSHADE by Nora Roberts—Murder and a runaway's disappearance force Colt Nightshade and Lt. Althea Grayson into an uneasy alliance....

December: LOST WARRIORS by Rachel Lee—With one war behind him, Medevac pilot Billy Joe Yuma still has the strength to fight off the affections of the one woman he can never have....

AMERICAN HEROES: Men who give all they've got for their country, their work—the women they love.

IMHER06

INTIMATE MOMENTS® Silhouette®

SILHOUETTE® Shadows™

NEW! FOR NOVEMBER

IT ALL BEGINS AT NIGHT....

The dark holds many secrets, and answers aren't easily found. In fact, in some cases the truth can be deadly. But Silhouette Shadows women aren't easily frightened....

Brave new authors Cheryl Emerson and Allie Harrison are about to see how scared *you* can get. These talented authors will entice you, bemuse you and thrill you!

#19 TREACHEROUS BEAUTIES by Cheryl Emerson
Widowed Anna Levee was out to discover who had mysteriously murdered her brother. Trouble was, the best suspect was slowly stealing Anna's heart. What if Jason Forrester decided he wanted her life as well?

#20 DREAM A DEADLY DREAM by Allie Harrison
Kate McCoy assured herself it was just a dream. The erotic fantasies she remembered were strictly her imagination. But when Jake Casperson knocked on her door, Kate discovered her nighttime visions were about to become reality....

Pick up your copy of our newest Silhouette Shadows books at your favorite retail outlet...and prepare to shiver!

SSHNE

TAKE A WALK ON THE
DARK SIDE OF LOVE WITH

Silhouette®

SHADOWS '93

October is the shivery season, when chill winds blow and shadows walk the night. Come along with us into a haunting world where love and danger go hand in hand, where passions will thrill you and dangers will chill you. Silhouette's second annual collection from the dark side of love brings you three perfectly haunting tales from three of our most bewitching authors:

Kathleen Korbel
Carla Cassidy
Lori Herter

Haunting a store near you this October.

Only from 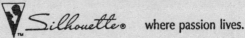 Silhouette® where passion lives.

SHAD93

ROMANTIC TRADITIONS

Marriages of convenience, secret babies, amnesia, brides left at the altar—these are the stuff of Romantic Traditions. And some of the finest Intimate Moments authors will bring these best-loved tales to you starting in October with ONCE UPON A WEDDING (IM #524), by award-winning author Paula Detmer Riggs.

To honor a promise and provide a stable home for an orphaned baby girl, staunch bachelor Jesse Dante asked Hazel O'Connor to marry him, underestimating the powers of passion and parenthood....

In January, look for Marilyn's Pappano's FINALLY A FATHER (IM #542), for a timely look at the ever-popular secret-baby plotline.

And ROMANTIC TRADITIONS doesn't stop there! In months to come we'll be bringing you more of your favorite stories, told the Intimate Moments way. So if you're the romantic type who appreciates tradition with a twist, come experience ROMANTIC TRADITIONS—only in

SIMRT1

INTIMATE MOMENTS®
Silhouette®

**You met them this month
and learned to love them!
They're the Rawlings family
of New Mexico!**

If you liked GABLE'S LADY (IM#523), don't miss his siblings' stories:

COOPER: He loves the ranch and his work there, but he's restless and the whole family can see it. Their solution: he needs a wife.

FLYNN: He's a lovable flirt who likes women too much to settle for just one.

KAT: She's always been her brothers' little sister but now that she's grown up—watch out!

Look for their stories as Linda Turner's exciting saga continues in

THE WILD WEST

Coming to you throughout 1994...only from Silhouette Intimate Moments.

WIL

**And now for
something completely different
from Silhouette....**

Every once in a while, Silhouette brings you a book that is truly unique and innovative, taking you into the world of paranormal happenings. And now these stories will carry our special "Spellbound" flash, letting you know that you're in for a truly exciting reading experience!

In October, look for *McLain's Law* (IM #528) by Kylie Brant

Lieutenant Detective Connor McLain believes only in what he can see—until Michele Easton's haunting visions help him solve a case...and her love opens his heart!

McLain's Law is also the Intimate Moments "Premiere" title, introducing you to a debut author, sure to be the star of tomorrow!

Available in October...only from Silhouette Intimate Moments

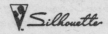